Agatha Webb

Anna Katharine Green

AGATHA WEBB

BY ANNA KATHARINE GREEN (MRS. CHARLES ROHLFS)

AUTHOR OF "THE LEAVENWORTH CASE, " "THAT AFFAIR NEXT DOOR" "LOST MAN'S LANE, " ETC.

THIS BOOK IS INSCRIBED TO MY FRIEND

PROFESSOR A. V. DICEY

OF OXFORD, ENGLAND

CONTENTS

BOOK I

THE PURPLE ORCHID

I.	A Cry on the Hill
II.	One Night's Work
III.	The Empty Drawer
IV.	The Full Drawer
V.	A Spot on the Lawn
VI.	"Breakfast is Served, Gentlemen!"
VII.	"Marry Me"
VIII.	"A Devil That Understands Men"
IX.	A Grand Woman
X.	Detective Knapp Arrives
XI.	The Man with a Beard
XII.	Wattles Comes
XIII.	Wattles Goes
XIV.	A Final Temptation
XV.	The Zabels Visited
XVI.	Local Talent at Work
XVII.	The Slippers, the Flower, and What Sweetwater Made of Them
XVIII.	Some Leading Questions
XIX.	Poor Philemon
XX.	A Surprise for Mr. Sutherland

BOOK II

THE MAN OF NO REPUTATION

I.	Sweetwater Reasons
II.	Sweetwater Acts
III.	A Sinister Pair
IV.	In the Shadow of the Mast
V.	In Extremity
VI.	The Adventure of the Parcel
VII.	The Adventure of the Scrap of Paper and the Three Words
VIII.	"Who Are You?"
IX.	Home Again

BOOK III

HAD BATSY LIVED!

 I. What Followed the Striking of the Clock
 II. A Witness Lost
 III. Why Agatha Webb will Never be Forgotten in Sutherlandtown
 IV. Father and Son
 V. "Not When They Are Young Girls"
 VI. Sweetwater Pays His Debt at Last to Mr. Sutherland

Agatha Webb

BOOK I

THE PURPLE ORCHID

I

A CRY ON THE HILL

The dance was over. From the great house on the hill the guests had all departed and only the musicians remained. As they filed out through the ample doorway, on their way home, the first faint streak of early dawn became visible in the east. One of them, a lank, plain-featured young man of ungainly aspect but penetrating eye, called the attention of the others to it.

"Look! " said he; "there is the daylight! This has been a gay night for Sutherlandtown. "

"Too gay, " muttered another, starting aside as the slight figure of a young man coming from the house behind them rushed hastily by. "Why, who's that? "

As they one and all had recognised the person thus alluded to, no one answered till he had dashed out of the gate and disappeared in the woods on the other side of the road. Then they all spoke at once.

"It's Mr. Frederick! "

"He seems in a desperate hurry. "

"He trod on my toes. "

"Did you hear the words he was muttering as he went by? "

As only the last question was calculated to rouse any interest, it alone received attention.

"No; what were they? I heard him say something, but I failed to catch the words. "

"He wasn't talking to you, or to me either, for that matter; but I have ears that can hear an eye wink. He said: 'Thank God, this night of horror is over! ' Think of that! After such a dance and such a spread, he calls the night horrible and thanks God that it is over. I thought he was the very man to enjoy this kind of thing. "

"So did I. "

"And so did I. "

The five musicians exchanged looks, then huddled in a group at the gate.

"He has quarrelled with his sweetheart, " suggested one.

"I'm not surprised at that, " declared another. "I never thought it would be a match. "

"Shame if it were! " muttered the ungainly youth who had spoken first.

As the subject of this comment was the son of the gentleman whose house they were just leaving, they necessarily spoke low; but their tones were rife with curiosity, and it was evident that the topic deeply interested them. One of the five who had not previously spoken now put in a word:

"I saw him when he first led out Miss Page to dance, and I saw him again when he stood up opposite her in the last quadrille, and I tell you, boys, there was a mighty deal of difference in the way he conducted himself toward her in the beginning of the evening and the last. You wouldn't have thought him the same man. Reckless young fellows like him are not to be caught by dimples only. They want cash. "

"Or family, at least; and she hasn't either. But what a pretty girl she is! Many a fellow as rich as he and as well connected would be satisfied with her good looks alone. "

"Good looks! " High scorn was observable in this exclamation, which was made by the young man whom I have before characterised as ungainly. "I refuse to acknowledge that she has any good looks. On the contrary, I consider her plain. "

"Oh! Oh!" burst in protest from more than one mouth. "And why does she have every fellow in the room dangling after her, then?" asked the player on the flageolet.

"She hasn't a regular feature."

"What difference does that make when it isn't her features you notice, but herself?"

"I don't like her."

A laugh followed this.

"That won't trouble her, Sweetwater. Sutherland does, if you don't, and that's much more to the point. And he'll marry her yet; he can't help it. Why, she'd witch the devil into leading her to the altar if she took a notion to have him for her bridegroom."

"There would be consistency in that," muttered the fellow just addressed. "But Mr. Frederick—"

"Hush! There's some one on the doorstep. Why, it's she!"

They all glanced back. The graceful figure of a young girl dressed in white was to be seen leaning toward them from the open doorway. Behind her shone a blaze of light—the candles not having been yet extinguished in the hall—and against this brilliant background her slight form, with all its bewitching outlines, stood out in plain relief.

"Who was that?" she began in a high, almost strident voice, totally out of keeping with the sensuous curves of her strange, sweet face. But the question remained unanswered, for at that moment her attention, as well as that of the men lingering at the gate, was attracted by the sound of hurrying feet and confused cries coming up the hill.

"Murder! Murder!" was the word panted out by more than one harsh voice; and in another instant a dozen men and boys came rushing into sight in a state of such excitement that the five musicians recoiled from the gate, and one of them went so far as to start back toward the house. As he did so he noticed a curious thing. The young woman whom they had all perceived standing in the door a moment before had vanished, yet she was known to possess the keenest curiosity of any one in town.

"Murder! Murder! " A terrible and unprecedented cry in this old, God-fearing town. Then came in hoarse explanation from the jostling group as they stopped at the gate: "Mrs. Webb has been killed! Stabbed with a knife! Tell Mr. Sutherland! "

Mrs. Webb!

As the musicians heard this name, so honoured and so universally beloved, they to a man uttered a cry. Mrs. Webb! Why, it was impossible. Shouting in their turn for Mr. Sutherland, they all crowded forward.

"Not Mrs. Webb! " they protested. "Who could have the daring or the heart to kill HER? "

"God knows, " answered a voice from the highway. "But she's dead— we've just seen her! "

"Then it's the old man's work, " quavered a piping voice. "I've always said he would turn on his best friend some day. 'Sylum's the best place for folks as has lost their wits. I—"

But here a hand was put over his mouth, and the rest of the words was lost in an inarticulate gurgle. Mr. Sutherland had just appeared on the porch.

He was a superb-looking man, with an expression of mingled kindness and dignity that invariably awakened both awe and admiration in the spectator. No man in the country—I was going to say no woman was more beloved, or held in higher esteem. Yet he could not control his only son, as everyone within ten miles of the hill well knew.

At this moment his face showed both pain and shock.

"What name are you shouting out there? " he brokenly demanded. "Agatha Webb? Is Agatha Webb hurt? "

"Yes, sir; killed, " repeated a half-dozen voices at once. "We've just come from the house. All the town is up. Some say her husband did it. "

"No, no! " was Mr. Sutherland's decisive though half-inaudible response. "Philemon Webb might end his own life, but not Agatha's. It was the money—"

Here he caught himself up, and, raising his voice, addressed the crowd of villagers more directly.

"Wait, " said he, "and I will go back with you. Where is Frederick? " he demanded of such members of his own household as stood about him.

No one knew.

"I wish some one would find my son. I want him to go into town with me. "

"He's over in the woods there, " volunteered a voice from without.

"In the woods! " repeated the father, in a surprised tone.

"Yes, sir; we all saw him go. Shall we sing out to him? "

"No, no; I will manage very well without him. " And taking up his hat Mr. Sutherland stepped out again upon the porch.

Suddenly he stopped. A hand had been laid on his arm and an insinuating voice was murmuring in his ear:

"Do you mind if I go with you? I will not make any trouble. "

It was the same young lady we have seen before.

The old gentleman frowned—he who never frowned and remarked shortly:

"A scene of murder is no place for women. "

The face upturned to his remained unmoved.

"I think I will go, " she quietly persisted. "I can easily mingle with the crowd."

He said not another word against it. Miss Page was under pay in his house, but for the last few weeks no one had undertaken to contradict her. In the interval since her first appearance on the porch, she had exchanged the light dress in which she had danced at the ball, for a darker and more serviceable one, and perhaps this token of her determination may have had its influence in silencing him. He joined the crowd, and together they moved down-hill. This was too much for the servants of the house. One by one they too left the house till it stood absolutely empty. Jerry snuffed out the candles and shut the front door, but the side entrance stood wide open, and into this entrance, as the last footstep died out on the hillside, passed a slight and resolute figure. It was that of the musician who had questioned Miss Page's attractions.

II

ONE NIGHT'S WORK

Sutherlandtown was a seaport. The village, which was a small one, consisted of one long street and numerous cross streets running down from the hillside and ending on the wharves. On one of the corners thus made, stood the Webb house, with its front door on the main street and its side door on one of the hillside lanes. As the group of men and boys who had been in search of Mr. Sutherland entered this last-mentioned lane, they could pick out this house from all the others, as it was the only one in which a light was still burning. Mr. Sutherland lost no time in entering upon the scene of tragedy. As his imposing figure emerged from the darkness and paused on the outskirts of the crowd that was blocking up every entrance to the house, a murmur of welcome went up, after which a way was made for him to the front door.

But before he could enter, some one plucked him by the sleeve.

"Look up! " whispered a voice into his ear.

He did so, and saw a woman's body hanging half out of an upper window. It hung limp, and the sight made him sick, notwithstanding his threescore years of experience.

"Who's that? " he cried. "That's not Agatha Webb. "

"No, that's Batsy, the cook. She's dead as well as her mistress. We left her where we found her for the coroner to see. "

"But this is horrible, " murmured Mr. Sutherland. "Has there been a butcher here? "

As he uttered these words, he felt another quick pressure on his arm. Looking down, he saw leaning against him the form of a young woman, but before he could address her she had started upright again and was moving on with the throng. It was Miss Page.

"It was the sight of this woman hanging from the window which first drew attention to the house, " volunteered a man who was standing as a sort of guardian at the main gateway. "Some of the sailors' wives who had been to the wharves to see their husbands off on the ship that sailed at daybreak, saw it as they came up the lane on their way home, and gave the alarm. Without that we might not have known to this hour what had happened."

"But Mrs. Webb?"

"Come in and see."

There was a board fence about the simple yard within which stood the humble house forever after to be pointed out as the scene of Sutherlandtown's most heartrending tragedy. In this fence was a gate, and through this gate now passed Mr. Sutherland, followed by his would-be companion, Miss Page. A path bordered by lilac bushes led up to the house, the door of which stood wide open. As soon as Mr. Sutherland entered upon this path a man approached him from the doorway. It was Amos Fenton, the constable.

"Ah, Mr. Sutherland," said he, "sad business, a very sad business! But what little girl have you there?"

"This is Miss Page, my housekeeper's niece. She would come. Inquisitiveness the cause. I do not approve of it."

"Miss Page must remain on the doorstep. We allow no one inside excepting yourself," he said respectfully, in recognition of the fact that nothing of importance was ever undertaken in Sutherland town without the presence of Mr. Sutherland.

Miss Page curtsied, looking so bewitching in the fresh morning light that the tough old constable scratched his chin in grudging admiration. But he did not reconsider his determination. Seeing this, she accepted her defeat gracefully, and moved aside to where the bushes offered her more or less protection from the curiosity of those about her. Meanwhile Mr. Sutherland had stepped into the house.

He found himself in a small hall with a staircase in front and an open door at the left. On the threshold of this open door a man stood, who at sight of him doffed his hat. Passing by this man, Mr. Sutherland entered the room beyond. A table spread with eatables met his view, beside which, in an attitude which struck him at the moment as peculiar, sat Philemon Webb, the well-known master of the house.

Astonished at seeing his old friend in this room and in such a position, he was about to address him, when Mr. Fenton stopped him.

"Wait! " said he. "Take a look at poor Philemon before you disturb him. When we broke into the house a half-hour ago he was sitting just as you see him now, and we have let him be for reasons you can easily appreciate. Examine him closely, Mr. Sutherland; he won't notice it. "

"But what ails him? Why does he sit crouched against the table? Is he hurt too? "

"No; look at his eyes. "

Mr. Sutherland stooped and pushed aside the long grey locks that half concealed the countenance of his aged friend.

"Why, " he cried, startled, "they are closed! He isn't dead? "

"No, he is asleep. "

"Asleep? "

"Yes. He was asleep when we came in and he is asleep yet. Some of the neighbours wanted to wake him, but I would not let them. His wits are not strong enough to bear a sudden shock. "

"No, no, poor Philemon! But that he should sit sleeping here while she—But what do these bottles mean and this parade of supper in a room they were not accustomed to eat in? "

"We don't know. It has not been eaten, you see. He has swallowed a glass of port, but that is all. The other glasses have had no wine in them, nor have the victuals been touched. "

"Seats set for three and only one occupied, " murmured Mr. Sutherland. "Strange! Could he have expected guests? "

"It looks like it. I didn't know that his wife allowed him such privileges; but she was always too good to him, and I fear has paid for it with her life. "

"Nonsense! he never killed her. Had his love been anything short of the worship it was, he stood in too much awe of her to lift his hand against her, even in his most demented moments."

"I don't trust men of uncertain wits," returned the other. "You have not noticed everything that is to be seen in this room."

Mr. Sutherland, recalled to himself by these words, looked quickly about him. With the exception of the table and what was on and by it there was nothing else in the room. Naturally his glance returned to Philemon Webb.

"I don't see anything but this poor sleeping man," he began.

"Look at his sleeve."

Mr. Sutherland, with a start, again bent down. The arm of his old friend lay crooked upon the table, and on its blue cotton sleeve there was a smear which might have been wine, but which was — blood.

As Mr. Sutherland became assured of this, he turned slightly pale and looked inquiringly at the two men who were intently watching him.

"This is bad," said he. "Any other marks of blood below stairs?"

"No; that one smear is all."

"Oh, Philemon!" burst from Mr. Sutherland, in deep emotion. Then, as he looked long and shudderingly at his friend, he added slowly:

"He has been in the room where she was killed; so much is evident. But that he understood what was done there I cannot believe, or he would not be sleeping here like a log. Come, let us go up-stairs."

Fenton, with an admonitory gesture toward his subordinate, turned directly toward the staircase. Mr. Sutherland followed him, and they at once proceeded to the upper hall and into the large front room which had been the scene of the tragedy.

It was the parlour or sitting-room of this small and unpretentious house. A rag carpet covered the floor and the furniture was of the plainest kind, but the woman who lay outstretched on the stiff, old-fashioned lounge opposite the door was far from being in accord with the homely type of her surroundings. Though the victim of a violent death, her face and form, both of a beauty seldom to be found among women of any station, were so majestic in their calm repose, that Mr. Sutherland, accustomed as he was to her noble appearance, experienced a shock of surprise that found vent in these words:

"Murdered! she? You have made some mistake, my friends. Look at her face!"

But even in the act of saying this his eyes fell on the blood which had dyed her cotton dress and he cried:

"Where was she struck and where is the weapon which has made this ghastly wound?"

"She was struck while standing or sitting at this table," returned the constable, pointing to two or three drops of blood on its smooth surface. "The weapon we have not found, but the wound shows that it was inflicted by a three-sided dagger."

"A three-sided dagger?"

"Yes."

"I didn't know there was such a thing in town. Philemon could have had no dagger."

"It does not seem so, but one can never tell. Simple cottages like these often contain the most unlooked-for articles."

"I cannot imagine a dagger being among its effects," declared Mr. Sutherland. "Where was the body of Mrs. Webb lying when you came in?"

"Where you see it now. Nothing has been moved or changed."

"She was found here, on this lounge, in the same position in which we see her now?"

"Yes, sir."

"But that is incredible. Look at the way she lies! Hands crossed, eyes closed, as though made ready for her burial. Only loving hands could have done this. What does it mean? "

"It means Philemon; that is what it means Philemon. "

Mr. Sutherland shuddered, but said nothing. He was dumbfounded by these evidences of a crazy man's work. Philemon Webb always seemed so harmless, though he had been failing in mind for the last ten years.

"But" cried Mr. Sutherland, suddenly rousing, "there is another victim. I saw old woman Batsy hanging from a window ledge, dead. "

"Yes, she is in this other room; but there is no wound on Batsy. "

"How was she killed, then? "

"That the doctors must tell us. "

Mr. Sutherland, guided by Mr. Fenton's gesture, entered a small room opening into the one in which they stood. His attention was at once attracted by the body of the woman he had seen from below, lying half in and half out of the open window. That she was dead was evident; but, as Mr. Fenton had said, no wound was to be seen upon her, nor were there any marks of blood on or about the place where she lay.

"This is a dreadful business, " groaned Mr. Sutherland, "the worst I have ever had anything to do with. Help me to lift the woman in; she has been long enough a show for the people outside. "

There was a bed in this room (indeed, it was Mrs. Webb's bedroom), and upon this poor Batsy was laid. As the face came uppermost both gentlemen started and looked at each other in amazement. The expression of terror and alarm which it showed was in striking contrast to the look of exaltation to be seen on the face of her dead mistress.

III

THE EMPTY DRAWER

As they re-entered the larger room, they were astonished to come upon Miss Page standing in the doorway. She was gazing at the recumbent figure of the dead woman, and for a moment seemed unconscious of their presence.

"How did you get in? Which of my men was weak enough to let you pass, against my express instructions? " asked the constable, who was of an irritable and suspicious nature.

She let the hood drop from her head, and, turning, surveyed him with a slow smile. There was witchery in that smile sufficient to affect a much more cultivated and callous nature than his, and though he had been proof against it once he could not quite resist the effect of its repetition.

"I insisted upon entering, " said she. "Do not blame the men; they did not want to use force against a woman. " She had not a good voice and she knew it; but she covered up this defect by a choice of intonations that carried her lightest speech to the heart. Hard-visaged Amos Fenton gave a grunt, which was as near an expression of approval as he ever gave to anyone.

"Well! well! " he growled, but not ill-naturedly, "it's a morbid curiosity that brings you here. Better drop it, girl; it won't do you any good in the eyes of sensible people. "

"Thank you, " was her demure reply, her lips dimpling at the corners in a way to shock the sensitive Mr. Sutherland.

Glancing from her to the still outlines of the noble figure on the couch, he remarked with an air of mild reproof:

"I do not understand you, Miss Page. If this solemn sight has no power to stop your coquetries, nothing can. As for your curiosity, it is both ill-timed and unwomanly. Let me see you leave this house at once, Miss Page; and if in the few hours which must elapse before breakfast you can find time to pack your trunks, you will still farther oblige me. "

"Oh, don't send me away, I entreat you."

It was a cry from her inner heart, which she probably regretted, for she instantly sought to cover up her inadvertent self-betrayal by a submissive bend of the head and a step backward. Neither Mr. Fenton nor Mr. Sutherland seemed to hear the one or see the other, their attention having returned to the more serious matter in hand.

"The dress which our poor friend wears shows her to have been struck before retiring," commented Mr. Sutherland, after another short survey of Mrs. Webb's figure. "If Philemon—"

"Excuse me, sir," interrupted the voice of the young man who had been left in the hall, "the lady is listening to what you say. She is still at the head of the stairs."

"She is, is she!" cried Fenton, sharply, his admiration for the fascinating stranger having oozed out at his companion's rebuff. "I will soon show her—" But the words melted into thin air as he reached the door. The young girl had disappeared, and only a faint perfume remained in the place where she had stood.

"A most extraordinary person," grumbled the constable, turning back, but stopping again as a faint murmur came up from below.

"The gentleman is waking," called up a voice whose lack of music was quite perceptible at a distance.

With a bound Mr. Fenton descended the stairs, followed by Mr. Sutherland.

Miss Page stood before the door of the room in which sat Philemon Webb. As they reached her side, she made a little bow that was half mocking, half deprecatory, and slipped from the house. An almost unbearable sensation of incongruity vanished with her, and Mr. Sutherland, for one, breathed like a man relieved.

"I wish the doctor would come," Fenton said, as they watched the slow lifting of Philemon Webb's head. "Our fastest rider has gone for him, but he's out Portchester way, and it may be an hour yet before he can get here."

"Philemon!"

Mr. Sutherland had advanced and was standing by his old friend's side.

"Philemon, what has become of your guests? You've waited for them here until morning."

The old man with a dazed look surveyed the two plates set on either side of him and shook his head.

"James and John are getting proud," said he, "or they forget, they forget."

James and John. He must mean the Zabels, yet there were many others answering to these names in town. Mr. Sutherland made another effort.

"Philemon, where is your wife? I do not see any place set here for her!"

"Agatha's sick, Agatha's cross; she don't care for a poor old man like me."

"Agatha's dead and you know it," thundered back the constable, with ill-judged severity. "Who killed her? tell me that. Who killed her?"

A sudden quenching of the last spark of intelligence in the old man's eye was the dreadful effect of these words. Laughing with that strange gurgle which proclaims an utterly irresponsible mind, he cried:

"The pussy cat! It was the pussy cat. Who's killed? I'm not killed. Let's go to Jericho."

Mr. Sutherland took him by the arm and led him up-stairs. Perhaps the sight of his dead wife would restore him. But he looked at her with the same indifference he showed to everything else.

"I don't like her calico dresses," said he. "She might have worn silk, but she wouldn't. Agatha, will you wear silk to my funeral?"

The experiment was too painful, and they drew him away. But the constable's curiosity had been roused, and after they had found some one to take care of him, he drew Mr. Sutherland aside and said:

"What did the old man mean by saying she might have worn silk? Are they better off than they seem? " Mr. Sutherland closed the door before replying.

"They are rich, " he declared, to the utter amazement of the other. "That is, they were; but they may have been robbed; if so, Philemon was not the wretch who killed her. I have been told that she kept her money in an old-fashioned cupboard. Do you suppose they alluded to that one? "

He pointed to a door set in the wall over the fireplace, and Mr. Fenton, perceiving a key sticking in the lock, stepped quickly across the floor and opened it. A row of books met his eyes, but on taking them down a couple of drawers were seen at the back.

"Are they locked? " asked Mr. Sutherland.

"One is and one is not. "

"Open the one that is unlocked. "

Mr. Fenton did so.

"It is empty, " said he.

Mr. Sutherland cast a look toward the dead woman, and again the perfect serenity of her countenance struck him.

"I do not know whether to regard her as the victim of her husband's imbecility or of some vile robber's cupidity. Can you find the key to the other drawer? "

"I will try. "

"Suppose you begin, then, by looking on her person. It should be in her pocket, if no marauder has been here. "

"It is not in her pocket. "

"Hanging to her neck, then, by a string?"

"No; there is a locket here, but no key. A very handsome locket, Mr. Sutherland, with a child's lock of golden hair—"

"Never mind, we will see that later; it is the key we want just now."

"Good heavens!"

"What is it?"

"It is in her hand; the one that lies underneath."

"Ah! A point, Fenton."

"A great point."

"Stand by her, Fenton. Don't let anyone rob her of that key till the coroner comes, and we are at liberty to take it."

"I will not leave her for an instant."

"Meanwhile, I will put back these books."

He had scarcely done so when a fresh arrival occurred. This time it was one of the village clergymen.

IV

THE FULL DRAWER

This gentleman had some information to give. It seems that at an early hour of this same night he had gone by this house on his way home from the bedside of a sick parishioner. As he was passing the gate he was run into by a man who came rushing out of the yard, in a state of violent agitation. In this man's hand was something that glittered, and though the encounter nearly upset them both, he had not stopped to utter an apology, but stumbled away out of sight with a hasty but infirm step, which showed he was neither young nor active. The minister had failed to see his face, but noticed the ends of a long beard blowing over his shoulder as he hurried away.

Philemon was a clean-shaven man.

Asked if he could give the time of this encounter, he replied that it was not far from midnight, as he was in his own house by half- past twelve.

"Did you glance up at these windows in passing? " asked Mr. Fenton.

"I must have; for I now remember they were both lighted. "

"Were the shades up? "

"I think not. I would have noticed it if they had been. "

"How were the shades when you broke into the house this morning? " inquired Mr. Sutherland of the constable.

"Just as they are now; we have moved nothing. The shades were both down—one of them over an open window. "

"Well, we may find this encounter of yours with this unknown man a matter of vital importance, Mr. Crane. "

"I wish I had seen his face. "

"What do you think the object was you saw glittering in his hand? "

"I should not like to say; I saw it but an instant. "

"Could it have been a knife or an old-fashioned dagger? "

"It might have been. "

"Alas! poor Agatha! That she, who so despised money, should fall a victim to man's cupidity! Unhappy life, unhappy death! Fenton, I shall always mourn for Agatha Webb. "

"Yet she seems to have found peace at last, " observed the minister. "I have never seen her look so contented. " And leading Mr. Sutherland aside, he whispered: "What is this you say about money? Had she, in spite of appearances, any considerable amount? I ask, because in spite of her humble home and simple manner of living, she always put more on the plate than any of her neighbours. Besides which, I have from time to time during my pastorate received anonymously certain contributions, which, as they were always for sick or suffering children—"

"Yes, yes; they came from her, I have no doubt of it. She was by no means poor, though I myself never knew the extent of her means till lately. Philemon was a good business man once; but they evidently preferred to live simply, having no children living—"

"They have lost six, I have been told. "

"So the Portchester folks say. They probably had no heart for display or for even the simplest luxuries. At all events, they did not indulge in them. "

"Philemon has long been past indulging in anything. "

"Oh, he likes his comfort, and he has had it too. Agatha never stinted him. "

"But why do you think her death was due to her having money? "

"She had a large sum in the house, and there are those in town who knew this. "

"And is it gone? "

"That we shall know later."

As the coroner arrived at this moment, the minister's curiosity had to wait. Fortunately for his equanimity, no one had the presumption to ask him to leave the room.

The coroner was a man of but few words, and but little given to emotion. Yet they were surprised at his first question:

"Who is the young woman standing outside there, the only one in the yard?"

Mr. Sutherland, moving rapidly to the window, drew aside the shade.

"It is Miss Page, my housekeeper's niece," he explained. "I do not understand her interest in this affair. She followed me here from the house and could hardly be got to leave this room, into which she intruded herself against my express command."

"But look at her attitude!" It was Mr. Fenton who spoke. "She's crazier than Philemon, it seems to me."

There was some reason for this remark. Guarded by the high fence from the gaze of the pushing crowd without, she stood upright and immovable in the middle of the yard, like one on watch. The hood, which she had dropped from her head when she thought her eyes and smile might be of use to her in the furtherance of her plans, had been drawn over it again, so that she looked more like a statue in grey than a living, breathing woman. Yet there was menace in her attitude and a purpose in the solitary stand she took in that circle of board-girded grass, which caused a thrill in the breasts of those who looked at her from that chamber of death.

"A mysterious young woman," muttered the minister.

"And one that I neither countenance nor under-stand," interpolated Mr. Sutherland. "I have just shown my displeasure at her actions by dismissing her from my house."

The coroner gave him a quick look, seemed about to speak, but changed his mind and turned toward the dead woman.

"We have a sad duty before us," said he.

The investigations which followed elicited one or two new facts. First, that all the doors of the house were found unlocked; and, secondly, that the constable had been among the first to enter, so that he could vouch that no disarrangement had been made in the rooms, with the exception of Batsy's removal to the bed.

Then, his attention being drawn to the dead woman, he discovered the key in her tightly closed hand.

"Where does this key belong?" he asked.

They showed him the drawers in the cupboard.

"One is empty," remarked Mi. Sutherland. "If the other is found to be in the same condition, then her money has been taken. That key she holds should open both these drawers."

"Then let it be made use of at once. It is important that we should know whether theft has been committed here as well as murder." And drawing the key out, he handed it to Mr. Fenton.

The constable immediately unlocked the drawer and brought it and its contents to the table.

"No money here," said he.

"But papers as good as money," announced the doctor. "See! here are deeds and more than one valuable bond. I judge she was a richer woman than any of us knew."

Mr. Sutherland, meantime, was looking with an air of disappointment into the now empty drawer.

"Just as I feared," said he. "She has been robbed of her ready money. It was doubtless in the other drawer."

"How came she by the key, then?"

"That is one of the mysteries of the affair; this murder is by no means a simple one. I begin to think we shall find it full of mysteries."

"Batsy's death, for instance?"

"O yes, Batsy! I forgot that she was found dead too."

"Without a wound, doctor."

"She had heart disease. I doctored her for it. The fright has killed her."

"The look of her face confirms that."

"Let me see! So it does; but we must have an autopsy to prove it."

"I would like to explain before any further measures are taken, how I came to know that Agatha Webb had money in her house," said Mr. Sutherland, as they stepped back into the other room. "Two days ago, as I was sitting with my family at table, old gossip Judy came in. Had Mrs. Sutherland been living, this old crone would not have presumed to intrude upon us at mealtime, but as we have no one now to uphold our dignity, this woman rushed into our presence panting with news, and told us all in one breath how she had just come from Mrs. Webb; that Mrs. Webb had money; that she had seen it, she herself; that, going into the house as usual without knocking, she had heard Agatha stepping overhead and had gone up; and finding the door of the sitting-room ajar, had looked in, and seen Agatha crossing the room with her hands full of bills; that these bills were big bills, for she heard Agatha cry, as she locked them up in the cupboard behind the book-shelves, 'A thousand dollars! That is too much money to have in one's house'; that she, Judy, thought so too, and being frightened at what she had seen, had crept away as silently as she had entered and run away to tell the neighbours. Happily, I was the first she found up that morning, but I have no doubt that, in spite of my express injunctions, she has since related the news to half the people in town."

"Was the young woman down yonder present when Judy told this story?" asked the coroner, pointing towards the yard.

Mr. Sutherland pondered. "Possibly; I do not remember. Frederick was seated at the table with me, and my housekeeper was pouring out the coffee, but it was early for Miss Page. She has been putting on great airs of late."

"Can it be possible he is trying to blind himself to the fact that his son Frederick wishes to marry this girl? " muttered the clergyman into the constable's ear.

The constable shook his head. Mr. Sutherland was one of those debonair men, whose very mildness makes them impenetrable.

V

A SPOT ON THE LAWN

The coroner, on leaving the house, was followed by Mr. Sutherland. As the fine figures of the two men appeared on the doorstep, a faint cheer was heard from the two or three favoured persons who were allowed to look through the gate. But to this token of welcome neither gentleman responded by so much as a look, all their attention being engrossed by the sight of the solitary figure of Miss Page, who still held her stand upon the lawn. Motionless as a statue, but with her eyes fixed upon their faces, she awaited their approach. When they were near her she thrust one hand from under her cloak, and pointing to the grass at her feet, said quietly:

"See this? "

They hastened towards her and bent down to examine the spot she indicated.

"What do you find there? " cried Mr. Sutherland, whose eyesight was not good.

"Blood, " responded the coroner, plucking up a blade of grass and surveying it closely.

"Blood, " echoed Miss Page, with so suggestive a glance that Mr. Sutherland stared at her in amazement, not understanding his own emotion.

"How were you able to discern a stain so nearly imperceptible? " asked the coroner.

"Imperceptible? It is the only thing I see in the whole yard, " she retorted, and with a slight bow, which was not without its element of mockery, she turned toward the gate.

"A most unaccountable girl, " commented the doctor. "But she is right about these stains. Abel, " he called to the man at the gate, "bring a box or barrel here and cover up this spot. I don't want it disturbed by trampling feet. "

Abel started to obey, just as the young girl laid her hand on the gate to open it.

"Won't you help me?" she asked. "The crowd is so great they won't let me through."

"Won't they?" The words came from without. "Just slip out as I slip in, and you'll find a place made for you."

Not recognising the voice, she hesitated for a moment, but seeing the gate swaying, she pushed against it just as a young man stepped through the gap. Necessarily they came face to face.

"Ah, it's you," he muttered, giving her a sharp glance.

"I do not know you," she haughtily declared, and slipped by him with such dexterity she was out of the gate before he could respond.

But he only snapped his finger and thumb mockingly at her, and smiled knowingly at Abel, who had lingered to watch the end of this encounter.

"Supple as a willow twig, eh?" he laughed. "Well, I have made whistles out of willows before now, and hallo! where did you get that?"

He was pointing to a rare flower that hung limp and faded from Abel's buttonhole.

"This? Oh, I found it in the house yonder. It was lying on the floor of the inner room, almost under Batsy's skirts. Curious sort of flower. I wonder where she got it?"

The intruder betrayed at once an unaccountable emotion. There was a strange glitter in his light green eyes that made Abel shift rather uneasily on his feet. "Was that before this pretty minx you have just let out came in here with Mr. Sutherland?"

"O yes; before anyone had started for the hill at all. Why, what has this young lady got to do with a flower dropped by Batsy?"

"She? Nothing. Only—and I have never given you bad advice, Abel— don't let that thing hang any longer from your buttonhole.

Put it into an envelope and keep it, and if you don't hear from me again in regard to it, write me out a fool and forget we were ever chums when little shavers. "

The man called Abel smiled, took out the flower, and went to cover up the grass as Dr. Talbot had requested. The stranger took his place at the gate, toward which the coroner and Mr. Sutherland were now advancing, with an air that showed his great anxiety to speak with them. He was the musician whom we saw secretly entering the last-mentioned gentleman's house after the departure of the servants.

As the coroner paused before him he spoke. "Dr. Talbot, " said he, dropping his eyes, which were apt to betray his thoughts too plainly, "you have often promised that you would give me a job if any matter came up where any nice detective work was wanted. Don't you think the time has come to remember me? "

"You, Sweetwater? I'm afraid the affair is too deep for an inexperienced man's first effort. I shall have to send to Boston for an expert. Another time, Sweetwater, when the complications are less serious. "

The young fellow, with a face white as milk, was turning away.

"But you'll let me stay around here? " he pleaded, pausing and giving the other an imploring look.

"O yes, " answered the good-natured coroner. "Fenton will have work enough for you and half a dozen others. Go and tell him I sent you. "

"Thank you, " returned the other, his face suddenly losing its aspect of acute disappointment. "Now I shall see where that flower fell, " he murmured.

VI

"BREAKFAST IS SERVED, GENTLEMEN! "

Mr. Sutherland returned home. As he entered the broad hall he met his son, Frederick. There was a look on the young man's face such as he had not seen there in years.

"Father, " faltered the youth, "may I have a few words with you? "

The father nodded kindly, though it is likely he would have much preferred his breakfast; and the young man led him into a little sitting-room littered with the faded garlands and other tokens of the preceding night's festivities.

"I have an apology to make, " Frederick began, "or rather, I have your forgiveness to ask. For years" he went on, stumbling over his words, though he gave no evidence of a wish to restrain them—"for years I have gone contrariwise to your wishes and caused my mother's heart to ache and you to wish I had never been born to be a curse to you and her. "

He had emphasised the word mother, and spoke altogether with force and deep intensity. Mr. Sutherland stood petrified; he had long ago given up this lad as lost.

"I—I wish to change. I wish to be as great a pride to you as I have been a shame and a dishonour. I may not succeed at once; but I am in earnest, and if you will give me your hand—"

The old man's arms were round the young man's shoulders at once.

"Frederick! " he cried, "my Frederick! "

"Do not make me too much ashamed, " murmured the youth, very pale and strangely discomposed. "With no excuse for my past, I suffer intolerable apprehension in regard to my future, lest my good intentions should fail or my self-control not hold out. But the knowledge that you are acquainted with my resolve, and regard it with an undeserved sympathy, may suffice to sustain me, and I should certainly be a base poltroon if I should disappoint you or her twice. "

He paused, drew himself from his father's arms, and glanced almost solemnly out of the window. "I swear that I will henceforth act as if she were still alive and watching me."

There was strange intensity in his manner. Mr. Sutherland regarded him with amazement. He had seen him in every mood natural to a reckless man, but never in so serious a one, never with a look of awe or purpose in his face. It gave him quite a new idea of Frederick.

"Yes," the young man went on, raising his right hand, but not removing his eyes from the distant prospect on which they were fixed, "I swear that I will henceforth do nothing to discredit her memory. Outwardly and inwardly, I will act as though her eye were still upon me and she could again suffer grief at my failures or thrill with pleasure at my success."

A portrait of Mrs. Sutherland, painted when Frederick was a lad of ten, hung within a few feet of him as he spoke. He did not glance at it, but Mr. Sutherland did, and with a look as if he expected to behold a responsive light beam from those pathetic features.

"She loved you very dearly," was his slow and earnest comment. "We have both loved you much more deeply than you have ever seemed to realise, Frederick."

"I believe it," responded the young man, turning with an expression of calm resolve to meet his father's eye. "As proof that I am no longer insensible to your affection, I have made up my mind to forego for your sake one of the dearest wishes of my heart. Father" he hesitated before he spoke the word, but he spoke it firmly at last, —"am I right in thinking you would not like Miss Page for a daughter?"

"Like my housekeeper's niece to take the place in this house once occupied by Marietta Sutherland? Frederick, I have always thought too well of you to believe you would carry your forgetfulness of me so far as that, even when I saw that you were influenced by her attractions."

"You did not do justice to my selfishness, father. I did mean to marry her, but I have given up living solely for myself, and she could never help me to live for others. Father, Amabel Page must not remain in this house to cause division between you and me."

"I have already intimated to her the desirability of her quitting a home where she is no longer respected, " the old gentleman declared. "She leaves on the 10.45 train. Her conduct this morning at the house of Mrs. Webb—who perhaps you do not know was most cruelly and foully murdered last night—was such as to cause comment and make her an undesirable adjunct to any gentleman's family. "

Frederick paled. Something in these words had caused him a great shock. Mr. Sutherland was fond enough to believe that it was the news of this extraordinary woman's death. But his son's words, as soon as lie could find any, showed that his mind was running on Amabel, whom he perhaps had found it difficult to connect even in the remotest way with crime.

"She at this place of death? How could that be? Who would take a young girl there? "

The father, experiencing, perhaps, more compassion for this soon-to-be-disillusioned lover than he thought it incumbent upon him to show, answered shortly, but without any compromise of the unhappy truth:

"She went; she was not taken. No one, not even myself, could keep her back after she had heard that a murder had been committed in the town. She even intruded into the house; and when ordered out of the room of death took up her stand in the yard in front, where she remained until she had the opportunity of pointing out to us a stain of blood on the grass, which might otherwise have escaped our attention. "

"Impossible! " Frederick's eye was staring; he looked like a man struck dumb by surprise or fear. "Amabel do this? You are mocking me, sir, or I may be dreaming, which may the good God grant. "

His father, who had not looked for so much emotion, eyed his son in surprise, which rapidly changed to alarm as the young man faltered and fell back against the wall.

"You are ill, Frederick; you are really ill. Let me call down Mrs. Harcourt. But no, I cannot summon her. She is this girl's aunt. "

Frederick made an effort and stood up.

"Do not call anybody, " he entreated. "I expect to suffer some in casting this fascinating girl out of my heart. Ultimately I will conquer the weakness; indeed I will. As for her interest in Mrs. Webb's death"—how low his voice sank and how he trembled! " she may have been better friends with her than we had any reason to suppose. I can think of no other motive for her conduct. Admiration for Mrs. Webb and horror—-"

"Breakfast is served, gentlemen! " cried a thrilling voice behind them. Amabel Page stood smiling in the doorway.

VII

"MARRY ME"

"Wait a moment, I must speak to you. " It was Amabel who was holding Frederick back. She had caught him by the arm as he was about leaving the room with his father, and he felt himself obliged to stop and listen.

"I start for Springfield to-day, " she announced. "I have another relative there living at the house. When shall I have the pleasure of seeing you in my new home? "

"Never. " It was said regretfully, and yet with a certain brusqueness, occasioned perhaps by over-excited feeling. "Hard as it is for me to say it, Amabel, it is but just for me to tell you that after our parting here to-day we will meet only as strangers. Friendship between us would be mockery, and any closer relationship has become impossible. "

It had cost him an immense effort to say these words, and he expected, fondly expected, I must admit, to see her colour change and her head droop. But instead of this she looked at him steadily for a moment, then slipped her hand down his arm till she reached his palm, which she pressed with sudden warmth, drawing him into the room as she did so, and shutting the door behind them. He was speechless, for she never had looked so handsome or so glowing. Instead of showing depression or humiliation even, she confronted him with a smile more dangerous than any display of grief, for it contained what it had hitherto lacked, positive and irresistible admiration. Her words were equally dangerous.

"I kiss your hand, as the Spaniards say. " And she almost did so, with a bend of her head, which just allowed him to catch a glimpse of two startling dimples.

He was astounded. He thought he knew this woman well, but at this moment she was as incomprehensible to him as if he had never made a study of her caprices and sought an explanation for her ever-shifting expressions.

"I am sensible of the honour, " said he, "but hardly understand how I have earned it. "

Still that incomprehensible look of admiration continued to illumine her face.

"I did not know I could ever think so well of you, " she declared. "If you do not take care, I shall end by loving you some day. "

"Ah! " he ejaculated, his face contracting with sudden pain; "your love, then, is but a potentiality. Very well, Amabel, keep it so and you will be spared much misery. As for me, who have not been as wise as you—-"

"Frederick! " She had come so near he did not have the strength to finish. Her face, with its indefinable charm, was raised to his, as she dropped these words one by one from her lips in lingering cadence: "Frederick—do you love me, then, so very much? "

He was angry; possibly because he felt his resolution failing him. "You know! " he hotly began, stepping back. Then with a sudden burst of feeling, that was almost like prayer, he resumed: "Do not tempt me, Amabel. I have trouble enough, without lamenting the failure of my first steadfast purpose. "

"Ah! " she said, stopping where she was, but drawing him toward her by every witchery of which her mobile features were capable; "your generous impulse has strengthened into a purpose, has it? Well, I'm not worth it, Frederick. "

More and more astounded, understanding her less than ever, but charmed by looks that would have moved an anchorite, he turned his head away in a vain attempt to escape an influence that was so rapidly undermining his determination.

She saw the movement, recognised the weakness it bespoke, and in the triumph of her heart allowed a low laugh to escape her.

Her voice, as I have before said, was unmusical though effective; but her laugh was deliciously sweet, especially when it was restrained to a mere ripple, as now.

"You will come to Springfield soon, " she avowed, slipping from before him so as to leave the way to the door open.

"Amabel! " His voice was strangely husky, and the involuntary opening and shutting of his hands revealed the emotion under which he was labouring. "Do you love me? You have acknowledged it now and then, but always as if you did not mean it. Now you acknowledge that you may some day, and this time as if you did mean it. What is the truth? Tell me, without coquetry or dissembling, for I am in dead earnest, and—-" He paused, choked, and turned toward the window where but a few minutes before he had taken that solemn oath. The remembrance of it seemed to come back with the movement. Flushing with a new agitation, he wheeled upon her sharply. "No, no, " he prayed, "say nothing. If you swore you did not love me I should not believe it, and if you swore that you did I should only find it harder to repeat what must again be said, that a union between us can never take place. I have given my solemn promise to—-"

"Well, well. Why do you stop? Am I so hard to talk to that the words will not leave your lips? "

"I have promised my father I will never marry you. He feels that he has grounds of complaint against you, and as I owe him everything—-"

He stopped amazed. She was looking at him intently, that same low laugh still on her lips.

"Tell the truth, " she whispered. "I know to what extent you consider your father's wishes. You think you ought not to marry me after what took place last night. Frederick, I like you for this evidence of consideration on your part, but do not struggle too relentlessly with your conscience. I can forgive much more in you than you think, and if you really love me—-"

"Stop! Let us understand each other. " He had turned mortally pale, and met her eyes with something akin to alarm. "What do you allude to in speaking of last night? I did not know there was anything said by us in our talk together—-"

"I do not allude to our talk. "

"Or—or in the one dance we had—-"

"Frederick, a dance is innocent."

The word seemed to strike him with the force of a blow.

"Innocent," he repeated, "innocent?" becoming paler still as the full weight of her meaning broke gradually upon him.

"I followed you into town," she whispered, coming closer, and breathing the words into his ear. "But what I saw you do there will not prevent me from obeying you if you say: 'Follow me wherever I go, Amabel; henceforth our lives are one.'"

"My God!"

It was all he said, but it seemed to create a gulf between them. In the silence that followed, the evil spirit latent beneath her beauty began to make itself evident even in the smile which no longer called into view the dimples which belong to guileless mirth, while upon his face, after the first paralysing effect of her words had passed, there appeared an expression of manly resistance that betrayed a virtue which as yet had never appeared in his selfish and altogether reckless life.

That this was more than a passing impulse he presently made evident by lifting his hand and pushing her slowly back.

"I do not know what you saw me do," said he; "but whatever it was, it can make no difference in our relations."

Her whisper, which had been but a breath before, became scarcely audible.

"I did not pause at the gate you entered," said she. "I went in after you."

A gasp of irresistible feeling escaped him, but he did not take his eyes from her face.

"It was a long time before you came out," she went on, "but previous to that time the shade of a certain window was thrust aside, and—-"

"Hush!" he commanded, in uncontrollable passion, pressing his hand with impulsive energy against her mouth. "Not another word of that, or I shall forget you are a woman or that I have ever loved you."

Her eyes, which were all she had remaining to plead with, took on a peculiar look of quiet satisfaction, and power. Seeing it, he let his hand fall and for the first time began to regard her with anything but a lover's eyes.

"I was the only person in sight at that time," she continued. "You have nothing to fear from the world at large."

"Fear?"

The word made its own echo; she had no need to emphasise it even by a smile. But she watched him as it sunk into his consciousness with an intentness it took all his strength to sustain. Suddenly her bearing and expression changed. The few remains of sweetness in her face vanished, and even the allurement which often lasts when the sweetness is gone, disappeared in the energy which now took possession of her whole threatening and inflexible personality.

"Marry me," she cried, "or I will proclaim you to be the murderer of Agatha Webb."

She had seen the death of love in his eyes.

VIII

"A DEVIL THAT UNDERSTANDS MEN"

Frederick Sutherland was a man of finer mental balance than he himself, perhaps, had ever realised. After the first few moments of stupefaction following the astounding alternative which had been given him, he broke out with the last sentence she probably expected to hear:

"What do you hope from a marriage with me, that to attain your wishes you thus sacrifice every womanly instinct?"

She met him on his own ground.

"What do I hope?" She actually glowed with the force of her secret desire. "Can you ask a poor girl like me, born in a tenement house, but with tastes and ambitions such as are usually only given to those who can gratify them? I want to be the rich Mr. Sutherland's daughter; acknowledged or unacknowledged, the wife of one who can enter any house in Boston as an equal. With a position like that I can rise to anything. I feel that I have the natural power and aptitude. I have felt it since I was a small child."

"And for that—-" he began.

"And for that," she broke in, "I am quite willing to overlook a blot on your record. Confident that you will never repeat the risk of last night, I am ready to share the burden of your secret through life. If you treat me well, I am sure I can make that burden light for you."

With a quick flush and an increase of self-assertion, probably not anticipated by her, he faced the daring girl with a desperate resolution that showed how handsome he could be if his soul once got control of his body.

"Woman," he cried, "they were right; you are little less than a devil."

Did she regard it as a compliment? Her smile would seem to say so.

"A devil that understands men, " she answered, with that slow dip of her dimples that made her smile so dangerous. "You will not hesitate long over this matter; a week, perhaps. "

"I shall not hesitate at all. Seeing you as you are, makes my course easy. You will never share any burden with me as my wife. "

Still she was not abashed.

"It is a pity, " she whispered; "it would have saved you such unnecessary struggle. But a week is not long to wait. I am certain of you then. This day week at twelve o'clock, Frederick. "

He seized her by the arm, and lost to everything but his rage, shook her with a desperate hand.

"Do you mean it? " he cried, a sudden horror showing itself in his face, notwithstanding his efforts to conceal it.

"I mean it so much, " she assured him, "that before I came home just now I paid a visit to the copse over the way. A certain hollow tree, where you and I have held more than one tryst, conceals within its depths a package containing over one thousand dollars. Frederick, I hold your life in my hands. "

The grasp with which he held her relaxed; a mortal despair settled upon his features, and recognising the impossibility of further concealing the effect of her words upon him, he sank into a chair and covered his face with his hands. She viewed him with an air of triumph, which brought back some of her beauty. When she spoke it was to say:

"If you wish to join me in Springfield before the time I have set, well and good. I am willing that the time of our separation should be shortened, but it must not be lengthened by so much as a day. Now, if you will excuse me, I will go and pack my trunks. "

He shuddered; her voice penetrated him to the quick.

Drawing herself up, she looked down on him with a strange mixture of passion and elation.

"You need fear no indiscretion on my part, so long as our armistice lasts, " said she. "No one can drag the truth from me while any hope remains of your doing your duty by me in the way I have suggested. "

And still he did not move.

"Frederick? "

Was it her voice that was thus murmuring his name? Can the tiger snarl one moment and fawn the next?

"Frederick, I have a final word to say—a last farewell. Up to this hour I have endured your attentions, or, let us say, accepted them, for I always found you handsome and agreeable, if not the master of my heart. But now it is love that I feel, love; and love with me is no fancy, but a passion—do you hear? —a passion which will make life a heaven or hell for the man who has inspired it. You should have thought of this when you opposed me. "

And with a look in which love and hatred contended for mastery, she bent and imprinted a kiss upon his forehead. Next moment she was gone.

Or so he thought. But when, after an interval of nameless recoil, he rose and attempted to stagger from the place, he discovered that she had been detained in the hall by two or three men who had just come in by the front door.

"Is this Miss Page? " they were asking.

"Yes, I am Miss Page—Amabel Page" she replied with suave politeness. "If you have any business with me, state it quickly, for I am about to leave town. "

"That is what we wish to prevent, " declared a tall, thin young man who seemed to take the lead. "Till the inquest has been held over the remains of Mrs. Webb, Coroner Talbot wishes you to regard yourself as a possible witness. "

"Me? " she cried, with an admirable gesture of surprise and a wide opening of her brown eyes that made her look like an astonished child. "What have I got to do with it? "

"You pointed out a certain spot of blood on the grass, and—well, the coroner's orders have to be obeyed, miss. You cannot leave the town without running the risk of arrest"

"Then I will stay in it, " she smiled. "I have no liking for arrests, " and the glint of her eye rested for a moment on Frederick. "Mr. Sutherland, " she continued, as that gentleman appeared at the dining-room door, "I shall have to impose upon your hospitality for a few days longer. These men here inform me that my innocent interest in pointing out to you that spot of blood on Mrs. Webb's lawn has awakened some curiosity, and that I am wanted as a witness by the coroner. "

Mr. Sutherland, with a quick stride, lessened the distance between himself and these unwelcome intruders. "The coroner's wishes are paramount just now, " said he, but the look he gave his son was not soon forgotten by the spectators.

IX

A GRAND WOMAN

There was but one topic discussed in the country-side that day, and that was the life and character of Agatha Webb.

Her history had not been a happy one. She and Philemon had come from Portchester some twenty or more years before to escape the sorrows associated with their native town. They had left behind them six small graves in Portchester churchyard; but though evidences of their affliction were always to be seen in the countenances of either, they had entered with so much purpose into the life of their adopted town that they had become persons of note there till Philemon's health began to fail, when Agatha quit all outside work and devoted herself exclusively to him. Of her character and winsome personality we can gather some idea from the various conversations carried on that day from Portchester Green to the shipyards in Sutherlandtown.

In Deacon Brainerd's cottage, the discussion was concerning Agatha's lack of vanity; a virtue not very common at that time among the women of this busy seaport.

"For a woman so handsome, " the good deacon was saying "(and I think I can safely call her the finest-featured woman who ever trod these streets), she showed as little interest in dress as anyone I ever knew. Calico at home and calico at church, yet she looked as much of a lady in her dark-sprigged gowns as Mrs. Webster in her silks or Mrs. Parsons in her thousand-dollar sealskin. "

As this was a topic within the scope of his eldest daughter's intelligence she at once spoke up: "I never thought she needed to dress so plainly. I don't believe in such a show of poverty myself. If one is too poor to go decent, all right; but they say she had more money than most anyone in town. I wonder who is going to get the benefit of it? "

"Why, Philemon, of course; that is, as long as he lives. He doubtless had the making of it. "

"Is it true that he's gone clean out of his head since her death? " interposed a neighbour who had happened in.

"So they say. I believe widow Jones has taken him into her house. "

"Do you think, " asked a second daughter with becoming hesitation, "that he had anything to do with her death? Some of the neighbours say he struck her while in one of his crazy fits, while others declare she was killed by some stranger, equally old and almost as infirm. "

"We won't discuss the subject, " objected the deacon. "Time will show who robbed us of the greatest-hearted and most capable woman in these parts. "

"And will time show who killed Batsy? " It was a morsel of a girl who spoke; the least one of the family, but the brightest. "I'm sorry for Batsy; she always gave me cookies when I went to see Mrs. Webb. "

"Batsy was a good girl for a Swede, " allowed the deacon's wife, who had not spoken till now. "When she first came into town on the spars of that wrecked ship we all remember, there was some struggle between Agatha and me as to which of us should have her. But I didn't like the task of teaching her the name of every pot and pan she had to use in the kitchen, so I gave her up to Agatha; and it was fortunate I did, for I've never been able to understand her talk to this day. "

"I could talk with her right well, " lisped the little one. "She never called things by their Swedish names unless she was worried; and I never worried her. "

"I wonder if she would have worshipped the ground under your feet, as she did that under Agatha's? " asked the deacon, eying his wife with just the suspicion of a malicious twinkle in his eye.

"I am not the greatest-hearted and most capable woman in town, " retorted his wife, clicking her needles as she went on knitting.

In Mr. Sprague's house on the opposite side of the road, Squire Fisher was relating some old tales of bygone Portchester days. "I knew Agatha when she was a girl, " he avowed. "She had the grandest manners and the most enchanting smile of any rich or poor man's daughter between the coast and Springfield. She did not dress in calico then. She wore the gayest clothes her father could buy. her, and old Jacob was not without means to make his daughter the leading figure in town. How we young fellows did adore her, and what lengths we went to win one of her glorious smiles! Two of us, John and James Zabel, have lived bachelors for her sake to this very day; but I hadn't courage enough for that; I married and"—something between a sigh and a chuckle filled out the sentence.

"What made Philemon carry off the prize? His good looks?"

"Yes, or his good luck. It wasn't his snap; of that you may be sure. James Zabel had the snap, and he was her first choice, too, but he got into some difficulty—I never knew just what it was, but it was regarded as serious at the time—and that match was broken off. Afterwards she married Philemon. You see, I was out of it altogether; had never been in it, perhaps; but there were three good years of my life in which I thought of little else than Agatha. I admired her spirit, you see. There was something more taking in her ways than in her beauty, wonderful as that was. She ruled us with a rod of iron, and yet we worshipped her. I have wondered to see her so meek of late. I never thought she would be satisfied with a brick-floored cottage and a husband of failing wits. But no one, to my knowledge, has ever heard a complaint from her lips; and the dignity of her afflicted wifehood has far transcended the haughtiness of those days when she had but to smile to have all the youth of Portchester at her feet."

"I suppose it was the loss of so many children that reconciled her to a quiet life. A woman cannot close the eyes of six children, one after the other, without some modification taking place in her character."

"Yes, she and Philemon have been unfortunate; but she was a splendid looking girl, boys. I never see such grand-looking women now."

In a little one-storied cottage on the hillside a woman was nursing a baby and talking at the same time of Agatha Webb.

"I shall never forget the night my first baby fell sick," she faltered; "I was just out of bed myself, and having no nearer neighbours then than now, I was all alone on the hillside, Alec being away at sea. I was too young to know much about sickness, but something told me that I must have help before morning or my baby would die. Though

I could just walk across the floor, I threw a shawl around me, took my baby in my arms, and opened the door. A blinding gust of rain blew in. A terrible storm was raging and I had not noticed it, I was so taken up with the child.

"I could not face that gale. Indeed, I was so weak I fell on my knees as it struck me and became dripping wet before I could drag myself inside. The baby began to moan and everything was turning dark before me, when I heard a strong, sweet voice cry out in the roadway:

"'Is there room in this house for me till the storm has blown by? I cannot see my way down the hillside.'

"With a bursting heart I looked up. A woman was standing in the doorway, with the look of an angel in her eyes. I did not know her, but her face was one to bring comfort to the saddest heart. Holding up my baby, I cried:

"'My baby is dying; I tried to go for the doctor, but my knees bent under me. Help me, as you are a mother—I—'

"I must have fallen again, for the next thing I remember I was lying by the hearth, looking up into her face, which was bending over me. She was white as the rag I had tied about my baby's throat, and by the way her breast heaved she was either very much frightened or very sorry.

"'I wish you had the help of anyone else,' said she. 'Babies perish in my arms and wither at my breast. I cannot touch it, much as I yearn to. But let me see its face; perhaps I can tell you what is the matter with it.'

"I showed her the baby's face, and she bent over it, trembling very much, almost as much indeed as myself.

"'It is very sick,' she said, 'but if you will use the remedies I advise, I think you can save it.' And she told me what to do, and helped me all she could; but she did not lay a finger on the little darling, though from the way she watched it I saw that her heart was set on his getting better. And he did; in an hour he was sleeping peacefully, and the terrible weight was gone from my heart and from hers. When the storm stopped, and she could leave the house, she gave me a kiss; but the look she gave him meant more than kisses. God must have forgotten her goodness to me that night when He let her die so pitiable a death. "

At the minister's house they were commenting upon the look of serenity observable in her dead face.

"I have known her for thirty years, " her pastor declared, "and never before have I seen her wear a look of real peace. It is wonderful, considering the circumstances. Do you think she was so weary of her life's long struggle that she hailed any release from it, even that of violence? "

A young man, a lawyer, visiting them from New York, was the only one to answer.

"I never saw the woman you are talking about, " said he, "and know nothing of the circumstances of her death beyond what you have told me. But from the very incongruity between her expression and the violent nature of her death, I argue that there are depths to this crime which have not yet been sounded. "

"What depths? It is a simple case of murder followed by theft. To be sure we do not yet know the criminal, but money was his motive; that is clear enough. "

"Are you ready to wager that that is all there is to it? "

This was a startling proposition to the minister.

"You forget my cloth, " said he.

The young man smiled. "That is true. Pardon me. I was only anxious to show how strong my conviction was against any such easy explanation of a crime marked by such contradictory features. "

Two children on the Portchester road were exchanging boyish confidences.

"Do you know what I think about it? " asked one.

"Naw! How should I? "

"Wall, I think old Mrs. Webb got the likes of what she sent. Don't you know she had six children once, and that she killed every one of them?"

"Killed 'em — she?"

"Yes, I heard her tell granny once all about it. She said there was a blight on her house — I don't know what that is; but I guess it's something big and heavy — and that it fell on every one of her children, as fast as they came, and killed 'em."

"Then I'm glad I ben't her child."

Very different were the recollections interchanged between two middle-aged Portchester women.

"She was drinking tea at my house when her sister Sairey came running in with the news that the baby she had left at home wasn't quite right. That was her first child, you know."

"Yes, yes, for I was with her when that baby came," broke in the other, "and such joy as she showed when they told her it was alive and well I never saw. I do not know why she didn't expect it to be alive, but she didn't, and her happiness was just wonderful to see."

"Well, she didn't enjoy it long. The poor little fellow died young. But I was telling you of the night when she first heard he was ailing. Philemon had been telling a good story, and we were all laughing, when Sairey came in. I can see Agatha now. She always had the most brilliant eyes in the county, but that day they were superbly dazzling. They changed, though, at the sight of Sairey's face, and she jumped to meet her just as if she knew what Sairey was going to say before ever a word left her lips. 'My baby!' (I can hear her yet.) 'Something is the matter with the baby!' And though Sairey made haste to tell her that he was only ailing and not at all ill, she turned upon Philemon with a look none of us ever quite understood; he changed so completely under it, just as she had under Sairey's; and to neither did the old happiness ever return, for the child died within a week, and when the next came it died also, and the next, till six small innocents lay buried in yonder old graveyard."

"I know; and sad enough it was too, especially as she and Philemon were both fond of children. Well, well, the ways of Providence are past rinding out! And now she is gone and Philemon—-"

"Ah, he'll follow her soon; he can't live without Agatha."

Nearer home, the old sexton was chattering about the six gravestones raised in Portchester churchyard to these six dead infants. He had been sent there to choose a spot in which to lay the mother, and was full of the shock it gave him to see that line of little stones, telling of a past with which the good people of Sutherlandtown found it hard to associate Philemon and Agatha Webb.

"I'm a digger of graves, " he mused, half to himself and half to his old wife watching him from the other side of the hearthstone. "I spend a good quarter of my time in the churchyard; but when I saw those six little mounds, and read the inscriptions over them, I couldn't help feeling queer. Think of this! On the first tiny headstone I read these words: "

STEPHEN,

Son of Philemon and Agatha Webb,

Died, Aged Six Weeks.

God be merciful to me a sinner!

"Now what does that mean? Did you ever hear anyone say? "

"No, " was his old wife's answer. "Perhaps she was one of those Calvinist folks who believe babies go to hell if they are not baptised. "

"But her children were all baptised. I've been told so; some of them before she was well out of her bed. 'God be merciful to me a sinner! ' And the chick not six weeks old! Something queer about that, dame, if it did happen more than thirty years ago. "

"What did you see over the grave of the child who was killed in her arms by lightning? "

"This:

"'And he was not, for God took him.'"

Farmer Waite had but one word to say:

"She came to me when my Sissy had the smallpox; the only person in town who would enter my doors. More than that; when Sissy was up and I went to pay the doctor's bill I found it had been settled. I did not know then who had enough money and compassion to do this for me; now I do."

Many an act of kindness which had been secretly performed in that town during the last twenty years came to light on that day, the most notable of which was the sending of a certain young lad to school and his subsequent education as a minister.

But other memories of a sweeter and more secret nature still came up likewise, among them the following:

A young girl, who was of a very timid but deeply sensitive nature, had been urged into an engagement with a man she did not like. Though the conflict this occasioned her and the misery which accompanied it were apparent to everybody, nobody stirred in her behalf but Agatha. She went to see her, and, though it was within a fortnight of the wedding, she did not hesitate to advise the girl to give him up, and when the poor child said she lacked the courage, Agatha herself went to the man and urged him into a display of generosity which saved the poor, timid thing from a life of misery. They say this was no easy task for Agatha, and that the man was sullen for a year. But the girl's gratitude was boundless.

Of her daring, which was always on the side of right and justice, the stories were numerous; so were the accounts, mostly among the women, of her rare tenderness and sympathy for the weak and the erring. Never was a man talked to as she talked to Jake Cobleigh the evening after he struck his mother, and if she had been in town on the day when Clarissa Mayhew ran away with that Philadelphia adventurer many said it would never have happened, for no girl could stand the admonition, or resist the pleading, of this childless mother.

It was reserved for Mr. Halliday and Mr. Sutherland to talk of her mental qualities. Her character was so marked and her manner so simple that few gave attention to the intellect that was the real basis of her power. The two mentioned gentlemen, however, appreciated her to the full, and it was while listening to their remarks that Frederick was suddenly startled by some one saying to him:

"You are the only person in town who have nothing to say about Agatha Webb. Didn't you ever exchange any words with her? —for I can hardly believe you could have met her eye to eye without having some remark to make about her beauty or her influence."

The speaker was Agnes Halliday, who had come in with her father for a social chat. She was one of Frederick's earliest playmates, but one with whom he had never assimilated and who did not like him. He knew this, as did everyone else in town, and it was with some hesitation he turned to answer her.

"I have but one recollection," he began, and for the moment got no farther, for in turning his head to address his young guest he had allowed his gaze to wander through the open window by which she sat, into the garden beyond, where Amabel could be seen picking flowers. As he spoke, Amabel lifted her face with one of her suggestive looks. She had doubtless heard Miss Halliday's remark.

Recovering himself with an effort, he repeated his words: "I have but one recollection of Mrs. Webb that I can give you. Years ago when I was a lad I was playing on the green with several other boys. We had had some dispute about a lost ball, and I was swearing angrily and loud when I suddenly perceived before me the tall form and compassionate face of Mrs. Webb. She was dressed in her usual simple way, and had a basket on her arm, but she looked so superior to any other woman I had ever met that I did not know whether to hide my face in her skirts or to follow my first impulse and run away. She saw the emotion she had aroused, and lifting up my face by the chin, she said: 'Little boy, I have buried six children, all of them younger than you, and now my husband and myself live alone. Often and often have I wished that one at least of these darling infants might have been spared us. But had God given me the choice of having them die young and innocent, or of growing up to swear as I have heard you to-day, I should have prayed God to take them, as He did. You have a mother. Do not break her heart by taking in vain the name of the God she reveres.' And with that she kissed me, and, strange as it may seem to you, in whatever folly or wickedness I have indulged, I have never made use of an oath from that day to this—and I thank God for it."

There was such unusual feeling in his voice, a feeling that none had ever suspected him capable of before, that Miss Halliday regarded him with astonishment and quite forgot to indulge in her usual banter. Even the gentlemen sat still, and there was a momentary silence, through which there presently broke the incongruous sound of a shrill and mocking laugh.

It came from Amabel, who had just finished gathering her bouquet in the garden outside.

X

DETECTIVE KNAPP ARRIVES

Meanwhile, in a small room at the court-house, a still more serious conversation was in progress. Dr. Talbot, Mr. Fenton, and a certain able lawyer in town by the name of Harvey, were in close discussion. The last had broken the silence of years, and was telling what he knew of Mrs. Webb's affairs.

He was a shrewd man, of unblemished reputation. When called upon to talk, he talked well, but he much preferred listening, and was, as now appeared, the safest repository of secrets to be found in all that region. He had been married three times, and could still count thirteen children around his board, one reason, perhaps, why he had learned to cultivate silence to such a degree. Happily, the time had come for him to talk, and he talked. This is what he said:

"Some fifteen years ago Philemon Webb came to me with a small sum of money, which he said he wished to have me invest for his wife. It was the fruit of a small speculation of his and he wanted it given unconditionally to her without her knowledge or that of the neighbours. I accordingly made out a deed of gift, which he signed with joyful alacrity, and then after due thought and careful investigation, I put the money into a new enterprise then being started in Boston. It was the best stroke of business I ever did in my life. At the end of a year it paid double, and after five had rolled away the accumulated interest had reached such a sum that both Philemon and myself thought it wisest to let her know what she was worth and what was being done with the money. I was in hopes it would lead her to make some change in her mode of living, which seemed to me out of keeping with her appearance and mental qualifications; while he, I imagine, looked for something more important still—a smile on the face which had somehow lost the trick of merriment, though it had never acquired that of ill nature. But we did not know Agatha; at least I did not. When she learned that she was rich, she looked at first awestruck and then heart-pierced. Forgetting me, or ignoring me, it makes no matter which, she threw herself into Philemon's arms and wept, while he, poor faithful fellow, looked as distressed as if he had brought news of failure instead of triumphant success. I suppose she thought of her buried children, and what the money would have been to her if they had lived; but she did not speak of them, nor am I quite sure they were in her thoughts when, after the first excitement was over, she drew back and said quietly, but in a tone of strong feeling, to Philemon: 'You meant me a happy surprise, and you must not be disappointed. This is heart money; we will use it to make our townsfolk happy. ' I saw him glance at her dress, which was a purple calico. I remember it because of that look and because of the sad smile with which she followed his glance. 'Can we not afford now, ' he ventured, 'a little show of luxury, or at least a ribbon or so for this beautiful throat of yours? ' She did not answer him; but her look had a rare compassion in it, a compassion, strange to say, that seemed to be expended upon him rather than upon herself. Philemon swallowed his disappointment. 'Agatha is right, ' he said to me. 'We do not need luxury. I do not know how I so far forgot myself as to mention it. ' That was ten years ago, and every day since then her property has increased. I did not know then, and I do not know now, why they were both so anxious that all knowledge of their good fortune should be kept from those about them; but that it was to be &o kept was made very evident to me; and, notwithstanding all temptations to the contrary, I have refrained from uttering a word likely to give away their secret. The money, which to all appearance was the cause of her tragic and untimely death, was interest money which I was delegated to deliver her. I took it to her day before yesterday, and it was all in crisp new notes, some of them twenties, but most of them tens and fives. I am free to say there was not such another roll of fresh money in town. "

"Warn all shopkeepers to keep a sharp lookout for new bills in the money they receive, " was Dr. Talbot's comment to the constable. "Fresh ten-and twenty-dollar bills are none too common in this town. And now about her will. Did you draw that up, Harvey? "

"No. I did not know she had made one. I often spoke to her about the advisability of her doing so, but she always put me off. And now it seems that she had it drawn up in Boston. Could not trust her old friend with too many secrets, I suppose. "

"So you don't know how her money has been left? "

"No more than you do. "

Here an interruption occurred. The door opened and a slim young man, wearing spectacles, came in. At sight of him they all rose.

"Well?" eagerly inquired Dr. Talbot.

"Nothing new," answered the young man, with a consequential air. "The elder woman died from loss of blood consequent upon a blow given by a small, three-sided, slender blade; the younger from a stroke of apoplexy, induced by fright."

"Good! I am glad to hear my instincts were not at fault. Loss of blood, eh? Death, then, was not instantaneous?"

"No."

"Strange!" fell from the lips of his two listeners. "She lived, yet gave no alarm."

"None that was heard," suggested the young doctor, who was from another town.

"Or, if heard, reached no ears but Philemon's," observed the constable. "Something must have taken him upstairs."

"I am not so sure," said the coroner, "that Philemon is not answerable for the whole crime, notwithstanding our failure to find the missing money anywhere in the house. How else account for the resignation with which she evidently met her death? Had a stranger struck her, Agatha Webb would have struggled. There is no sign of struggle in the room."

"She would have struggled against Philemon had she had strength to struggle. I think she was asleep when she was struck."

"Ah! And was not standing by the table? How about the blood there, then?"

"Shaken from the murderer's fingers in fright or disgust."

"There was no blood on Philemon's fingers."

"No; he wiped them on his sleeve."

"If he was the one to use the dagger against her, where is the dagger? Should we not be able to find it somewhere about the premises?"

"He may have buried it outside. Crazy men are super naturally cunning."

"When you can produce it from any place inside that board fence, I will consider your theory. At present I limit my suspicions of Philemon to the half-unconscious attentions which a man of disordered intellect might give a wife bleeding and dying under his eyes. My idea on the subject is—-"

"Would you be so kind as not to give utterance to your ideas until I have been able to form some for myself?" interrupted a voice from the doorway.

As this voice was unexpected, they all turned. A small man with sleek dark hair and expressionless features stood before them. Behind him was Abel, carrying a hand-bag and umbrella.

"The detective from Boston," announced the latter. Coroner Talbot rose.

"You are in good time," he remarked. "We have work of no ordinary nature for you."

The man failed to look interested. But then his countenance was not one to show emotion.

"My name is Knapp," said he. "I have had my supper, and am ready to go to work. I have read the newspapers; all I want now is any additional facts that have come to light since the telegraphic dispatches were sent to Boston. Facts, mind you; not theories. I never allow myself to be hampered by other persons' theories."

Not liking his manner, which was brusque and too self-important for a man of such insignificant appearance, Coroner Talbot referred him to Mr. Fenton, who immediately proceeded to give him the result of such investigations as he and his men had been able to make; which done, Mr. Knapp put on his hat and turned toward the door.

"I will go to the house and see for myself what is to be learned there," said he. "May I ask the privilege of going alone?" he added, as Mr. Fenton moved. "Abel will see that I am given admittance."

"Show me your credentials," said the coroner. He did so. "They seem all right, and you should be a man who understands his business. Go alone, if you prefer, but bring your conclusions here. They may need some correcting."

"Oh, I will return," Knapp nonchalantly remarked, and went out, having made anything but a favourable impression upon the assembled gentlemen.

"I wish we had shown more grit and tried to handle this thing ourselves," observed Mr. Fenton. "I cannot bear to think of that cold, bloodless creature hovering over our beloved Agatha."

"I wonder at Carson. Why should he send us such a man? Could he not see the matter demanded extraordinary skill and judgment?"

"Oh, this fellow may have skill. But he is so unpleasant. I hate to deal with folks of such fish-like characteristics. But who is this?" he asked as a gentle tap was heard at the door. "Why, it's Loton. What can he want here?"

The man whose presence in the doorway had called out this exclamation started at the sound of the doctor's heavy voice, and came very hesitatingly forward. He was of a weak, irritable type, and seemed to be in a state of great excitement.

"I beg pardon," said he, "for showing myself. I don't like to intrude into such company, but I have something to tell you which may be of use, sirs, though it isn't any great thing, either."

"Something about the murder which has taken place?" asked the coroner, in a milder tone. He knew Loton well, and realised the advisability of encouragement in his case.

"The murder! Oh, I wouldn't presume to say anything about the murder. I'm not the man to stir up any such subject as that. It's about the money—or some money—more money than usually falls into my till. It—it was rather queer, sirs, and I have felt the flutter of it all day. Shall I tell you about it? It happened last night, late last night, sirs, so late that I was in bed with my wife, and had been snoring, she said, four hours."

"What money? New money? Crisp, fresh bills, Loton?" eagerly questioned Mr. Fenton.

Loton, who was the keeper of a small confectionery and bakery store on one of the side streets leading up the hill, shifted uneasily between his two interrogators, and finally addressed himself to the coroner:

"It was new money. I thought it felt so at night, but I was sure of it in the morning. A brand-new bill, sir, a—But that isn't the queerest thing about it. I was asleep, sir, sound asleep, and dreaming of my courting days (for I asked Sally at the circus, sirs, and the band playing on the hill made me think of it), when I was suddenly shook awake by Sally herself, who says she hadn't slept a wink for listening to the music and wishing she was a girl again. 'There's a man at the shop door, ' cries she. 'He's a- calling of you; go and see what he wants. ' I was mad at being wakened. Dreaming is pleasant, specially when clowns and kissing get mixed up in it, but duty is duty, and so into the shop I stumbled, swearing a bit perhaps, for I hadn't stopped for a light and it was as dark as double shutters could make it. The hammering had become deafening. No let up till I reached the door, when it suddenly ceased.

"'What is it? ' I cried. 'Who's there and what do you want? '

"A trembling voice answered me. 'Let me in, ' it said. 'I want to buy something to eat. For God's sake, open the door! '

"I don't know why I obeyed, for it was late, and I did not know the voice, but something in the impatient rattling of the door which accompanied the words affected me in spite of myself, and I slowly opened my shop to this midnight customer.

"'You must be hungry, ' I began. But the person who had crowded in as soon as the opening was large enough wouldn't let me finish.

"'Bread! I want bread, or crackers, or anything that you can find easiest, ' he gasped, like a man who had been running. 'Here's money'; and he poked into my hand a bill so stiff that it rattled. 'It's more than enough, ' he hastened to say, as I hesitated over it, 'but never mind that; I'll come for the change in the morning. '

"'Who are you? I cried. 'You are not Blind Willy, I'm sure. '

"But his only answer was 'Bread! ' while he leaned so hard against the counter I felt it shake.

"I could not stand that cry of 'Bread! ' so I groped about in the dark, and found him a stale loaf, which I put into his arms, with a short, 'There! Now tell me what your name is. '

"But at this he seemed to shrink into himself; and muttering something that might pass for thanks, he stumbled towards the door and rushed hastily out. Running after him, I listened eagerly to his steps. They went up the hill. "

"And the money? What about the money? " asked the coroner. "Didn't he come back for the change? "

"No. I put it in the till, thinking it was a dollar bill. But when I came to look at it in the morning, it was a twenty; yes, sirs, a twenty! "

This was startling. The coroner and the constable looked at each other before looking again at him.

"And where is that bill now? " asked the former. "Have you brought it with you? "

"I have, sir. It's been in and out of the till twenty times to-day. I haven't known what to do with it. I don't like to think wrong of anybody, but when I heard that Mrs. Webb (God bless her!) was murdered last night for money, I couldn't rest for the weight of this thing on my conscience. Here's the bill, sir. I wish I had let the old man rap on my door till morning before I had taken it from him. "

They did not share this feeling. A distinct and valuable clew seemed to be afforded them by the fresh, crisp bill they saw in his hand. Silently Dr. Talbot took it, while Mr. Fenton, with a shrewd look, asked:

"What reasons have you for calling this mysterious customer old? I thought it was so dark you could not see him. "

The man, who looked relieved since he had rid himself of the bill, eyed the constable in some perplexity.

"I didn't see a feature of his face, " said he, "and yet I'm sure he was old. I never thought of him as being anything else. "

"Well, we will see. And is that all you have to tell us? "

His nod was expressive, and they let him go.

An hour or so later Detective Knapp made his reappearance.

"Well, " asked the coroner, as he came quietly in and closed the door behind him, "what's your opinion? "

"Simple case, sir. Murdered for money. Find the man with a flowing beard. "

XI

THE MAN WITH A BEARD

There were but few men in town who wore long beards. A list was made of these and handed to the coroner, who regarded it with a grim smile.

"Not a man whose name is here would be guilty of a misdemeanour, let alone a crime. You must look outside of our village population for the murderer of Agatha Webb."

"Very likely, but tell me something first about these persons," urged Knapp. "Who is Edward Hope?"

"A watch repairer; a man of estimable character."

"And Sylvester Chubb?"

"A farmer who, to support his mother, wife, and seven children, works from morning till sundown on his farm, and from sundown till 11 o'clock at night on little fancy articles he cuts out from wood and sells in Boston."

"John Barker, Thomas Elder, Timothy Sinn?"

"All good men; I can vouch for every one of them."

"And John Zabel, James Zabel?"

"Irreproachable, both of them. Famous shipbuilders once, but the change to iron shipbuilding has thrown them out of business. Pity, too, for they were remarkable builders. By the by, Fenton, we don't see them at church or on the docks any more."

"No, they keep very much to themselves; getting old, like ourselves, Talbot."

"Lively boys once. We must hunt them up, Fenton. Can't bear to see old friends drop away from good company. But this isn't business. You need not pause over their names, Knapp."

Agatha Webb

But Knapp had slipped out.

We will follow him.

Walking briskly down the street, he went up the steps of a certain house and rang the bell. A gentleman with a face not entirely unknown to us came to the door.

The detective did not pause for preliminaries.

"Are you Mr. Crane? " he asked, —"the gentleman who ran against a man coming out of Mrs. Webb's house last night? "

"I am Mr. Crane, " was the slightly surprised rejoinder, "and I was run against by a man there, yes. "

"Very well, " remarked the detective, quietly, "my name is Knapp. I have been sent from Boston to look into this matter, and I have an idea that you can help me more than any other man here in Sutherlandtown. Who was this person who came in contact with you so violently? You know, even if you have been careful not to mention any names. "

"You are mistaken. I don't know; I can't know. He wore a sweeping beard, and walked and acted like a man no longer young, but beyond that—-"

"Mr. Crane, excuse me, but I know men. If you had no suspicion as to whom that person was you would not look so embarrassed. You suspect, or, at least, associate in your own mind a name with the man you met. Was it either of these you see written here? "

Mr. Crane glanced at the card on which the other had scribbled a couple of names, and started perceptibly.

"You have me, " said he; "you must be a man of remarkable perspicacity. "

The detective smiled and pocketed his card. The names he thus concealed were John Zabel, James Zabel.

"You have not said which of the two it was, " Knapp quietly suggested.

"No, " returned the minister, "and I have not even thought. Indeed, I am not sure that I have not made a dreadful mistake in thinking it was either. A glimpse such as I had is far from satisfactory; and they are both such excellent men—-"

"Eight! You did make a mistake, of course, I have not the least doubt of it. So don't think of the matter again. I will find out who the real man was; rest easy. "

And with the lightest of bows, Knapp drew off and passed as quickly as he could, without attracting attention, round the corner to the confectioner's.

Here his attack was warier. Sally Loton was behind the counter with her husband, and they had evidently been talking the matter over very confidentially. But Knapp was not to be awed by her small, keen eye or strident voice, and presently succeeded in surprising a knowing look on the lady's face, which convinced him that in the confidences between husband and wife a name had been used which she appeared to be less unwilling to impart than he. Knapp, consequently, turned his full attention towards her, using in his attack that oldest and subtlest weapon against the sex—flattery.

"My dear madam, " said he, "your good heart is apparent; your husband has confided to you a name which you, out of fear of some mistake, hesitate to repeat. A neighbourly spirit, ma'am, a very neighbourly spirit; but you should not allow your goodness to defeat the ends of justice. If you simply told us whom this man resembled we would be able to get some idea of his appearance. "

"He didn't resemble anyone I know, " growled Loton. "It was too dark for me to see how he looked. "

"His voice, then? People are traced by their voices. "

"I didn't recognise his voice. "

Knapp smiled, his eye still on the woman.

"Yet you have thought of someone he reminded you of? "

The man was silent, but the wife tossed her head ever so lightly.

"Now, you must have had your reasons for that. No one thinks of a good and respectable neighbour in connection with the buying of a loaf of bread at mid-night with a twenty-dollar bill, without some positive reason."

"The man wore a beard. I felt it brush my hand as he took the loaf."

"Good! That is a point."

"Which made me think of other men who wore beards."

"As, for instance—-"

The detective had taken from his pocket the card which he had used with such effect at the minister's, and as he said these words twirled it so that the two names written upon it fell under Sally Loton's inquisitive eyes. The look with which she read them was enough. John Zabel, James Zabel.

"Who told you it was either of these men?" she asked.

"You did," he retorted, pocketing the card with a smile.

"La, now! Samuel, I never spoke a word," she insisted, in anxious protest to her husband, as the detective slid quietly from the store.

XII

WATTLES COMES

The Hallidays lived but a few rods from the Sutherlands. Yet as it was dusk when Miss Halliday rose to depart, Frederick naturally offered his services as her escort.

She accepted them with a slight blush, the first he had ever seen on her face, or at least had ever noted there. It caused him such surprise that he forgot Amabel's presence in the garden till they came upon her at the gate.

"A pleasant evening, " observed that young girl in her high, unmusical voice.

"Very, " was Miss Halliday's short reply; and for a moment the two faces were in line as he held open the gate before his departing guest.

They were very different faces in feature and expression, and till that night he had never thought of comparing them. Indeed, the fascination which beamed from Amabel Page's far from regular features had put all others out of his mind, but now, as he surveyed the two girls, the candour and purity which marked Agnes's countenance came out so strongly under his glance that Amabel lost all attraction for him, and he drew his young neighbour hastily away.

Amabel noted the movement and smiled. Her contempt for Agnes Halliday's charms amounted to disdain.

She might have felt less confidence in her own had she been in a position to note the frequent glances Frederick cast at his old playmate as they proceeded slowly up the road. Not that there was any passion in them—he was too full of care for that; but the curiosity which could prompt him to turn his head a dozen times in the course of so short a walk, to see why Agnes Halliday held her face so persistently away from him, had an element of feeling in it that was more or less significant. As for Agnes, she was so unlike her accustomed self as to astonish even herself. Whereas she had never before walked a dozen steps with him without indulging in some sharp saying, she found herself disinclined to speak at all, much less to speak lightly. In mutual silence, then, they reached the gateway leading into the Halliday grounds. But Agnes having passed in, they both stopped and for the first time looked squarely at each other. Her eyes fell first, perhaps because his had changed in his contemplation of her. He smiled as he saw this, and in a half-careless, half-wistful tone, said quietly:

"Agnes, what would you think of a man who, after having committed little else but folly all his life, suddenly made up his mind to turn absolutely toward the right and to pursue it in face of every obstacle and every discouragement?"

"I should think," she slowly replied, with one quick lift of her eyes toward his face, "that he had entered upon the noblest effort of which man is capable, and the hardest. I should have great sympathy for that man, Frederick."

"Would you?" he said, recalling Amabel's face with bitter aversion as he gazed into the womanly countenance he had hitherto slighted as uninteresting. "It is the first kind word you have ever given me, Agnes. Possibly it is the first I have ever deserved."

And without another word he doffed his hat, saluted her, and vanished down the hillside.

She remained; remained so long that it was nearly nine when she entered the family parlour. As she came in her mother looked up and was startled at her unaccustomed pallor.

"Why, Agnes," cried her mother, "what is the matter?"

Her answer was inaudible. What was the matter? She dreaded, even feared, to ask herself.

Meantime a strange scene was taking place in the woods toward which she had seen Frederick go. The moon, which was particularly bright that night, shone upon a certain hollow where a huge tree lay. Around it the underbrush was thick and the shadow dark, but in this especial place the opening was large enough for the rays to enter freely. Into this circlet of light Frederick Sutherland had come. Alone and without the restraint imposed upon him by watching eyes, he showed a countenance so wan and full of trouble that it was well it could not be seen by either of the two women whose thoughts were at that moment fixed upon him. To Amabel it would have given a throb of selfish hope, while to Agnes it would have brought a pang of despair which might have somewhat too suddenly interpreted to her the mystery of her own sensations.

He had bent at once to the hollow space made by the outspreading roots just mentioned, and was feeling with an air of confidence along the ground for something he had every reason to expect to find, when the shock of a sudden distrust seized him, and he flung himself down in terror, feeling and feeling again among the fallen leaves and broken twigs, till a full realisation of his misfortune reached him, and he was obliged to acknowledge that the place was empty.

Overwhelmed at his loss, aghast at the consequences it must entail upon him, he rose in a trembling sweat, crying out in his anger and dismay:

"She has been here! She has taken it! " And realising for the first time the subtlety and strength of the antagonist pitted against him, he forgot his new resolutions and even that old promise made in his childhood to Agatha Webb, and uttered oath after oath, cursing himself, the woman, and what she had done, till a casual glance at the heavens overhead, in which the liquid moon hung calm and beautiful, recalled him to himself. With a sense of shame, the keener that it was a new sensation in his breast, he ceased his vain repinings, and turning from the unhallowed spot, made his way with deeper and deeper misgivings toward a home made hateful to him now by the presence of the woman who was thus bent upon his ruin.

He understood her now. He rated at its full value both her determination and her power, and had she been so unfortunate as to have carried her imprudence to the point of surprising him by her presence, it would have taken more than the memory of that day's solemn resolves to have kept him from using his strength against her. But she was wise, and did not intrude upon him in his hour of anger, though who could say she was not near enough to hear the sigh which broke irresistibly from his lips as he emerged from the wood and approached his father's house?

A lamp was still burning in Mr. Sutherland's study over the front door, and the sight of it seemed to change for a moment the current of Frederick's thoughts. Pausing at the gate, he considered with himself, and then with a freer countenance and a lighter step was about to proceed inward, when he heard the sound of a heavy breather coming up the hill, and hesitated—why he hardly knew, except that every advancing step occasioned him more or less apprehension.

The person, whoever it was, stopped before reaching the brow of the hill, and, panting heavily, muttered an oath which Frederick heard. Though it was no more profane than those which had just escaped his own lips in the forest, it produced an effect upon him which was only second in intensity to the terror of the discovery that the money he had so safely hidden was gone.

Trembling in every limb, he dashed down the hill and confronted the person standing there.

"You! " he cried, "you! " And for a moment he looked as if he would like to fell to the ground the man before him.

But this man was a heavyweight of no ordinary physical strength and adroitness, and only smiled at Frederick's heat and threatening attitude.

"I thought I would be made welcome, " he smiled, with just the hint of sinister meaning in his tone. Then, before Frederick could speak: "I have merely saved you a trip to Boston; why so much anger, friend? You have the money; of that I am positive. "

"Hush! We can't talk here, " whispered Frederick. "Come into the grounds, or, what would be better, into the woods over there. "

"I don't go into any woods with you, " laughed the other; "not after last night, my friend. But I will talk low; that's no more than fair; I don't want to put you into any other man's power, especially if you have the money. "

"Wattles, "—Frederick's tone was broken, almost unintelligible, — "what do you mean by your allusion to last night? Have you dared to connect me—-"

"Pooh! Pooh! " interrupted the other, good-humouredly. "Don't let us waste words over a chance expression I may have dropped. I don't care anything about last night's work, or who was concerned in it. That's nothing to me. All I want, my boy, is the money, and that I want devilish bad, or I would not have run up here from Boston, when I might have made half a hundred off a countryman Lewis brought in from the Canada wilds this morning."

"Wattles, I swear—-"

But the hand he had raised was quickly drawn down by the other.

"Don't," said the older man, shortly. "It won't pay, Sutherland. Stage-talk never passed for anything with me. Besides, your white face tells a truer story than your lips, and time is precious. I want to take the 11 o'clock train back. So down with the cash. Nine hundred and fifty-five it is, but, being friends, we will let the odd five go."

"Wattles, I was to bring it to you to-morrow, or was it the next day? I do not want to give it to you to-night; indeed, I cannot, but—Wattles, wait, stop! Where are you going?"

"To see your father. I want to tell him that his son owes me a debt; that this debt was incurred in a way that lays him liable to arrest for forgery; that, bad as he thinks you, there are facts which can be picked up in Boston which would render Frederick Sutherland's continued residence under the parental roof impossible; that, in fact, you are a scamp of the first water, and that only my friendship for you has kept you out of prison so long. Won't that make a nice story for the old gentleman's ears!"

"Wattles—I—oh, my God! Wattles, stop a minute and listen to me. I have not got the money. I had enough this morning to pay you, had it legitimately, Wattles, but it has been stolen from me and—-"

"I will also tell him," the other broke in, as quietly as if Frederick had not uttered a word, "that in a certain visit to Boston you lost five hundred dollars on one hand; that you lost it unfairly, not having a dollar to pay with; that to prevent scandal I be came your security, with the understanding that I was to be paid at the end of ten days from that night; that you thereupon played again and lost four hundred and odd more, so that your debt amounted to nine hundred and fifty-five dollars; that the ten days passed without payment; that, wanting money, I pressed you and even resorted to a threat or two; and that, seeing me in earnest, you swore that the dollars should be mine within five days; that instead of remaining in Boston to get them, you came here; and that this morning at a very early hour you telegraphed that the funds were to hand and that you would bring them down to me to- morrow. The old gentleman may draw conclusions from this, Sutherland, which may make his position as your father anything but grateful to him. He may even— Ah, you would try that game, would you? "

The young man had flung himself at the older man's throat as if he would choke off the words he saw trembling on his lips. But the struggle thus begun was short. In a moment both stood panting, and Frederick, with lowered head, was saying humbly:

"I beg pardon, Wattles, but you drive me mad with your suggestions and conclusions. I have not got the money, but I will try and get it. Wait here. "

"For ten minutes, Sutherland; no longer! The moon is bright, and I can see the hands of my watch distinctly. At a quarter to ten, you will return here with the amount I have mentioned, or I will seek it at your father's hands in his own study. "

Frederick made a hurried gesture and vanished up the walk. Next moment he was at his father's study door.

XIII

WATTLES GOES

Mr. Sutherland was busily engaged with a law paper when his son entered his presence, but at sigh of that son's face, he dropped the paper with an alacrity which Frederick was too much engaged with his own thoughts to notice.

"Father, " he began without preamble or excuse, "I am in serious and immediate need of nine hundred and fifty dollars. I want it so much that I ask you to make me a check for that amount to-night, conscious though I am that you have every right to deny me this request, and that my debt to you already passes the bound of presumption on my part and indulgence on yours. I cannot tell you why I want it or for what. That belongs to my past life, the consequences of which I have not yet escaped, but I feel bound to state that you will not be the loser by this material proof of confidence in me, as I shall soon be in a position to repay all my debts, among which this will necessarily stand foremost. "

The old gentleman looked startled and nervously fingered the paper he had let fall. "Why do you say you will soon be in a position to repay me? What do you mean by that? "

The flash, which had not yet subsided from the young man's face, ebbed slowly away as he encountered his father's eye.

"I mean to work, " he murmured. "I mean to make a man of myself as soon as possible. "

The look which Mr. Sutherland gave him was more inquiring than sympathetic.

"And you need this money for a start? " said he.

Frederick bowed; he seemed to be losing the faculty of speech. The clock over the mantel had told off five of the precious moments.

"I will give it to you, " said his father, and drew out his check-book. But he did not hasten to open it; his eyes still rested on his son.

"Now, " murmured the young man. "There is a train leaving soon. I wish to get it away on that train. "

His father frowned with natural distrust.

"I wish you would confide in me, " said he.

Frederick did not answer. The hands of the clock were moving on.

"I will give it to you; but I should like to know what for. "

"It is impossible for me to tell you, " groaned the young man, starting as he heard a step on the walk without.

"Your need has become strangely imperative, " proceeded the other. "Has Miss Page—-"

Frederick took a step forward and laid his hand on his father's arm.

"It is not for her, " he whispered. "It goes into other hands. "

Mr. Sutherland, who had turned over the document as his son approached, breathed more easily. Taking up his pen, he dipped it in the ink. Frederick watched him with constantly whitening cheek. The step on the walk had mounted to the front door.

"Nine hundred and fifty? " inquired the father.

"Nine hundred and fifty, " answered the son.

The judge, with a last look, stooped over the book. The hands of the clock pointed to a quarter to ten.

"Father, I have my whole future in which to thank you, " cried Frederick, seizing the check his father held out to him and making rapidly for the door. "I will be back before midnight. " And he flung himself down-stairs just as the front door opened and Wattles stepped in.

"Ah, " exclaimed the latter, as his eye fell on the paper fluttering in the other's hand, "I expected money, not paper. "

"The paper is good," answered Frederick, drawing him swiftly out of the house. "It has my father's signature upon it."

"Your father's signature?"

"Yes."

Wattles gave it a look, then slowly shook his head at Frederick.

"Is it as well done as the one you tried to pass off on Brady?"

Frederick cringed, and for a moment looked as if the struggle was too much for him. Then he rallied and eying Wattles firmly, said:

"You have a right to distrust me, but you are on the wrong track, Wattles. What I did once, I can never do again; and I hope I may live to prove myself a changed man. As for that check, I will soon prove its value in your eyes. Follow me up-stairs to my father."

His energy—the energy of despair, no doubt seemed to make an impression on the other.

"You might as well proclaim yourself a forger outright, as to force your father to declare this to be his signature," he observed.

"I know it," said Frederick.

"Yet you will run that risk?"

"If you oblige me."

Wattles shrugged his shoulders. He was a magnificent-looking man and towered in that old colonial hall like a youthful giant.

"I bear you no ill will," said he. "If this represents money, I am satisfied, and I begin to think it does. But listen, Sutherland. Something has happened to you. A week ago you would have put a bullet through my head before you would have been willing to have so compromised yourself. I think I know what that something is. To save yourself from being thought guilty of a big crime you are willing to incur suspicion of a small one. It's a wise move, my boy, but look out! No tricks with me or my friendship may not hold.

Meantime, I cash this check to-morrow." And he swung away through the night with a grand-opera selection on his lips.

XIV

A FINAL TEMPTATION

Frederick looked like a man thoroughly exhausted when the final echo of this hateful voice died away on the hillside. For the last twenty hours he had been the prey of one harrowing emotion after another, and human nature could endure no more without rest.

But rest would not come. The position in which he found himself, between Amabel and the man who had just left, was of too threatening a nature for him to ignore. But one means of escape presented itself. It was a cowardly one; but anything was better than to make an attempt to stand his ground against two such merciless antagonists; so he resolved upon flight.

Packing up a few necessaries and leaving a letter behind him for his father, he made his way down the stairs of the now darkened house to a door opening upon the garden. To his astonishment he found it unlocked, but, giving little heed to this in his excitement, he opened it with caution, and, with a parting sigh for the sheltering home he was about to leave forever, stepped from the house he no longer felt worthy to inhabit.

His intention was to take the train at Portchester, and that he might reach that place without inconvenient encounters, he decided to proceed by a short cut through the fields. This led him north along the ridge that overlooks the road running around the base of the hill. He did not think of this road, however, or of anything, in fact, but the necessity of taking the very earliest train out of Portchester. As this left at 3.30 A. M., he realised that he must hasten in order to reach it. But he was not destined to take it or any other train out of Portchester that night, for when he reached the fence dividing Mr. Sutherland's grounds from those of his adjoining neighbour, he saw, drawn up in the moonlight just at the point where he had intended to leap the fence, the form of a woman with one hand held out to stop him.

It was Amabel.

Confounded by this check and filled with an anger that was nigh to dangerous, he fell back and then immediately sprang forward.

"What are you doing here? " he cried. "Don't you know that it is eleven o'clock and that my father requires the house to be closed at that hour? "

"And you? " was her sole retort; "what are you doing here? Are you searching for flowers in the woods, and is that valise you carry the receptacle in which you hope to put your botanical specimens? "

With a savage gesture he dropped the valise and took her fiercely by the shoulders.

"Where have you hidden my money? " he hissed. "Tell me, or —-"

"Or what? " she asked, smiling into his face in a way that made him lose his grip.

"Or—or I cannot answer for myself, " he proceeded, stammering. "Do you. think I can endure everything from you because you are a woman? No; I will have those bills, every one of them, or show myself your master. Where are they, you incarnate fiend? "

It was an unwise word to use, but she did not seem to heed it.

"Ah, " she said softly, and with a lingering accent, as if his grasp of her had been a caress to which she was not entirely averse. "I did not think you would discover its loss so soon. When did you go to the woods, Frederick? And was Miss Halliday with you? "

He had a disposition to strike her, but controlled himself. Blows would not avail against the softness of this suave, yet merciless, being. Only a will as strong as her own could hope to cope with this smiling fury; and this he was determined to show, though, alas! he had everything to lose in a struggle that robbed her of nothing but a hope which was but a baseless fabric at best; for he was more than ever determined never to marry her.

"A man does not need to wait long to miss his own, " said he. "And if you have taken this money, which, you do not deny, you have shown yourself very short-sighted, for danger lies closer to the person holding this money than to the one you vilify by your threats. This you will find, Amabel, when you come to make use of the weapon with which you have thought to arm yourself. "

"Tut, tut! " was her contemptuous reply. "Do you consider me a child? Do I look like a babbling infant, Frederick? "

Her face, which had been lifted to his in saying this, was so illumined, both by her smile, which was strangely enchanting for one so evil, and by the moon-light, which so etherialises all that it touches, that he found himself forced to recall that other purer, truer face he had left at the honeysuckle porch to keep down a last wild impulse toward her, which would have been his undoing, both in this world and the next, as he knew.

"Or do I look simply like a woman? " she went on, seeing the impression she had made, and playing upon it. "A woman who understands herself and you and all the secret perils of the game we are both playing? If I am a child, treat me as a child; but if I am a woman—-"

"Stand out of my way! " he cried, catching up his valise and striding furiously by her. "Woman or child, know that I will not be your plaything to be damned in this world and in the next. "

"Are you bound for the city of destruction? " she laughed, not moving, but showing such confidence in her power to hold him back that he stopped in spite of himself. "If so, you are taking the direct road there and have only to hasten. But you had better remain in your father's house; even if you are something of a prisoner there, like my very insignificant self. The outcome will be more satisfactory, even if you have to share your future with me. "

"And what course will you take, " he asked, pausing with his hand on the fence, "if I decide to choose destruction without you, rather than perdition with you? "

"What course? Why, I shall tell Dr. Talbot just enough to show you to be as desirable a witness in the impending inquest as myself. The result I leave to your judgment. But you will not drive me to this extremity. You will come back and—"

"Woman, I will never come back. I shall have to dare your worst in a week and will begin by daring you now. I—"

But he did not leap the fence, though he made a move to do so, for at that moment a party of men came hurrying by on the lower road, one of whom was heard to say:

"I will bet my head that we will put our hand on Agatha Webb's murderer to-night. The man who shoves twenty-dollar bills around so heedlessly should not wear a beard so long it leads to detection."

It was the coroner, the constable, Knapp, and Abel on their way to the forest road on which lived John and James Zabel.

Frederick and Amabel confronted each other, and after a moment's silence returned as if by a common impulse towards the house.

"What have they got in their heads?" queried she. "Whatever it is, it may serve to occupy them till the week of your probation is over."

He did not answer. A new and overwhelming complication had been added to the difficulties of his situation.

XV

THE ZABELS VISITED

Let us follow the party now winding up the hillside.

In a deeply wooded spot on a side road stood the little house to which John and James Zabel had removed when their business on the docks had terminated. There was no other dwelling of greater or lesser pretension on the road, which may account for the fact that none of the persons now approaching it had been in that neighbourhood for years, though it was by no means a long walk from the village in which they all led such busy lives.

The heavy shadows cast by the woods through which the road meandered were not without their effect upon the spirits of the four men passing through them, so that long before they reached the opening in which the Zabel cottage stood, silence had fallen upon the whole party. Dr. Talbot especially looked as if he little relished this late visit to his old friends, and not till they caught a glimpse of the long sloping roof and heavy chimney of the Zabel cottage did he shake off the gloom incident to the nature of his errand.

"Gentlemen," said he, coming to a sudden halt, "let us understand each other. We are about to make a call on two of our oldest and most respectable townsfolk. If in the course of that call I choose to make mention of the twenty-dollar bill left with Loton, well and good, but if not, you are to take my reticence as proof of my own belief that they had nothing to do with it."

Two of the party bowed; Knapp, only, made no sign.

"There is no light in the window," observed Abel. "What if we find them gone to bed?"

"We will wake them," said the constable. "I cannot go back without being myself assured that no more money like that given to Loton remains in the house."

"Very well," remarked Knapp, and going up to the door before him, he struck a resounding knock sufficiently startling in that place of silence.

But loud as the summons was it brought no answer. Not only the moon-lighted door, but the little windows on each side of it remained shut, and there was no evidence that the knock had been heard.

"Zabel! John Zabel! " shouted the constable, stepping around the side of the house. "Get up, my good friends, and let an old crony in. James! John! Late as it is, we have business with you. Open the door; don't stop to dress. "

But this appeal received no more recognition than the first, and after rapping on the window against which he had flung the words, he came back and looked up and down the front of the house.

It had a solitary aspect and was much less comfortable-looking than he had expected. Indeed, there were signs of poverty, or at least of neglect, about the place that astonished him. Not only had the weeds been allowed to grow over the doorstep, but from the unpainted front itself bits of boards had rotted away, leaving great gaps about the window-ledges and at the base of the sunken and well-nigh toppling chimney. The moon flooding the roof showed up all these imperfections with pitiless insistence, and the torn edges of the green paper shades that half concealed the rooms within were plainly to be seen, as well as the dismantled knocker which hung by one nail to the old cracked door. The vision of Knapp with his ear laid against this door added to the forlorn and sinister aspect of the scene, and gave to the constable, who remembered the brothers in their palmy days when they were the life and pride of the town, a by no means agreeable sensation, as he advanced toward the detective and asked him what they should do now.

"Break down the door! " was the uncompromising reply. "Or, wait! The windows of country houses are seldom fastened; let me see if I cannot enter by some one of them. "

"Better not, " said the coroner, with considerable feeling. "Let us exhaust all other means first. " And he took hold of the knob of the door to shake it, when to his surprise it turned and the door opened. It had not been locked.

Rather taken aback by this, he hesitated. But Knapp showed less scruple. Without waiting for any man's permission, he glided in and stepped cautiously, but without any delay, into a room the door of which stood wide open before him. The constable was about to follow when he saw Knapp come stumbling back.

"Devilish work, " he muttered, and drew the others in to see.

Never will any of these men forget the sight that there met their eyes.

On the floor near the entrance lay one brother, in a streak of moonlight, which showed every feature of his worn and lifeless face, and at a table drawn up in the centre of the room sat the other, rigid in death, with a book clutched in his hand.

Both, had been dead some time, and on the faces and in the aspects of both was visible a misery that added its own gloom to the pitiable and gruesome scene, and made the shining of the great white moon, which filled every corner of the bare room, seem a mockery well-nigh unendurable to those who contemplated it. John, dead in his chair! James, dead on the floor!

Knapp, who of all present was least likely to feel the awesome nature of the tragedy, was naturally the first to speak.

"Both wear long beards, " said he, "but the one lying on the floor was doubtless Loton's customer. Ah! " he cried, pointing at the table, as he carefully crossed the floor. "Here is the bread, and- -" Even he had his moments of feeling. The appearance of that loaf had stunned him; one corner of it had been gnawed off.

"A light! let us have a light! " cried Mr. Fenton, speaking for the first time since his entrance. "These moonbeams are horrible; see how they cling to the bodies as if they delighted in lighting up these wasted and shrunken forms. "

"Could it have been hunger? " began Abel, tremblingly following Knapp's every movement as he struck a match and lit a lantern which he had brought in his pocket.

"God help us all if it was! " said Fenton, in a secret remorse no one but Dr. Talbot understood. "But who could have believed it of men who were once so prosperous? Are you sure that one of them has gnawed this bread? Could it not have been—"

"These are the marks of human teeth, " observed Knapp, who was examining the loaf carefully. "I declare, it makes me very uncomfortable, notwithstanding it's in the line of regular experiences. " And he laid the bread down hurriedly.

Meantime, Mr. Fenton, who had been bending over another portion of the table, turned and walked away to the window.

"I am glad they are dead, " he muttered. "They have at least shared the fate of their victims. Take a look under that old handkerchief lying beside the newspaper, Knapp. "

The detective did so. A three-edged dagger, with a curiously wrought handle, met his eye. It had blood dried on its point, and was, as all could see, the weapon with which Agatha Webb had been killed.

XVI

LOCAL TALENT AT WORK

"Gentlemen, we have reached the conclusion of this business sooner than I expected, " announced Knapp. "If you will give me just ten minutes I will endeavour to find that large remainder of money we have every reason to think is hidden away in this house. "

"Stop a minute, " said the coroner. "Let me see what book John is holding so tightly. Why, " he exclaimed, drawing it out and giving it one glance, "it is a Bible. "

Laying it reverently down he met the detective's astonished glance and seriously remarked:

"There is some incongruity between the presence of this book and the deed we believe to have been performed down yonder. "

"None at all, " quoth the detective. "It was not the man in the chair, but the one on the floor, who made use of that dagger. But I wish you had left it to me to remove that book, sir. "

"You? and why? What difference would it have made? "

"I would have noticed between what pages his finger was inserted. Nothing like making yourself acquainted with every detail in a case like this. "

Dr. Talbot gazed wistfully at the book. He would have liked to know himself on what especial passage his friend's eyes had last rested.

"I will stand aside, " said he, "and hear your report when you are done. "

The detective had already begun his investigations.

"Here is a spot of blood, " said he. "See! on the right trouser leg of the one you call James. This connects him indisputably with the crime in which this dagger was used. No signs of violence on his body. She was the only one to receive a blow. His death is the result of God's providence. "

"Or man's neglect," muttered the constable.

"There is no money in any of their pockets, or on either wasted figure," the detective continued, after a few minutes of silent search. "It must be hidden in the room, or—look through that Bible, sirs."

The coroner, glad of an opportunity to do something, took up the book, and ran hurriedly through its leaves, then turned it and shook it out over the table. Nothing fell out; the bills must be looked for elsewhere.

"The furniture is scanty," Abel observed, with an inquiring look about him.

"Very, very scanty," assented the constable, still with that biting remorse at his heart.

"There is nothing in this cupboard," pursued the detective, swinging open a door in the wall, "but a set of old china more or less nicked."

Abel started. An old recollection had come up. Some weeks before, he had been present when James had made an effort to sell this set. They were all in Warner's store, and James Zabel (he could see his easy attitude yet, and hear the off-hand tones with which he tried to carry the affair off) had said, quite as if he had never thought of it before: "By the by, I have a set of china at the house which came over in the Mayflower. John likes it, but it has grown to be an eyesore to me, and if you hear of anybody who has a fancy for such things, send him up to the cottage. I will let it go for a song." Nobody answered, and James disappeared. It was the last time, Abel remembered, that he had been seen about town.

"I can't stand it," cried the lad. "I can't stand it. If they died of hunger I must know it. I am going to take a look at their larder." And before anyone could stop him he dashed to the rear of the house.

The constable would have liked to follow him, but he looked about the walls of the room instead. John and James had been fond of pictures and had once indulged their fancy to the verge of extravagance, but there were no pictures on the walls now, nor was there so much as a candlestick on the empty and dust-covered mantel. Only on a bracket in one corner there was a worthless trinket made out of cloves and beads which had doubtless been given them by some country damsel in their young bachelor days. But nothing of any value anywhere, and Mr. Fenton felt that he now knew why they had made so many visits to Boston at one time, and why they always returned with a thinner valise than they took away. He was still dwelling on the thought of the depths of misery to which highly respectable folks can sink without the knowledge of the nearest neighbours, when Abel came back looking greatly troubled.

"It is the saddest thing I ever heard of, " said he. "These men must have been driven wild by misery. This room is sumptuous in comparison to the ones at the back; and as for the pantry, there is not even a scrap there a mouse could eat. I struck a match and glanced into the flour barrel. It looked as if it had been licked. I declare, it makes a fellow feel sick. "

The constable, with a shudder, withdrew towards the door.

"The atmosphere here is stifling, " said he. "I must have a breath of out-door air. "

But he was not destined to any such immediate relief. As he moved down the hall the form of a man darkened the doorway and he heard an anxious voice exclaim:

"Ah, Mr. Fenton, is that you? I have been looking for you everywhere. "

It was Sweetwater, the young man who had previously shown so much anxiety to be of service to the coroner.

Mr. Fenton looked displeased.

"And how came you to find me here? " he asked.

"Oh, some men saw you take this road, and I guessed the rest. "

"Oh, ah, very good. And what do you want, Sweetwater? "

The young man, who was glowing with pride and all alive with an enthusiasm which he had kept suppressed for hours, slipped up to the constable and whispered in his ear: "I have made a discovery, sir.

I know you will excuse the presumption, but I couldn't bring myself to keep quiet and follow in that other fellow's wake. I had to make investigations on my own account, and — and" — stammering in his eagerness "they have been successful, sir. I have found out who was the murderer of Agatha Webb. "

The constable, compassionating the disappointment in store for him, shook his head, with a solemn look toward the room from which he had just emerged. "You are late, Sweetwater, " said he. "We have found him out ourselves, and he lies there, dead. "

It was dark where they stood and Sweetwater's back was to the moonlight, so that the blank look which must have crossed his face at this announcement was lost upon the constable. But his consternation was evident from the way he thrust out either hand to steady himself against the walls of the narrow passageway, and Mr. Fenton was not at all surprised to hear him stammer out:

"Dead! He! Whom do you mean by he, Mr. Fenton? "

"The man in whose house we now are, " returned the other. "Is there anyone else who can be suspected of this crime? "

Sweetwater gave a gulp that seemed to restore him to himself.

"There are two men living here, both very good men, I have heard. Which of them do you mean, and why do you think that either John or James Zabel killed Agatha Webb? "

For reply Mr. Fenton drew him toward the room in which such a great heart-tragedy had taken place.

"Look, " said he, "and see what can happen in a Christian land, in the midst of Christian people living not fifty rods away. These men are dead, Sweetwater, dead from hunger. The loaf of bread you see there came too late. It was bought with a twenty-dollar bill, taken from Agatha Webb's cupboard drawer. "

Sweetwater, to whom the whole scene seemed like some horrible nightmare, stared at the figure of James lying on the floor, and then at the figure of John seated at the table, as if his mind had failed to take in the constable's words.

"Dead! " he murmured. "Dead! John and James Zabel. What will happen next? Is the town under a curse? " And he fell on his knees before the prostrate form of James, only to start up again as he saw the eyes of Knapp resting on him.

"Ah, " he muttered, "the detective! " And after giving the man from Boston a close look he turned toward Mr. Fenton.

"You said something about this good old man having killed Agatha Webb. What was it? I was too dazed to take it in. "

Mr. Fenton, not understanding the young man's eagerness, but willing enough to enlighten him as to the situation, told him what reasons there were for ascribing the crime in the Webb cottage to the mad need of these starving men. Sweetwater listened with open eyes and confused bearing, only controlling himself when his eyes by chance fell upon the quiet figure of the detective, now moving softly to and fro through the room.

"But why murder when he could have had his loaf for the asking? " remonstrated Sweetwater. "Agatha Webb would have gone without a meal any time to feed a wandering tramp; how much more to supply the necessities of two of her oldest and dearest friends! "

"Yes, " remarked Fenton, "but you forget or perhaps never knew that the master passion of these men was pride. James Zabel ask for bread! I can much sooner imagine him stealing it; yes, or striking a blow for it, so that the blow shut forever the eyes that saw him do it. "

"You don't believe your own words, Mr. Fenton. How can you? " Sweetwater's hand was on the breast of the accused man as he spoke, and his manner was almost solemn. "You must not take it for granted, " he went on, his green eyes twinkling with a curious light, "that all wisdom comes from Boston. We in Sutherlandtown have some sparks of it, if they have not yet been recognised. You are satisfied"—here he addressed himself to Knapp—"that the blow which killed Agatha Webb was struck by this respectable old man?"

Knapp smiled as if a child had asked him this question; but he answered him good-humouredly enough.

"You see the dagger lying here with which the deed was done, and you see the bread that was bought from Loton with a twenty-dollar bill of Agatha Webb's money. In these you can read my answer."

"Good evidence," acknowledged Sweetwater—"very good evidence, especially when we remember that Mr. Crane met an old man rushing from her gateway with something glittering in his hand. I never was so beat in my life, and yet—and yet—if I could have a few minutes of quiet thought all by myself I am certain I could show you that there is more to this matter than you think. Indeed, I know that there is, but I do not like to give my reasons till I have conquered the difficulties presented by these men having had the twenty-dollar bill."

"What fellow is this?" suddenly broke in Knapp.

"A fiddler, a nobody," quietly whispered Mr. Fenton in his ear.

Sweetwater heard him and changed in a twinkling from the uncertain, half-baffled, wholly humble person they had just seen, to a man with a purpose strong enough to make him hold up his head with the best.

"I am a musician," he admitted, "and I play on the violin for money whenever the occasion offers, something which you will yet congratulate yourselves upon if you wish to reach the root of this mysterious and dastardly crime. But that I am a nobody I deny, and I even dare to hope that you will agree with me in this estimate of myself before this very night is over. Only give me an opportunity for considering this subject, and the permission to walk for a few minutes about this house."

"That is my prerogative," protested the detective firmly, but without any display of feeling. "I am the man employed to pick up whatever clews the place may present."

"Have you picked up all that are to be found in this room?" asked Sweetwater calmly.

Knapp shrugged his shoulders. He was very well satisfied with himself.

"Then give me a chance, " prayed Sweetwater. "Mr. Fenton, " he urged more earnestly, "I am not the fool you take me for. I feel, I know, I have a genius for this kind of thing, and though I am not prepossessing to look at, and though I do play the fiddle, I swear there are depths to this affair which none of you have as yet sounded. Sirs, where are the nine hundred and eighty dollars in bills which go to make up the clean thousand that was taken from the small drawer at the back of Agatha Webb's cupboard? "

"They are in some secret hiding-place, no doubt, which we will presently come upon as we go through the house, " answered Knapp.

"Umph! Then I advise you to put your hand on them as soon as possible, " retorted Sweetwater. "I will confine myself to going over the ground you have already investigated. " And with a sudden ignoring of the others' presence, which could only have sprung from an intense egotism or from an overwhelming belief in his own theory, he began an investigation of the room that threw the other's more commonplace efforts entirely in the shade.

Knapp, with a slight compression of his lips, which was the sole expression of anger he ever allowed himself, took up his hat and made his bow to Mr. Fenton.

"I see, " said he, "that the sympathy of those present is with local talent. Let local talent work, then, sir, and when you feel the need of a man of training and experience, send to the tavern on the docks, where I will be found till I am notified that my services are no longer required. "

"No, no! " protested Mr. Fenton. "This boy's enthusiasm will soon evaporate. Let him fuss away if he will. His petty business need not interrupt us. "

"But he understands himself, " whispered Knapp. "I should think he had been on our own force for years. "

"All the more reason to see what he's up to. Wait, if only to satisfy your curiosity. I shan't let many minutes go by before I pull him up. "

Knapp, who was really of a cold and unimpressionable temperament, refrained from further argument, and confined himself to watching the young man, whose movements seemed to fascinate him.

"Astonishing! " Mr. Fenton heard him mutter to himself. "He's more like an eel than a man. " And indeed the way Sweetwater wound himself out and in through that room, seeing everything that came under his eye, was a sight well worth any professional's attention. Pausing before the dead man on the floor, he held the lantern close to the white, worn face. "Ha! " said he, picking something from the long beard, "here's a crumb of that same bread. Did you see that, Mr. Knapp? "

The question was so sudden and so sharp that the detective came near replying to it; but he bethought himself, and said nothing.

"That settles which of the two gnawed the loaf, " continued Sweetwater.

The next minute he was hovering over the still more pathetic figure of John, sitting in the chair.

"Sad! Sad! " he murmured.

Suddenly he laid his finger on a small rent in the old man's faded vest. "You saw this, of course, " said he, with a quick glance over his shoulder at the silent detective.

No answer, as before.

"It's a new slit, " declared the officious youth, looking closer, "and — yes — there's blood on its edges. Here, take the lantern, Mr. Fenton, I must see how the skin looks underneath. Oh, gentlemen, no shirt! The poorest dockhand has a shirt! Brocaded vest and no shirt; but he's past our pity now. Ah, only a bruise over the heart. Sirs, what did you make out of this? "

As none of them had even seen it, Knapp was not the only one to remain silent.

"Shall I tell you what I make out of it? " said the lad, rising hurriedly from the floor, which he had as hurriedly examined. "This old man has tried to take his life with the dagger already wet with the blood of Agatha Webb. But his arm was too feeble. The point only pierced the vest, wiping off a little blood in its passage, then the weapon fell from his hand and struck the floor, as you will see by the fresh dent in the old board I am standing on. Have you anything to say against these simple deductions? "

Again the detective opened his lips and might have spoken, but Sweetwater gave him no chance.

"Where is the letter he was writing? " he demanded. "Have any of you seen any paper lying about here? "

"He was not writing, " objected Knapp; "he was reading; reading in that old Bible you see there. "

Sweetwater caught up the book, looked it over, and laid it down, with that same curious twinkle of his eye they had noted in him before.

"He was writing, " he insisted. "See, here is his pencil. " And he showed them the battered end of a small lead-pencil lying on the edge of his chair.

"Writing at some time, " admitted Knapp.

"Writing just before the deed, " insisted Sweetwater. "Look at the fingers of his right hand. They have not moved since the pencil fell out of them. "

"The letter, or whatever it was, shall be looked for, " declared the constable.

Sweetwater bowed, his eyes roving restlessly into every nook and corner of the room.

"James was the stronger of the two, " he remarked; "yet there is no evidence that he made any attempt at suicide. "

"How do you know that it was suicide John attempted? " asked someone. "Why might not the dagger have fallen from James's hand in an effort to kill his brother? "

"Because the dent in the floor would have been to the right of the chair instead of to the left, " he returned. "Besides, James's hand would not have failed so utterly, since he had strength to pick up the weapon afterward and lay it where you found it."

"True, we found it lying on the table," observed Abel, scratching his head in forced admiration of his old schoolmate.

"All easy, very easy," Sweetwater remarked, seeing the wonder in every eye. "Matters like those are for a child's reading, but what is difficult, and what I find hard to come by, is how the twenty-dollar bill got into the old man's hand. He found it here, but how—"

"Found it here? How do you know that?"

"Gentlemen, that is a point I will make clear to you later, when I have laid my hand on a certain clew I am anxiously seeking. You know this is new work for me and I have to advance warily. Did any of you gentlemen, when you came into this room, detect the faintest odour of any kind of perfume?"

"Perfume?" echoed Abel, with a glance about the musty apartment. "Rats, rather."

Sweetwater shook his head with a discouraged air, but suddenly brightened, and stepping quickly across the floor, paused at one of the windows. It was that one in which the shade had been drawn.

Peering at this shade he gave a grunt.

"You must excuse me for a minute," said he; "I have not found what I wanted in this room and now must look outside for it. Will someone bring the lantern?"

"I will," volunteered Knapp, with grim good humour. Indeed, the situation was almost ludicrous to him.

"Bring it round the house, then, to the ground under this window," ordered Sweetwater, without giving any sign that he noticed or even recognised the other's air of condescension. "And, gentlemen, please don't follow. It's footsteps I am after, and the fewer we make ourselves, the easier will it be for me to establish the clew I am after."

Mr. Fenton stared. What had got into the fellow?

The lantern gone, the room resumed its former appearance.

Abel, who had been much struck by Sweetwater's mysterious manoeuvres, drew near Dr. Talbot and whispered in his ear: "We might have done without that fellow from Boston."

To which the coroner replied:

"Perhaps so, and perhaps not. Sweetwater has not yet proved his case; let us wait till he explains himself." Then, turning to the constable, he showed him an old-fashioned miniature, which he had found lying on James's breast, when he made his first examination. It was set with pearls and backed with gold and was worth many meals, for the lack of which its devoted owner had perished.

"Agatha Webb's portrait," explained Talbot, "or rather Agatha Gilchrist's; for I presume this was painted when she and James were lovers."

"She was certainly a beauty," commented Fenton, as he bent over the miniature in the moonlight. "I do not wonder she queened it over the whole country."

"He must have worn it where I found it for the last forty years," mused the doctor. "And yet men say that love is a fleeting passion. Well, after coming upon this proof of devotion, I find it impossible to believe James Zabel accountable for the death of one so fondly remembered. Sweetwater's instinct was truer than Knapp's."

"Or ours," muttered Fenton.

"Gentlemen," interposed Abel, pointing to a bright spot that just then made its appearance in the dark outline of the shade before alluded to, "do you see that hole? It was the sight of that prick in the shade which sent Sweetwater outside looking for footprints. See! Now his eye is to it" (as the bright spot became suddenly eclipsed). "We are under examination, sirs, and the next thing we will hear is that he's not the only person who's been peering into this room through that hole."

He was so far right that the first words of Sweetwater on his re-entrance were: "It's all O. K., sirs. I have found my missing clew. James Zabel was not the only person who came up here from the

Webb cottage last night. " And turning to Knapp, who was losing some of his supercilious manner, he asked, with significant emphasis: "If, of the full amount stolen from Agatha Webb, you found twenty dollars in the possession of one man and nine hundred and eighty dollars in the possession of another, upon which of the two would you fix as the probable murderer of the good woman?"

"Upon him who held the lion's share, of course."

"Very good; then it is not in this cottage you will find the person most wanted. You must look—But there! first let me give you a glimpse of the money. Is there anyone here ready to accompany me in search of it? I shall have to take him a quarter of a mile farther up-hill."

"You have seen the money? You know where it is?" asked Dr. Talbot and Mr. Fenton in one breath.

"Gentlemen, I can put my hand on it in ten minutes."

At this unexpected and somewhat startling statement Knapp looked at Dr. Talbot and Dr. Talbot looked at the constable, but only the last spoke.

"That is saying a good deal. But no matter. I am willing to credit the assertion. Lead on, Sweetwater; I'll go with you."

Sweetwater seemed to grow an inch taller in his satisfied vanity. "And Dr. Talbot?" he suggested.

But the coroner's duty held him to the house and he decided not to accompany them. Knapp and Abel, however, yielded to the curiosity which had been aroused by these extraordinary promises, and presently the four men mentioned started on their small expedition up the hill.

Sweetwater headed the procession. He had admonished silence, and his wish in this regard was so well carried out that they looked more like a group of spectres moving up the moon-lighted road, than a party of eager and impatient men. Not till they turned into the main thoroughfare did anyone speak. Then Abel could no longer restrain himself and he cried out:

"We are going to Mr. Sutherland's."

But Sweetwater quickly undeceived him.

"No," said he, "only into the woods opposite his house."

But at this Mr. Fenton drew him back.

"Are you sure of yourself?" he said. "Have you really seen this money and is it concealed in this forest?"

"I have seen the money," Sweetwater solemnly declared, "and it is hidden in these woods."

Mr. Fenton dropped his arm, and they moved on till their way was blocked by the huge trunk of a fallen tree.

"It is here we are to look," cried Sweetwater, pausing and motioning Knapp to turn his lantern on the spot where the shadows lay thickest. "Now, what do you see?" he asked.

"The upturned roots of a great tree," said Mr. Fenton.

"And under them?"

"A hole, or, rather, the entrance to one."

"Very good; the money is in that hole. Pull it out, Mr. Fenton."

The assurance with which Sweetwater spoke was such that Mr. Fenton at once stooped and plunged his hand into the hole. But when, after a hurried search, he drew it out again, there was nothing in it; the place was empty. Sweetwater stared at Mr. Fenton amazed.

"Don't you find anything?" he asked. "Isn't there a roll of bills in that hole?"

"No," was the gloomy answer, after a renewed attempt and a second disappointment. "There is nothing to be found here. You are labouring under some misapprehension, Sweetwater."

"But I can't be. I saw the money; saw it in the hand of the person who hid it there. Let me look for it, constable. I will not give up the search till I have turned the place topsy-turvy."

Kneeling down in Mr. Fenton's place, he thrust his hand into the hole. On either side of him peered the faces of Mr. Fenton and Knapp. (Abel had slipped away at a whisper from Sweetwater.) They were lit with a similar expression of anxious interest and growing doubt. His own countenance was a study of conflicting and by no means cheerful emotions. Suddenly his aspect changed. With a quick twist of his lithe, if awkward, body, he threw himself lengthwise on the ground, and began tearing at the earth inside the hole, like a burrowing animal.

"I cannot be mistaken. Nothing will make me believe it is not here. It has simply been buried deeper than I thought. Ah! What did I tell you? See here! And see here!"

Bringing his hands into the full blaze of the light, he showed two rolls of new, crisp bills.

"They were lying under half a foot of earth," said he, "but if they had been buried as deep as Grannie Fuller's well, I'd have unearthed them."

Meantime Mr. Fenton was rapidly counting one roll and Knapp the other. The result was an aggregate sum of nine hundred and eighty dollars, just the amount Sweetwater had promised to show them.

"A good stroke of business," cried Mr. Fenton. "And now, Sweetwater, whose is the hand that buried this treasure? Nothing is to be gained by preserving silence on this point any longer."

Instantly the young man became very grave. With a quick glance around which seemed to embrace the secret recesses of the forest rather than the eager faces bending towards him, he lowered his voice and quietly said:

"The hand that buried this money under the roots of this old tree is the same which you saw pointing downward at the spot of blood in Agatha Webb's front yard."

"You do not mean Annabel Page! " cried Mr. Fenton, with natural surprise.

"Yes, I do; and I am glad it is you who have named her. "

XVII

THE SLIPPERS, THE FLOWER, AND WHAT SWEETWATER MADE OF THEM

A half-hour later these men were all closeted with Dr. Talbot in the Zabel kitchen. Abel had rejoined them, and Sweetwater was telling his story with great earnestness and no little show of pride.

"Gentlemen, when I charge a young woman of respectable appearance and connections with such a revolting crime as murder, I do so with good reason, as I hope presently to make plain to you all.

"Gentlemen, on the night and at the hour Agatha Webb was killed, I was playing with four other musicians in Mr. Sutherland's hallway. From the place where I sat I could see what went on in the parlour and also have a clear view of the passageway leading down to the garden door. As the dancing was going on in the parlour I naturally looked that way most, and this is how I came to note the eagerness with which, during the first part of the evening, Frederick Sutherland and Amabel Page came together in the quadrilles and country dances. Sometimes she spoke as she passed him, and sometimes he answered, but not always, although he never failed to show he was pleased with her or would have been if something—perhaps it was his lack of confidence in her, sirs—had not stood in the way of a perfect understanding. She seemed to notice that he did not always respond, and after a while showed less inclination to speak herself, though she did not fail to watch him, and that intently. But she did not watch him any more closely than I did her, though I little thought at the time what would come of my espionage. She wore a white dress and white shoes, and was as coquettish and seductive as the evil one makes them. Suddenly I missed her. She was in the middle of the dance one minute and entirely out of it the next. Naturally I supposed her to have slipped aside with Frederick Sutherland, but he was still in sight, looking so pale and so abstracted, however, I was sure the young miss was up to some sort of mischief. But what mischief? Watching and waiting, but no longer confining my attention to the parlour, I presently espied her stealing along the passageway I have mentioned, carrying a long cloak which she rolled up and hid behind the open door. Then she came back humming a gay little song which didn't deceive me for a moment. 'Good!' thought I, 'she and that cloak will soon join company.' And they did. As we were playing the Harebell mazurka I again caught sight of her stealthy white figure in that distant doorway. Seizing the cloak, she wrapped it round her, and with just one furtive look backwards, seen, I warrant, by no one but myself, she vanished in the outside dark. 'Now to note who follows her! ' But nobody followed her. This struck me as strange, and having a natural love for detective work, in spite of my devotion to the arts, I consulted the clock at the foot of the stairs, and noting that it was half-past eleven, scribbled the hour on the margin of my music, with the intention of seeing how long my lady would linger outside alone. Gentlemen, it was two hours before I saw her face again. How she got back into the house I do not know. It was not by the garden door, for my eye seldom left it; yet at or near half-past one I heard her voice on the stair above me and saw her descend and melt into the crowd as if she had not been absent from it for more than five minutes. A half-hour later I saw her with Frederick again. They were dancing, but not with the same spirit as before, and even while I watched them they separated. Now where was Miss Page during those two long hours? I think I know, and it is time I unburdened myself to the police.

"But first I must inform you of a small discovery I made while the dance was still in progress. Miss Page had descended the stairs, as I have said, from what I now know to have been her own room. Her dress was, in all respects, the same as before, with one exception — her white slippers had been exchanged for blue ones. This seemed to show that they had been rendered unserviceable, or at least unsightly, by the walk she had taken. This in itself was not remarkable nor would her peculiar escapade have made more than a temporary impression upon my curiosity if she had not afterward shown in my presence such an unaccountable and extraordinary interest in the murder which had taken place in the town below during the very hours of her absence from Mr. Sutherland's ball. This, in consideration of her sex, and her being a stranger to the person attacked, was remarkable, and, though perhaps I had no business to do what I did, I no sooner saw the house emptied of master and servants than I stole softly back, and climbed the stairs to her room. Had no good followed this intrusion, which, I am quite ready to acknowledge, was a trifle presumptuous, I would have held my peace in regard to it; but as I did make a discovery there, which has, as I believe, an important bearing on this affair, I have forced myself to mention it. The lights in the house having been left burning, I had no difficulty in finding her apartment. I knew it by the folderols scattered about. But I did not stop to look at them. I was on a search for her slippers, and presently came upon them, thrust behind an old picture in the dimmest corner of the room. Taking them down, I examined them closely. They were not only soiled, gentlemen, but dreadfully cut and rubbed. In short, they were ruined, and, thinking that the young lady herself would be glad to be rid of them, I quietly put them into my pocket, and carried them to my own home. Abel has just been for them, so you can see them for yourselves, and if your judgment coincides with mine, you will discover something more on them than mud."

Dr. Talbot, though he stared a little at the young man's confessed theft, took the slippers Abel was holding out and carefully turned them over. They were, as Sweetwater had said, grievously torn and soiled, and showed, beside several deep earth-stains, a mark or two of a bright red colour, quite unmistakable in its character.

"Blood," declared the coroner. "There is no doubt about it. Miss Page was where blood was spilled last night."

"I have another proof against her," Sweetwater went on, in full enjoyment of his prominence amongst these men, who, up to now, had barely recognised his existence. "When, full of the suspicion that Miss Page had had a hand in the theft which had taken place at Mrs. Webb's house, if not in the murder that accompanied it, I hastened down to the scene of the tragedy, I met this young woman issuing from the front gate. She had just been making herself conspicuous by pointing out a trail of blood on the grass plot. Dr. Talbot, who was there, will remember how she looked on that occasion; but I doubt if he noticed how Abel here looked, or so much as remarked the faded flower the silly boy had stuck in his buttonhole."

"—me if I did!" ejaculated the coroner.

"Yet that flower has a very important bearing on this case. He had found it, as he will tell you, on the floor near Batsy's skirts, and as soon as I saw it in his coat, I bade him take it out and keep it, for, gentlemen, it was a very uncommon flower, the like of which can only be found in this town in Mr. Sutherland's conservatory. I remember seeing such a one in Miss Page's hair, early in the evening. Have you that flower about you, Abel?"

Abel had, and being filled with importance too, showed it to the doctor and to Mr. Fenton. It was withered and faded in hue, but it was unmistakably an orchid of the rarest description.

"It was lying near Batsy, " explained Abel. "I drew Mr. Fenton's attention to it at the time, but he scarcely noticed it. "

"I will make up for my indifference now, " said that gentleman.

"I should have been shown that flower, " put in Knapp.

"So you should, " acknowledged Sweetwater, "but when the detective instinct is aroused it is hard for a man to be just to his rivals; besides, I was otherwise occupied. I had Miss Page to watch. Happily for me, you had decided that she should not be allowed to leave town till after the inquest, and so my task became easy. This whole day I have spent in sight of Mr. Sutherland's house, and at nightfall I was rewarded by detecting her end a prolonged walk in the garden by a hurried dash into the woods opposite. I followed her and noted carefully all that she did. As she had just seen Frederick Sutherland and Miss Halliday disappear up the road together, she probably felt free to do as she liked, for she walked very directly to the old tree we have just come from, and kneeling down beside it pulled from the hole underneath something which rattled in her hand with that peculiar sound we associate with fresh bank-notes. I had approached her as near as I dared, and was peering around a tree trunk, when she stooped down again and plunged both hands into the hole. She remained in this position so long that I did not know what to make of it. But she rose at last and turned toward home, laughing to herself in a wicked but pleased way that did not tend to make me think any more of her. The moon was shining very brightly by this time and I could readily perceive every detail of her person. She held her hands out before her and shook them more than once as she trod by me, so I was sure there was nothing in them, and this is why I was so confident we should find the money still in the hole.

"When I saw her enter the house, I set out to find you, but the courthouse room was empty, and it was a long time before I learned where to look for you. But at last a fellow at Brighton's corner said he saw four men go by on their way to Zabel's cottage, and on the chance of finding you amongst them, I turned down here. The shock you gave me in announcing that you had discovered the murderer of

Agatha Webb knocked me over for a moment, but now I hope you realise, as I do, that this wretched man could never have had an active hand in her death, notwithstanding the fact that one of the stolen bills has been found in his possession. For, and here is my great point, the proof is not wanting that Miss Page visited this house as well as Mrs. Webb's during her famous escapade; or at least stood under the window beneath which I have just been searching. A footprint can be seen there, sirs, a very plain footprint, and if Dr. Talbot will take the trouble to compare it with the slipper he holds in his hand, he will find it to have been made by the foot that wore that slipper."

The coroner, with a quick glance from the slipper in his hand up to Sweetwater's eager face, showed a decided disposition to make the experiment thus suggested. But Mr. Fenton, whose mind was full of the Zabel tragedy, interrupted them with the question:

"But how do you explain by this hypothesis the fact of James Zabel trying to pass one of the twenty-dollar bills stolen from Mrs. Webb's cupboard? Do you consider Miss Page generous enough to give him that money?"

"You ask ME that, Mr. Fenton. Do you wish to know what *I* think of the connection between these two great tragedies?"

"Yes; you have earned a voice in this matter; speak, Sweetwater."

"Well, then, I think Miss Page has made an effort to throw the blame of her own misdoing on one or both of these unfortunate old men. She is sufficiently cold-blooded and calculating to do so; and circumstances certainly favoured her. Shall I show how?"

Mr. Fenton consulted Knapp, who nodded his head. The Boston detective was not without curiosity as to how Sweetwater would prove the case.

"Old James Zabel had seen his brother sinking rapidly from inanition; this their condition amply shows. He was weak himself, but John was weaker, and in a moment of desperation he rushed out to ask a crumb of bread from Agatha Webb, or possibly—for I have heard some whispers of an old custom of theirs to join Philemon at his yearly merry-making and so obtain in a natural way the bite for himself and brother he perhaps had not the courage to ask for outright. But death had been in the Webb cottage before him, which awful circumstance, acting on his already weakened nerves, drove him half insane from the house and sent him wandering blindly about the streets for a good half-hour before he reappeared in his own house. How do I know this? From a very simple fact. Abel here has been to inquire, among other things, if Mr. Crane remembers the tune we were playing at the great house when he came down the main street from visiting old widow Walker. Fortunately he does, for the trip, trip, trip in it struck his fancy, and he has found himself humming it over more than once since. Well, that waltz was played by us at a quarter after midnight, which fixes the time of the encounter at Mrs. Webb's gateway pretty accurately. But, as you will soon see, it was ten minutes to one before James Zabel knocked at Loton's door. How do I know this? By the same method of reasoning by which I determined the time of Mr. Crane's encounter. Mrs. Loton was greatly pleased with the music played that night, and had all her windows open in order to hear it, and she says we were playing 'Money Musk' when that knocking came to disturb her. Now, gentlemen, we played 'Money Musk' just before we were called out to supper, and as we went to supper promptly at one, you can see just how my calculation was made. Thirty-five minutes, then, passed between the moment James Zabel was seen rushing from Mrs. Webb's gateway and that in which he appeared at Loton's bakery, demanding a loaf of bread, and offering in exchange one of the bills which had been stolen from the murdered woman's drawer. Thirty-five minutes! And he and his brother were starving. Does it look, then, as if that money was in his possession when he left Mrs. Webb's house? Would any man who felt the pangs of hunger as he did, or who saw a brother perishing for food before his eyes, allow thirty-five minutes to elapse before he made use of the money that rightfully or wrongfully had come into his hand? No; and so I say that he did not have it when Mr. Crane met him. That, instead of committing crime to obtain it, he found it in his own home, lying on his table, when, after his frenzied absence, he returned to tell his dreadful news to the brother he had left behind him. But how did it come there? you ask. Gentlemen, remember the footprints under the window. Amabel Page brought it. Having seen or perhaps met this old man roaming in or near the Webb cottage during the time she was there herself, she conceived the plan of throwing upon him the onus of the crime she had herself committed, and with a slyness to be expected from one so crafty, stole up to his home, made a hole in the shade hanging over an open window, looked into the room where John sat, saw that he was there alone and asleep, and, creeping in by the front door, laid on the table beside him the twenty-dollar bill and the bloody dagger with which she had just slain Agatha Webb. Then she stole out again, and in twenty minutes more was leading the dance in Mr. Sutherland's parlour."

"Well reasoned!" murmured Abel, expecting the others to echo him. But, though Mr. Fenton and Dr. Talbot looked almost convinced, they said nothing, while Knapp, of course, was quiet as an oyster.

Sweetwater, with an easy smile calculated to hide his disappointment, went on as if perfectly satisfied.

"Meanwhile John awakes, sees the dagger, and thinks to end his misery with it, but finds himself too feeble. The cut in his vest, the dent in the floor, prove this, but if you call for further proof, a little fact, which some, if not all, of you seem to have overlooked, will amply satisfy you that this one at least of my conclusions is correct. Open the Bible, Abel; open it, not to shake it for what will never fall from between its leaves, but to find in the Bible itself the lines I have declared to you he wrote as a dying legacy with that tightly clutched pencil. Have you found them?"

"No," was Abel's perplexed retort; "I cannot see any sign of writing on flyleaf or margin."

"Are those the only blank places in the sacred book? Search the leaves devoted to the family record. Now! what do you find there?"

Knapp, who was losing some of his indifference, drew nearer and read for himself the scrawl which now appeared to every eye on the discoloured page which Abel here turned uppermost.

"Almost illegible," he said; "one can just make out these words: 'Forgive me, James—tried to use dagger—found lying—but hand wouldn't—dying without—don't grieve—true men—haven't disgraced ourselves—God bless—' That is all."

"The effort must have overcome him," resumed Sweetwater in a voice from which he carefully excluded all signs of secret triumph, "and when James returned, as he did a few minutes later, he was evidently unable to ask questions, even if John was in a condition to answer them. But the fallen dagger told its own story, for James picked it up and put it back on the table, and it was at this minute he saw, what John had not, the twenty-dollar bill lying there with its promise of life and comfort. Hope revives; he catches up the bill, flies down to Loton's, procures a loaf of bread, and comes frantically back, gnawing it as he runs; for his own hunger is more than he can endure. Re-entering his brother's presence, he rushes forward with the bread. But the relief has come too late; John has died in his absence; and James, dizzy with the shock, reels back and succumbs to his own misery. Gentlemen, have you anything to say in contradiction to these various suppositions? "

For a moment Dr. Talbot, Mr. Fenton, and even Knapp stood silent; then the last remarked, with pardonable dryness:

"All this is ingenious, but, unfortunately, it is up set by a little fact which you yourself have overlooked. Have you examined attentively the dagger of which you have so often spoken, Mr. Sweetwater? "

"Not as I would like to, but I noticed it had blood on its edge, and was of the shape and size necessary to inflict the wound from which Mrs. Webb died. "

"Very good, but there is something else of interest to be observed on it. Fetch it, Abel. "

Abel, hurrying from the room, soon brought back the weapon in question. Sweetwater, with a vague sense of disappointment disturbing him, took it eagerly and studied it very closely. But he only shook his head.

"Bring it nearer to the light, " suggested Knapp, "and examine the little scroll near the top of the handle. "

Sweetwater did so, and at once changed colour. In the midst of the scroll were two very small but yet perfectly distinct letters; they were J. Z.

"How did Amabel Page come by a dagger marked with the Zabel initials? " questioned Knapp. "Do you think her foresight went so far as to provide herself with a dagger ostensibly belonging to one of these brothers? And then, have you forgotten that when Mr. Crane met the old man at Mrs. Webb's gateway he saw in his hand something that glistened? Now what was that, if not this dagger? "

Sweetwater was more disturbed than he cared to acknowledge.

"That just shows my lack of experience, " he grumbled. "I thought I had turned this subject so thoroughly over in my mind that no one could bring an objection against it. "

Knapp shook his head and smiled. "Young enthusiasts like yourself are great at forming theories which well-seasoned men like myself must regard as fantastical. However, " he went on, "there is no doubt that Miss Page was a witness to, even if she has not profited by, the murder we have been considering. But, with this palpable proof of the Zabels' direct connection with the affair, I would not recommend her arrest as yet. "

"She should be under surveillance, though, " intimated the coroner.

"Most certainly, " acquiesced Knapp.

As for Sweetwater, he remained silent till the opportunity came for him to whisper apart to Dr. Talbot, when he said:

"For all the palpable proof of which Mr. Knapp speaks—the J. Z. on the dagger, and the possibility of this being the object he was seen carrying out of Philemon Webb's gate—I maintain that this old man in his moribund condition never struck the blow that killed Agatha Webb. He hadn't strength enough, even if his lifelong love for her had not been sufficient to prevent him. "

The coroner looked thoughtful.

"You are right, " said he; "he hadn't strength enough. But don't expend too much energy in talk. Wait and see what a few direct questions will elicit from Miss Page. "

XVIII

SOME LEADING QUESTIONS

Frederick rose early. He had slept but little. The words he had overheard at the end of the lot the night before were still ringing in his ears. Going down the back stairs, in his anxiety to avoid Amabel, he came upon one of the stablemen.

"Been to the village this morning? " he asked.

"No, sir, but Lem has. There's great news there. I wonder if anyone has told Mr. Sutherland. "

"What news, Jake? I don't think my father is up yet. "

"Why, sir, there were two more deaths in town last night—the brothers Zabel; and folks do say (Lem heard it a dozen times between the grocery and the fish market) that it was one of these old men who killed Mrs. Webb. The dagger has been found in their house, and most of the money. Why, sir, what's the matter? Are you sick? "

Frederick made an effort and stood upright. He had nearly fallen.

"No; that is, I am not quite myself. So many horrors, Jake. What did they die of? You say they are both dead—both? "

"Yes, sir, and it's dreadful to think of, but it was hunger, sir. Bread came too late. Both men are mere skeletons to look at. They have kept themselves close for weeks now, and nobody knew how bad off they were. I don't wonder it upset you, sir. We all feel it a bit, and I just dread to tell Mr. Sutherland. "

Frederick staggered away. He had never in his life been so near mental and physical collapse. At the threshold of the sitting-room door he met his father. Mr. Sutherland was looking both troubled and anxious; more so, Frederick thought, than when he signed the check for him on the previous night. As their eyes met, both showed embarrassment, but Frederick, whose nerves had been highly strung by what he had just heard, soon controlled himself, and surveying his father with forced calmness, began:

"This is dreadful news, sir. "

But his father, intent on his own thought, hurriedly interrupted him.

"You told me yesterday that everything was broken off between you and Miss Page. Yet I saw you reenter the house together last night a little while after I gave you the money you asked for. "

"I know, and it must have had a bad appearance. I entreat you, however, to believe that this meeting between Miss Page and myself was against my wish, and that the relations between us have not been affected by anything that passed between us. "

"I am glad to hear it, my son. You could not do worse by yourself than to return to your old devotion. "

"I agree with you, sir. " And then, because he could not help it, Frederick inquired if he had heard the news.

Mr. Sutherland, evidently startled, asked what news; to which Frederick replied:

"The news about the Zabels. They are both dead, sir, —dead from hunger. Can you imagine it! "

This was something so different from what his father had expected to hear, that he did not take it in at first. When he did, his surprise and grief were even greater than Frederick had anticipated. Seeing him so affected, Frederick, who thought that the whole truth would be no harder to bear than the half, added the suspicion which had been attached to the younger one's name, and then stood back, scarcely daring to be a witness to the outraged feelings which such a communication could not fail to awaken in one of his father's temperament.

But though he thus escaped the shocked look which crossed his father's countenance, he could not fail to hear the indignant exclamation which burst from his lips, nor help perceiving that it would take more than the most complete circumstantial evidence to convince his father of the guilt of men he had known and respected for so many years.

For some reason Frederick experienced great relief at this, and was bracing himself to meet the fire of questions which his statement must necessarily call forth, when the sound of approaching steps drew the attention of both towards a party of men coming up the hillside.

Among them was Mr. Courtney, Prosecuting Attorney for the district, and as Mr. Sutherland recognised him he sprang forward, saying, "There's Courtney; he will explain this. "

Frederick followed, anxious and bewildered, and soon had the doubtful pleasure of seeing his father enter his study in company with the four men considered to be most interested in the elucidation of the Webb mystery.

As he was lingering in an undecided mood in the small passageway leading up-stairs he felt the pressure of a finger on his shoulder. Looking up, he met the eyes of Amabel, who was leaning toward him over the banisters. She was smiling, and, though her face was not without evidences of physical languor, there was a charm about her person which would have been sufficiently enthralling to him twenty-four hours before, but which now caused him such a physical repulsion that he started back in the effort to rid his shoulder from her disturbing touch.

She frowned. It was an instantaneous expression of displeasure which was soon lost in one of her gurgling laughs.

"Is my touch so burdensome? " she demanded. "If the pressure of one finger is so unbearable to your sensitive nerves, how will you relish the weight of my whole hand? "

There was a fierceness in her tone, a purpose in her look, that for the first time in his struggle with her revealed the full depth of her dark nature. Shrinking from her appalled, he put up his hand in protest, at which she changed again in a twinkling, and with a cautious gesture toward the room into which Mr. Sutherland and his friends had disappeared, she whispered significantly:

"We may not have another chance to confer together. Understand, then, that it will not be necessary for you to tell me, in so many words, that you are ready to link your fortunes to mine; the taking off of the ring you wear and your slow putting of it on again, in my presence, will be understood by me as a token that you have reconsidered your present attitude and desire my silence and—myself."

Frederick could not repress a shudder.

For an instant he was tempted to succumb on the spot and have the long agony over. Then his horror of the woman rose to such a pitch that he uttered an execration, and, turning away from her face, which was rapidly growing loathsome to him, he ran out of the passageway into the garden, seeing as he ran a persistent vision of himself pulling off the ring and putting it back again, under the spell of a look he rebelled against even while he yielded to its influence.

"I will not wear a ring, I will not subject myself to the possibility of obeying her behest under a sudden stress of fear or fascination," he exclaimed, pausing by the well-curb and looking over it at his reflection in the water beneath. "If I drop it here I at least lose the horror of doing what she suggests, under some involuntary impulse." But the thought that the mere absence of the ring from his finger would not stand in the way of his going through the motions to which she had just given such significance, deterred him from the sacrifice of a valuable family jewel, and he left the spot with an air of frenzy such as a man displays when he feels himself on the verge of a doom he can neither meet nor avert.

As he re-entered the house, he felt himself enveloped in the atmosphere of a coming crisis. He could hear voices in the upper hall, and amongst them he caught the accents of her he had learned so lately to fear. Impelled by something deeper than curiosity and more potent even than dread, he hastened toward the stairs. When half-way up, he caught sight of Amabel. She was leaning back against the balustrade that ran across the upper hall, with her hands gripping the rail on either side of her and her face turned toward the five men who had evidently issued from Mr. Sutherland's study to interview her.

As her back was to Frederick he could not judge of the expression of that face save by the effect it had upon the different men confronting her. But to see them was enough. From their looks he could perceive that this young girl was in one of her baffling moods, and that from his father down, not one of the men present knew what to make of her.

At the sound his feet made, a relaxation took place in her body and she lost something of the defiant attitude she had before maintained. Presently he heard her voice:

"I am willing to answer any questions you may choose to put to me here; but I cannot consent to shut myself in with you in that small study; I should suffocate. "

Frederick could perceive the looks which passed between the five men assembled before her, and was astonished to note that the insignificant fellow they called Sweetwater was the first to answer.

"Very well, " said he; "if you enjoy the publicity of the open hall, no one here will object. Is not that so, gentlemen? "

Her two little fingers, which were turned towards Frederick, ran up and down the rail, making a peculiar rasping noise, which for a moment was the only sound to be heard. Then Mr. Courtney said:

"How came you to have the handling of the money taken from Agatha Webb's private drawer? "

It was a startling question, but it seemed to affect Amabel less than it did Frederick. It made him start, but she only turned her head a trifle aside, so that the peculiar smile with which she prepared to answer could be seen by anyone standing below.

"Suppose you ask something less leading than that, to begin with, " she suggested, in her high, unmusical voice. "From the searching nature of this inquiry, you evidently believe I have information of an important character to give you concerning Mrs. Webb's unhappy death. Ask me about that; the other question I will answer later. "

The aplomb with which this was said, mixed as it was with a feminine allurement of more than ordinary subtlety, made Mr. Sutherland frown and Dr. Talbot look perplexed, but it did not embarrass Mr. Courtney, who made haste to respond in his dryest accents:

"Very well, I am not particular as to what you answer first. A flower worn by you at the dance was found near Batsy's skirts, before she was lifted up that morning. Can you explain this, or, rather, will you? "

Agatha Webb

"You are not obliged to, you know, " put in Mr. Sutherland, with his inexorable sense of justice. "Still, if you would, it might rob these gentlemen of suspicions you certainly cannot wish them to entertain. "

"What I say, " she remarked slowly, "will be as true to the facts as if I stood here on my oath. I can explain how a flower from my hair came to be in Mrs. Webb's house, but not how it came to be found under Batsy's feet. That someone else must clear up. " Her little finger, lifted from the rail, pointed toward Frederick, but no one saw this, unless it was that gentleman himself. "I wore a purple orchid in my hair that night, and there would be nothing strange in its being afterward picked up in Mrs. Webb's house, because I was in that house at or near the time she was murdered. "

"You in that house? "

"Yes, as far as the ground floor; no farther. " Here the little finger stopped pointing. "I am ready to tell you about it, sirs, and only regret I have delayed doing so so long, but I wished to be sure it was necessary. Your presence here and your first question show that it is. "

There was suavity in her tone now, not unmixed with candour. Sweetwater did not seem to relish this, for he moved uneasily and lost a shade of his self-satisfied attitude. He had still to be made acquainted with all the ins and outs of this woman's remarkable nature.

"We are waiting, " suggested Dr. Talbot.

She turned to face this new speaker, and Frederick was relieved from the sight of her tantalising smile.

"I will tell my story simply, " said she, "with the simple suggestion that you believe me; otherwise you will make a mistake. While I was resting from a dance the other night, I heard two of the young people talking about the Zabels. One of them was laughing at the old men, and the other was trying to relate some half-forgotten story of early love which had been the cause, she thought, of their strange and melancholy lives. I was listening to them, but I did not take in much of what they were saying till I heard behind me an irascible voice exclaiming: 'You laugh, do you? I wonder if you would laugh so easily if you knew that these two poor old men haven't had a decent meal in a fortnight? ' I didn't know the speaker, but I was thrilled by his words. Not had a good meal, these men, for a fortnight! I felt as if personally guilty of their suffering, and, happening to raise my eyes at this minute and seeing through an open door the bountiful refreshments prepared for us in the supper room, I felt guiltier than ever. Suddenly I took a resolution. It was a queer one, and may serve to show you some of the oddities of my nature. Though I was engaged for the next dance, and though I was dressed in the flimsy garments suitable to the occasion, I decided to leave the ball and carry some sandwiches down to these old men. Procuring a bit of paper, I made up a bundle and stole out of the house without having said a word to anybody of my intention. Not wishing to be seen, I went out by the garden door, which is at the end of the dark hall—"

"Just as the band was playing the Harebell mazurka, " interpolated Sweetwater.

Startled for the first time from her careless composure by an interruption of which it was impossible for her at that time to measure either the motive or the meaning, she ceased to play with her fingers on the baluster rail and let her eyes rest for a moment on the man who had thus spoken, as if she hesitated between her desire to annihilate him for his impertinence and a fear of the cold hate she saw actuating his every word and look. Then she went on, as if no one had spoken:

"I ran down the hill recklessly. I was bent on my errand and not at all afraid of the dark. When I reached that part of the road where the streets branch off, I heard footsteps in front of me. I had overtaken someone. Slackening my pace, so that I should not pass this person, whom I instinctively knew to be a man, I followed him till I came to a high board fence. It was that surrounding Agatha Webb's house, and when I saw it I could not help connecting the rather stealthy gait of the man in front of me with a story I had lately heard of the large sum of money she was known to keep in her house. Whether this was before or after this person disappeared round the corner I cannot say, but no sooner had I become certain that he was bent upon entering this house than my impulse to follow him became greater than my precaution, and turning aside from the direct path to the Zabels', I hurried down High Street just in time to see the man enter Mrs. Webb's front gateway.

"It was a late hour for visiting, but as the house had lights in both its lower and upper stories, I should by good rights have taken it for granted that he was an expected guest and gone on my way to the Zabels'. But I did not. The softness with which this person stepped and the skulking way in which he hesitated at the front gate aroused my worst fears, and after he had opened that gate and slid in, I was so pursued by the idea that he was there for no good that I stepped inside the gate myself and took my stand in the deep shadow cast by the old pear tree on the right-hand side of the walk. Did anyone speak?"

There was a unanimous denial from the five gentlemen before her, yet she did not look satisfied.

"I thought I heard someone make a remark, " she repeated, and paused again for a half-minute, during which her smile was a study, it was so cold and in such startling contrast to the vivid glances she threw everywhere except behind her on the landing where Frederick stood listening to her every word.

"We are very much interested, " remarked Mr. Courtney. "Pray, go on. "

Drawing her left hand from the balustrade where it had rested, she looked at one of her fingers with an odd backward gesture.

"I will, " she said, and her tone was hard and threatening. "Five minutes, no longer, passed, when I was startled by a loud and terrible cry from the house, and looking up at the second-story window from which the sound proceeded, I saw a woman's figure hanging out in a seemingly pulseless condition. Too terrified to move, I clung trembling to the tree, hearing and not hearing the shouts and laughter of a dozen or more men, who at that minute passed by the corner on their way to the wharves. I was dazed, I was choking, and only came to myself when, sooner or later, I do not know how soon or how late, a fresh horror happened. The woman whom I had just seen fall almost from the window was a serving woman, but when I heard another scream I knew that the mistress of the house was being attacked, and rivetting my eyes on those windows, I beheld the shade of one of them thrown back and a hand appear, flinging out something which fell in the grass on the opposite side of the lawn. Then the shade fell again, and hearing nothing further, I ran to where the object flung out had fallen, and feeling for it, found and picked up an old-fashioned dagger, dripping with blood. Horrified beyond all expression, I dropped the weapon and retreated into my former place of concealment.

"But I was not satisfied to remain there. A curiosity, a determination even, to see the man who had committed this dastardly deed, attacked me with such force that I was induced to leave my hiding-place and even to enter the house where in all probability he was counting the gains he had just obtained at the price of so much precious blood. The door, which he had not perfectly closed behind him, seemed to invite me in, and before I had realised my own temerity, I was standing in the hall of this ill-fated house."

The interest, which up to this moment had been breathless, now expressed itself in hurried ejaculations and broken words; and Mr. Sutherland, who had listened like one in a dream, exclaimed eagerly, and in a tone which proved that he, for the moment at least, believed this more than improbable tale:

"Then you can tell us if Philemon was in the little room at the moment when you entered the house?"

As everyone there present realised the importance of this question, a general movement took place and each and all drew nearer as she met their eyes and answered placidly:

"Yes; Mr. Webb was sitting in a chair asleep. He was the only person I saw."

"Oh, I know he never committed this crime," gasped his old friend, in a relief so great that one and all seemed to share it.

"Now I have courage for the rest. Go on, Miss Page."

But Miss Page paused again to look at her finger, and give that sideways toss to her head that seemed so uncalled for by the situation to any who did not know of the compact between herself and the listening man below.

"I hate to go back to that moment," said she; "for when I saw the candles burning on the table, and the husband of the woman who at that very instant was possibly breathing her last breath in the room overhead, sitting there in unconscious apathy, I felt something rise in my throat that made me deathly sick for a moment. Then I went right in where he was, and was about to shake his arm and wake him, when I detected a spot of blood on my finger from the dagger I had handled. That gave me another turn, and led me to wipe off my finger on his sleeve."

"It's a pity you did not wipe off your slippers too," murmured Sweetwater.

Again she looked at him, again her eyes opened in terror upon the face of this man, once so plain and insignificant in her eyes, but now so filled with menace she inwardly quaked before it, for all her apparent scorn.

"Slippers," she murmured.

"Did not your feet as well as your hands pass through the blood on the grass?"

She disdained to answer him.

"I have accounted for the blood on my hand," she said, not looking at him, but at Mr. Courtney. "If there is any on my slippers it can be accounted for in the same way." And she rapidly resumed her narrative. "I had no sooner made my little finger clean I never thought of anyone suspecting the old gentleman when I heard steps on the stairs and knew that the murderer was coming down, and in another instant would pass the open door before which I stood.

"Though I had been courageous enough up to that minute, I was seized by a sudden panic at the prospect of meeting face to face one whose hands were perhaps dripping with the blood of his victim. To confront him there and then might mean death to me, and I did not want to die, but to live, for I am young, sirs, and not without a prospect of happiness before me. So I sprang back, and seeing no other place of concealment in the whole bare room, crouched down in the shadow of the man you call Philemon. For one, two minutes, I knelt there in a state of mortal terror, while the feet descended, paused, started to enter the room where I was, hesitated, turned, and finally left the house."

"Miss Page, wait, wait," put in the coroner. "You saw him; you can tell who this man was?"

The eagerness of this appeal seemed to excite her. A slight colour appeared in her cheeks and she took a step forward, but before the words for which they so anxiously waited could leave her lips, she gave a start and drew back with, an ejaculation which left a more or less sinister echo in the ears of all who heard it.

Frederick had just shown himself at the top of the staircase.

"Good-morning, gentlemen, " said he, advancing into their midst with an air whose unexpected manliness disguised his inward agitation. "The few words I have just heard Miss Page say interest me so much, I find it impossible not to join you. "

Amabel, upon whose lips a faint complacent smile had appeared as he stepped by her, glanced up at these words in secret astonishment at the indifference they showed, and then dropped her eyes to his hands with an intent gaze which seemed to affect him unpleasantly, for he thrust them immediately behind him, though he did not lower his head or lose his air of determination.

"Is my presence here undesirable? " he inquired, with a glance towards his father.

Sweetwater looked as if he thought it was, but he did not presume to say anything, and the others being too interested in the developments of Miss Page's story to waste any time on lesser matters, Frederick remained, greatly to Miss Page's evident satisfaction.

"Did you see this man's face? " Mr. Courtney now broke in, in urgent inquiry.

Her answer came slowly, after another long look in Frederick's direction.

"No, I did not dare to make the effort. I was obliged to crouch too close to the floor. I simply heard his footsteps. "

"See, now! " muttered Sweetwater, but in so low a tone she did not hear him. "She condemns herself. There isn't a woman living who would fail to look up under such circumstances, even at the risk of her life. "

Knapp seemed to agree with him, but Mr. Courtney, following his one idea, pressed his former question, saying:

"Was it an old man's step?"

"It was not an agile one."

"And you did not catch the least glimpse of the man's face or figure?"

"Not a glimpse."

"So you are in no position to identify him?"

"If by any chance I should hear those same footsteps coming down a flight of stairs, I think I should be able to recognise them," she allowed, in the sweetest tones at her command.

"She knows it is too late for her to hear those of the two dead Zabels," growled the man from Boston.

"We are no nearer the solution of this mystery than we were in the beginning," remarked the coroner.

"Gentlemen, I have not yet finished my story," intimated Amabel, sweetly. "Perhaps what I have yet to tell may give you some clew to the identity of this man."

"Ah, yes; go on, go on. You have not yet explained how you came to be in possession of Agatha's money."

"Just so," she answered, with another quick look at Frederick, the last she gave him for some time. "As soon, then, as I dared, I ran out of the house into the yard. The moon, which had been under a cloud, was now shining brightly, and by its light I saw that the space before me was empty and that I might venture to enter the street. But before doing so I looked about for the dagger I had thrown from me before going in, but I could not find it. It had been picked up by the fugitive and carried away. Annoyed at the cowardice which had led me to lose such a valuable piece of evidence through a purely womanish emotion, I was about to leave the yard, when my eyes fell on the little bundle of sandwiches which I had brought down from the hill and which I had let fall under the pear tree, at the first scream I had heard from the house. It had burst open and two or three of the sandwiches lay broken on the ground. But those that were intact I picked up, and being more than ever anxious to cover up by some ostensible errand my absence from the party, I rushed away toward the lonely road where these brothers lived, meaning to leave such fragments as remained on the old doorstep, beyond which I had been told such suffering existed.

"It was now late, very late, for a girl like myself to be out, but, under the excitement of what I had just seen and heard, I became oblivious to fear, and rushed into those dismal shadows as into transparent daylight. Perhaps the shouts and stray sounds of laughter that came up from the wharves where a ship was getting under way gave me a certain sense of companionship. Perhaps—but it is folly for me to dilate upon my feelings; it is my errand you are interested in, and what happened when I approached the Zabels' dreary dwelling."

The look with which she paused, ostensibly to take breath, but in reality to weigh and criticise the looks of those about her, was one of those wholly indescribable ones with which she was accustomed to control the judgment of men who allowed themselves to watch too closely the ever-changing expression of her weird yet charming face. But it fell upon men steeled against her fascinations, and realising her inability to move them, she proceeded with her story before even the most anxious of her hearers could request her to do so.

"I had come along the road very quietly," said she, "for my feet were lightly shod, and the moonlight was too bright for me to make a misstep. But as I cleared the trees and came into the open place where the house stands I stumbled with surprise at seeing a figure crouching on the doorstep I had anticipated finding as empty as the road. It was an old man's figure, and as I paused in my embarrassment he slowly and with great feebleness rose to his feet and began to grope about for the door. As he did so, I heard a sharp tinkling sound, as of something metallic falling on the doorstone, and, taking a quick step forward, I looked over his shoulder and espied in the moonlight at his feet a dagger so like the one I had lately handled in Mrs. Webb's yard that I was overwhelmed with astonishment, and surveyed the aged and feeble form of the man who had dropped it with a sensation difficult to describe. The next moment he was stooping for the weapon, with a startled air that has impressed itself distinctly upon my memory, and when, after many feeble attempts, he succeeded in grasping it, he vanished into the house so suddenly that I could not be sure whether or not he had seen me standing there.

"All this was more than surprising to me, for I had never thought of associating an old man with this crime. Indeed, I was so astonished to find him in possession of this weapon that I forgot all about my errand and only wondered how I could see and know more. Fearing detection, I slid in amongst the bushes and soon found myself under one of the windows. The shade was down and I was about to push it aside when I heard someone moving about inside and stopped. But I could not restrain my curiosity, so pulling a hairpin from my hair, I worked a little hole in the shade and through this I looked into a room brightly illumined by the moon which shone in through an adjoining window. And what did I see there? " Her eye turned on Frederick. His right hand had stolen toward his left, but it paused under her look and remained motionless. "Only an old man sitting at a table and—" Why did she pause, and why did she cover up that pause with a wholly inconsequential sentence? Perhaps Frederick could have told, Frederick, whose hand had now fallen at his side. But Frederick volunteered nothing, and no one, not even Sweetwater, guessed all that lay beyond that AND which was left hovering in the air to be finished—-when? Alas! had she not set the day and the hour?

What she did say was in seeming explanation of her previous sentence. "It was not the same old man I had seen on the doorstep, and while I was looking at him I became aware of someone leaving the house and passing me on the road up-hill. Of course this ended my interest in what went on within, and turning as quickly as I could I hurried into the road and followed the shadow I could just perceive disappearing in the woods above me. I was bound, gentlemen, as you see, to follow out my adventure to the end. But my task now became very difficult, for the moon was high and shone down upon the road so distinctly that I could not follow the person before me as closely as I wished without running the risk of being discovered by him. I therefore trusted more to my ear than to my eye, and as long as I could hear his steps in front of me I was satisfied. But presently, as we turned up this very hill, I ceased to hear these steps and so became confident that he had taken to the woods. I was so sure of this that I did not hesitate to enter them myself, and, knowing the paths well, as I have every opportunity of doing, living, as we do, directly opposite this forest, I easily found my way to the little clearing that I have reason to think you gentlemen have since become acquainted with. But though from the sounds I heard I was assured that the person I was following was not far in advance of me, I did not dare to enter this brilliantly illumined space, especially as there was every indication of this person having completed whatever task he had set for himself. Indeed, I was sure that I heard his steps coming back. So, for the second time, I crouched down in the darkest place I could find and let this mysterious person pass me. When he had quite disappeared, I made my own retreat, for it was late, and I was afraid of being missed at the ball. But later, or rather the next day, I recrossed the road and began a search for the money which I was confident had been left in the woods opposite, by the person I had been following. I found it, and when the man here present who, though a mere fiddler, has presumed to take a leading part in this interview, came upon me with the bills in my hand, I was but burying deeper the ill-gotten gains I had come upon."

"Ah, and so making them your own, " quoth Sweetwater, stung by the sarcasm in that word fiddler.

But with a suavity against which every attack fell powerless, she met his significant look with one fully as significant, and quietly said:

"If I had wanted the money for myself I would not have risked leaving it where the murderer could find it by digging up a few handfuls of mould and a bunch of sodden leaves. No, I had another motive for my action, a motive with which few, if any, of you will be willing to credit me. I wished to save the murderer, whom I had some reason, as you see, for thinking I knew, from the consequences of his own action."

Mr. Courtney, Dr. Talbot, and even Mr. Sutherland, who naturally believed she referred to Zabel, and who, one and all, had a lingering tenderness for this unfortunate old man, which not even this seeming act of madness on his part could quite destroy, felt a species of reaction at this, and surveyed the singular being before them with, perhaps, the slightest shade of relenting in their severity. Sweetwater alone betrayed restlessness, Knapp showed no feeling at all, while Frederick stood like one petrified, and moved neither hand nor foot.

"Crime is despicable when it results from cupidity only, " she went on, with a deliberateness so hard that the more susceptible of her auditors shuddered. "But crime that springs from some imperative and overpowering necessity of the mind or body might well awaken sympathy, and I am not ashamed of having been sorry for this frenzied and suffering man. Weak and impulsive as you may consider me, I did not want him to suffer on account of a moment's madness, as he undoubtedly would if he were ever found with Agatha Webb's money in his possession, so I plunged it deeper into the soil and trusted to the confusion which crime always awakens even in the strongest mind, for him not to discover its hiding-place till the danger connected with it was over."

"Ha! wonderful! Devilish subtle, eh? Clever, too clever!" were some of the whispered exclamations which this curious explanation on her part brought out. Yet only Sweetwater showed his open and entire disbelief of the story, the others possibly remembering that for such natures as hers there is no governing law and no commonplace interpretation.

To Sweetwater, however, this was but so much display of feminine resource and subtlety. Though he felt he should keep still in the presence of men so greatly his superiors, he could not resist saying:

"Truth is sometimes stranger than fiction. I should never have attributed any such motive as you mention to the young girl I saw leaving this spot with many a backward glance at the hole from which we afterwards extracted the large sum of money in question. But say that this reburying of stolen funds was out of consideration for the feeble old man you describe as having carried them there, do you not see that by this act you can be held as an accessory after the fact?"

Her eyebrows went up and the delicate curve of her lips was not without menace as she said:

"You hate me, Mr. Sweetwater. Do you wish me to tell these gentlemen why?"

The flush which, notwithstanding this peculiar young man's nerve, instantly crimsoned his features, was a surprise to Frederick. So was it to the others, who saw in it a possible hint as to the real cause of his persistent pursuit of this young girl, which they had hitherto ascribed entirely to his love of justice. Slighted love makes some hearts venomous. Could this ungainly fellow have once loved and been disdained by this bewitching piece of unreliability?

It was a very possible assumption, though Sweetwater's blush was the only answer he gave to her question, which nevertheless had amply served its turn.

To fill the gap caused by his silence, Mr. Sutherland made an effort and addressed her himself.

"Your conduct, " said he, "has not been that of a strictly honourable person. Why did you fail to give the alarm when you re- entered my house after being witness to this double tragedy? "

Her serenity was not to be disturbed.

"I have just explained, " she reminded him, "that I had sympathy for the criminal. "

"We all have sympathy for James Zabel, but—"

"I do not believe one word of this story, " interposed Sweetwater, in reckless disregard of proprieties. "A hungry, feeble old man, like Zabel, on the verge of death, could not have found his way into these woods. You carried the money there yourself, miss; you are the—"

"Hush! " interposed the coroner, authoritatively; "do not let us go too fast—yet. Miss Page has an air of speaking the truth, strange and unaccountable as it may seem. Zabel was an admirable man once, and if he was led into theft and murder, it was not until his faculties had been weakened by his own suffering and that of his much-loved brother. "

"Thank you, " was her simple reply; and for the first time every man there thrilled at her tone. Seeing it, all the dangerous fascination of her look and manner returned upon her with double force. "I have been unwise, " said she, "and let my sympathy run away with my judgment. Women have impulses of this kind sometimes, and men blame them for it, till they themselves come to the point of feeling the need of just such blind devotion. I am sure I regret my short-sightedness now, for I have lost esteem by it, while he—" With a wave of the hand she dismissed the subject, and Dr. Talbot, watching her, felt a shade of his distrust leave him, and in its place a species of admiration for the lithe, graceful, bewitching personality before them, with her childish impulses and womanly wit which half mystified and half imposed upon them.

Mr. Sutherland, on the contrary, was neither charmed from his antagonism nor convinced of her honesty. There was something in this matter that could not be explained away by her argument, and his suspicion of that something he felt perfectly sure was shared by his son, toward whose cold, set face he had frequently cast the most uneasy glances. He was not ready, however, to probe into the subject more deeply, nor could he, for the sake of Frederick, urge on to any further confession a young woman whom his unhappy son professed to love, and in whose discretion he had so little confidence. As for Sweetwater, he had now fully recovered his self-possession, and bore himself with great discretion when Dr. Talbot finally said:

"Well, gentlemen, we have got more than we expected when we came here this morning. There remains, however, a point regarding which we have received no explanation. Miss Page, how came that orchid, which I am told you wore in your hair at the dance, to be found lying near the hem of Batsy's skirts? You distinctly told us that you did not go up-stairs when you were in Mrs. Webb's house."

"Ah, that's so!" acquiesced the Boston detective dryly. "How came that flower on the scene of the murder?"

She smiled and seemed equal to the emergency.

"That is a mystery for us all to solve," she said quietly, frankly meeting the eyes of her questioner.

"A mystery it is your business to solve," corrected the district attorney. "Nothing that you have told us in support of your innocence would, in the eyes of the law, weigh for one instant against the complicity shown by that one piece of circumstantial evidence against you."

Her smile carried a certain high-handed denial of this to one heart there, at least. But her words were humble enough.

"I am aware of that," said she. Then, turning to where Sweetwater stood lowering upon her from out his half-closed eyes, she impetuously exclaimed: "You, sir, who, with no excuse an honourable person can recognise, have seen fit to arrogate to yourself duties wholly out of your province, prove yourself equal to your presumption by ferreting out, alone and unassisted, the secret of this mystery. It can be done, for, mark, *I* did not carry that flower into the room where it was found. This I am ready to assert before God and before man! "

Her hand was raised, her whole attitude spoke defiance and—hard as it was for Sweetwater to acknowledge it—truth. He felt that he had received a challenge, and with a quick glance at Knapp, who barely responded by a shrug, he shifted over to the side of Dr. Talbot.

Amabel at once dropped her hand.

"May I go? " she now cried appealingly to Mr. Courtney. "I really have no more to say, and I am tired. "

"Did you see the figure of the man who brushed by you in the wood? Was it that of the old man you saw on the doorstep? "

At this direct question Frederick quivered in spite of his dogged self-control. But she, with her face upturned to meet the scrutiny of the speaker, showed only a childish kind of wonder. "Why do you ask that? Is there any doubt about its being the same? "

What an actress she was! Frederick stood appalled. He had been amazed at the skill with which she had manipulated her story so as to keep her promise to him, and yet leave the way open for that further confession which would alter the whole into a denunciation of himself which he would find it difficult, if not impossible, to meet. But this extreme dissimulation made him lose heart. It showed her to be an antagonist of almost illimitable resource and secret determination.

"I did not suppose there could be any doubt, " she added, in such a natural tone of surprise that Mr. Courtney dropped the subject, and Dr. Talbot turned to Sweetwater, who for the moment seemed to have robbed Knapp of his rightful place as the coroner's confidant.

"Shall we let her go for the present? " he whispered. "She does look tired, poor girl. "

The public challenge which Sweetwater had received made him wary, and his reply was a guarded one:

"I do not trust her, yet there is much to confirm her story. Those sandwiches, now. She says she dropped them in Mrs. Webb's yard under the pear tree, and that the bag that held them burst open. Gentlemen, the birds were so busy there on the morning after the murder that I could not but notice them, notwithstanding my absorption in greater matters. I remember wondering what they were all pecking at so eagerly. But how about the flower whose presence on the scene of guilt she challenges me to explain? And the money so deftly reburied by her? Can any explanation make her other than accessory to a crime on whose fruits she lays her hand in a way tending solely to concealment? No, sirs; and so I shall not relax my vigilance over her, even if, in order to be faithful to it, I have to suggest that a warrant be made out for her imprisonment."

"You are right," acquiesced the coroner, and turning to Miss Page, he told her she was too valuable a witness to be lost sight of, and requested her to prepare to accompany him into town.

She made no objection. On the contrary her cheeks dimpled, and she turned away with alacrity towards her room. But before the door closed on her she looked back, and, with a persuasive smile, remarked that she had told all she knew, or thought she knew at the time. But that perhaps, after thinking the matter carefully over, she might remember some detail that would throw some extra light on the subject.

"Call her back!" cried Mr. Courtney. "She is withholding something. Let us hear it all."

But Mr. Sutherland, with a side look at Frederick, persuaded the district attorney to postpone all further examination of this artful girl until they were alone. The anxious father had noted, what the rest were too preoccupied to observe, that Frederick had reached the limit of his strength and could not be trusted to preserve his composure any longer in face of this searching examination into the conduct of a woman from whom he had so lately detached himself.

XIX

POOR PHILEMON

The next day was the day of Agatha's funeral. She was to be buried in Portchester, by the side of her six children, and, as the day was fine, the whole town, as by common consent, assembled in the road along which the humble cortege was to make its way to the spot indicated.

From the windows of farmhouses, from between the trees of the few scattered thickets along the way, saddened and curious faces looked forth till Sweetwater, who walked as near as he dared to the immediate friends of the deceased, felt the impossibility of remembering them all and gave up the task in despair.

Before one house, about a mile out of town, the procession paused, and at a gesture from the minister everyone within sight took off their hats, amid a hush which made almost painfully apparent the twittering of birds and the other sounds of animate and inanimate nature, which are inseparable from a country road. They had reached widow Jones's cottage in which Philemon was then staying.

The front door was closed, and so were the lower windows, but in one of the upper casements a movement was perceptible, and in another instant there came into view a woman and man, supporting between them the impassive form of Agatha's husband. Holding him up in plain sight of the almost breathless throng below, the woman pointed to where his darling lay and appeared to say something to him.

Then there was to be seen a strange sight. The old man, with his thin white locks fluttering in the breeze, leaned forward with a smile, and holding out his arms, cried in a faint but joyful tone: "Agatha!" Then, as if realising for the first time that it was death he looked upon, and that the crowd below was a funeral procession, his face altered and he fell back with a low heartbroken moan into the arms of those who supported him.

As his white head disappeared from sight, the procession moved on, and from only one pair of lips went up that groan of sorrow with which every heart seemed surcharged. One groan. From whose lips did it come? Sweetwater endeavoured to ascertain, but was not able, nor could anyone inform him, unless it was Mr. Sutherland, whom he dared not approach.

This gentleman was on foot like the rest, with his arm fast linked in that of his son Frederick. He had meant to ride, for the distance was long for men past sixty; but finding the latter resolved to walk, he had consented to do the same rather than be separated from his son.

He had fears for Frederick—he could hardly have told why; and as the ceremony proceeded and Agatha was solemnly laid away in the place prepared for her, his sympathies grew upon him to such an extent that he found it difficult to quit the young man for a moment, or even to turn his eyes away from the face he had never seemed to know till now. But as friends and strangers were now leaving the yard, he controlled himself, and assuming a more natural demeanour, asked his son if he were now ready to ride back. But, to his astonishment, Frederick replied that he did not intend to return to Sutherland town at present; that he had business in Portchester, and that he was doubtful as to when he would be ready to return. As the old gentleman did not wish to raise a controversy, he said nothing, but as soon as he saw Frederick disappear up the road, he sent back the carriage he had ordered, saying that he would return in a Portchester gig as soon as he had settled some affairs of his own, which might and might not detain him there till evening.

Then he proceeded to a little inn, where he hired a room with windows that looked out on the high-road. In one of these windows he sat all day, watching for Frederick, who had gone farther up the road.

But no Frederick appeared, and with vague misgivings, for which as yet he had no name, he left the window and set out on foot for home.

It was now dark, but a silvery gleam on the horizon gave promise of the speedy rising of a full moon. Otherwise he would not have attempted to walk over a road proverbially dark and dismal.

The churchyard in which they had just laid away Agatha lay in his course. As he approached it he felt his heart fail, and stopping a moment at the stone wall that separated it from the highroad, he leaned against the trunk of a huge elm that guarded the gate of entrance. As he did so he heard a sound of repressed sobbing from some spot not very far away, and, moved by some undefinable impulse stronger than his will, he pushed open the gate and entered the sacred precincts.

Instantly the weirdness and desolation of the spot struck him. He wished, yet dreaded, to advance. Something in the grief of the mourner whose sobs he had heard had seized upon his heart-strings, and yet, as he hesitated, the sounds came again, and forgetting that his intrusion might not prove altogether welcome, he pressed forward, till he came within a few feet of the spot from which the sobs issued.

He had moved quietly, feeling the awesomeness of the place, and when he paused it was with a sensation of dread, not to be entirely explained by the sad and dismal surroundings. Dark as it was, he discerned the outline of a form lying stretched in speechless misery across a grave; but when, impelled by an almost irresistible compassion, he strove to speak, his tongue clove to the roof of his mouth and he only drew back farther into the shadow.

He had recognised the mourner and the grave. The mourner was Frederick and the grave that of Agatha Webb.

A few minutes later Mr. Sutherland reappeared at the door of the inn, and asked for a gig and driver to take him back to Sutherlandtown. He said, in excuse for his indecision, that he had undertaken to walk, but had found his strength inadequate to the exertion. He was looking very pale, and trembled so that the landlord, who took his order, asked him if he were ill. But Mr. Sutherland insisted that he was quite well, only in a hurry, and showed the greatest impatience till he was again started upon the road.

For the first half-mile he sat perfectly silent. The moon was now up, and the road stretched before them, flooded with light. As long as no one was to be seen on this road, or on the path running beside it, Mr. Sutherland held himself erect, his eyes fixed before him, in an attitude of anxious inquiry. But as soon as any sound came to break the silence, or there appeared in the distance ahead of them the least appearance of a plodding wayfarer, he drew back, and hid himself in the recesses of the vehicle. This happened several times. Then his whole manner changed. They had just passed Frederick, walking, with bowed head, toward Sutherlandtown.

But he was not the only person on the road at this time. A few minutes previously they had passed another man walking in the same direction. As Mr. Sutherland mused over this he found himself peering through the small window at the back of the buggy, striving to catch another glimpse of the two men plodding behind him. He could see them both, his son's form throwing its long shadow over the moonlit road, followed only too closely by the man whose ungainly shape he feared to acknowledge to himself was growing only too familiar in his eyes.

Falling into a troubled reverie, he beheld the well-known houses, and the great trees under whose shadow he had grown from youth to manhood, flit by him like phantoms in a dream. But suddenly one house and one place drew his attention with a force that startled him again into an erect attitude, and seizing with one hand the arm of the driver, he pointed with the other at the door of the cottage they were passing, saying in choked tones:

"See! see! Something dreadful has happened since we passed by here this morning. That is crape, Samuel, crape, hanging from the doorpost yonder! "

"Yes, it is crape, " answered the driver, jumping out and running up the path to look. "Philemon must be dead; the good Philemon. "

Here was a fresh blow. Mr. Sutherland bowed before it for a moment, then he rose hurriedly and stepped down into the road beside the driver.

"Get in again, " said he, "and drive on. Ride a half-mile, then come back for me. I must see the widow Jones. "

The driver, awed both by the occasion and the feeling it had called up in Mr. Sutherland, did as he was bid and drove away. Mr. Sutherland, with a glance back at the road lie had just traversed, walked painfully up the path to Mrs. Jones's door.

A moment's conversation with the woman who answered his summons proved the driver's supposition to be correct. Philemon had passed away. He had never rallied from the shock he had received. He had joined his beloved Agatha on the day of her burial, and the long tragedy of their mutual life was over.

"It is a mercy that no inheritor of their misfortune remains, " quoth the good woman, as she saw the affliction her tidings caused in this much-revered friend.

The assent Mr. Sutherland gave was mechanical. He was anxiously studying the road leading toward Portchester.

Suddenly he stepped hastily into the house.

"Will you be so good as to let me sit down in your parlour for a few minutes? " he asked. "I should like to rest there for an instant alone. This final blow has upset me. "

The good woman bowed. Mr. Sutherland's word was law in that town. She did not even dare to protest against the ALONE which he had so pointedly emphasised, but left him after making him, as she said, comfortable, and went back to her duties in the room above.

It was fortunate she was so amenable to his wishes, for no sooner had her steps ceased to be heard than Mr. Sutherland rose from the easy-chair in which he had been seated, and, putting out the lamp widow Jones had insisted on lighting, passed directly to the window, through which he began to peer with looks of the deepest anxiety.

A man was coming up the road, a young man, Frederick. As Mr. Sutherland recognised him he leaned forward with increased anxiety, till at the appearance of his son in front his scrutiny grew so strained and penetrating that it seemed to exercise a magnetic influence upon Frederick, causing him to look up.

The glance he gave the house was but momentary, but in that glance the father saw all that he had secretly dreaded. As his son's eye fell on that fluttering bit of crape, testifying to another death in this already much-bereaved community, he staggered wildly, then in a pause of doubt drew nearer and nearer till his fingers grasped this symbol of mourning and clung there. Next moment he was far down the road, plunging toward home in a state of great mental disorder.

A half-hour afterwards Mr. Sutherland reached home. He had not overtaken Frederick again, or even his accompanying shadow. Ascertaining at his own door that his son had not yet come in, but had been seen going farther up the hill, he turned back again into the road and proceeded after him on foot.

The next place to his own was occupied by Mr. Halliday. As he approached it he caught sight of a man standing half in and half out of the honeysuckle porch, whom he at first thought to be Frederick. But he soon saw that it was the fellow who had been following his son all the way from Portchester, and, controlling his first movement of dislike, he stepped up to him and quietly said:

"Sweetwater, is this you? "

The young man fell back and showed a most extraordinary agitation, quickly suppressed, however. "Yes, sir, it is no one else. Do you know what I am doing here? "

"I fear I do. You have been to Portchester. You have seen my son— "

Sweetwater made a hurried, almost an entreating, gesture.

"Never mind that, Mr. Sutherland. I had rather you wouldn't say anything about that. I am as much broken up by what I have seen as you are. I never suspected him of having any direct connection with this murder; only the girl to whom he has so unfortunately attached himself. But after what I have seen, what am I to think? what am I to do? I honour you; I would not grieve you; but—but— oh, sir, perhaps you can help me out of the maze into which I have stumbled. Perhaps you can assure me that Mr. Frederick did not leave the ball at the time she did. I missed him from among the dancers. I did not see him between twelve and three, but perhaps you did; and—and—"

His voice broke. He was almost as profoundly agitated as Mr. Sutherland. As for the latter, who found himself unable to reassure the other on this very vital point, having no remembrance himself of having seen Frederick among his guests during those fatal hours, he stood speechless, lost in abysses, the depth and horror of which only a father can appreciate. Sweetwater respected his anguish and for a moment was silent himself. Then he burst out:

"I had rather never lived to see this day than be the cause of shame or suffering to you. Tell me what to do. Shall I be deaf, dumb—"

Here Mr. Sutherland found voice.

"You make too much of what you saw, " said he. "My boy has faults and has lived anything but a satisfactory life, but he is not as bad as you would intimate. He can never have taken life. That would be incredible, monstrous, in one brought up as he has been. Besides, if he were so far gone in evil as to be willing to attempt crime, he had no motive to do so; Sweetwater, he had no motive. A few hundred dollars but these he could have got from me, and did, but—"

Why did the wretched father stop? Did he recall the circumstances under which Frederick had obtained these last hundreds from him? They were not ordinary circumstances, and Frederick had been in no ordinary strait. Mr. Sutherland could not but acknowledge to himself that there was something in this whole matter which contradicted the very plea he was making, and not being able to establish the conviction of his son's innocence in his own mind, he was too honourable to try to establish it in that of another. His next words betrayed the depth of his struggle:

"It is that girl who has ruined him, Sweetwater. He loves but doubts her, as who could help doing after the story she told us day before yesterday? Indeed, he has doubted her ever since that fatal night, and it is this which has broken his heart, and not— not—" Again the old gentleman paused; again he recovered himself, this time with a touch of his usual dignity and self-command. "Leave me, " he cried. "Nothing that you have seen has escaped me; but our interpretations of it may differ. I will watch over my son from this hour, and you may trust my vigilance. "

Sweetwater bowed.

"You have a right to command me, " said he. "You may have forgotten, but I have not, that I owe my life to you. Years ago— perhaps you can recall it—it was at the Black Pond—I was going down for the third time and my mother was screaming in terror on the bank, when you plunged in and—Well, sir, such things are never forgotten, and, as I said before, you have only to command me. " He turned to go, but suddenly came back. There were signs of mental conflict in his face and voice. "Mr. Sutherland, I am not a talkative man. If I trust your vigilance you may trust my discretion. Only I must have your word that you will convey no warning to your son. "

Mr. Sutherland made an indefinable gesture, and Sweetwater again disappeared, this time not to return. As for Mr. Sutherland, he remained standing before Mr. Halliday's door. What had the young man meant by this emphatic repetition of his former suggestion? That he would be quiet, also, and not speak of what he had seen? Why, then—But to the hope thus given, this honest-hearted gentleman would yield no quarter, and seeing a duty before him, a duty he dare not shirk, he brought his emotions, violent as they were, into complete and absolute subjection, and, opening Mr. Halliday's door, entered the house. They were old neighbours, and ceremony was ignored between them.

Finding the hall empty and the parlour door open he walked immediately into the latter room. The sight that met his eyes never left his memory. Agnes, his little Agnes, whom he had always loved and whom he had vainly longed to call by the endearing name of daughter, sat with her face towards him, looking up at Frederick. That young gentleman had just spoken to her, or she had just received something from his hand for her own was held out and her expression was one of gratitude and acceptance. She was not a beautiful girl, but she had a beautiful look, and at this moment it was exalted by a feeling the old gentleman had once longed, but now dreaded inexpressibly, to see there. What could it mean? Why did she show at this unhappy crisis, interest, devotion, passion almost, for one she had regarded with open scorn when it was the dearest wish of his heart to see them united? It was one of the contradictions of our mysterious human nature, and at this crisis and in this moment of secret heart-break and miserable doubt it made the old gentleman shrink, with his first feeling of actual despair.

The next moment Agnes had risen and they were both facing him.

"Good-evening, Agnes."

Mr. Sutherland forced himself to speak lightly.

"Ah, Frederick, do I find you here?" The latter question had more constraint in it.

Frederick smiled. There was an air of relief about him, almost of cheerfulness.

"I was just leaving," said he. "I was the bearer of a message to Miss Halliday." He had always called her Agnes before.

Mr. Sutherland, who had found his faculties confused by the expression he had surprised on the young girl's face, answered with a divided attention:

"And I have a message to give you. Wait outside on the porch for me, Frederick, till I exchange a word with our little friend here. "

Agnes, who had thrust something she held into a box that lay beside her on a table, turned with a confused blush to listen.

Mr. Sutherland waited till Frederick had stepped into the hall. Then he drew Agnes to one side and remorselessly, persistently, raised her face toward him till she was forced to meet his benevolent but searching regard.

"Do you know, " he whispered, in what he endeavoured to make a bantering tone, "how very few days it is since that unhappy boy yonder confessed his love for a young lady whose name I cannot bring myself to utter in your presence? "

The intent was kind, but the effect was unexpectedly cruel. With a droop of her head and a hurried gasp which conveyed a mixture of entreaty and reproach, Agnes drew back in a vague endeavour to hide her sudden uneasiness. He saw his mistake, and let his hands drop.

"Don't, my dear, " he whispered. "I had no idea it would hurt you to hear this. You have always seemed indifferent, hard even, toward my scapegrace son. And this was right, for—for—" What could he say, how express one-tenth of that with which his breast was labouring! He could not, he dared not, so ended, as we have intimated, by a confused stammering.

Agnes, who had never before seen this object of her lifelong admiration under any serious emotion, felt an impulse of remorse, as if she herself had been guilty of occasioning him embarrassment. Plucking up her courage, she wistfully eyed him.

"Did you imagine, " she murmured, "that I needed any warning against Frederick, who has never honoured me with his regard, as he has the young lady you cannot mention? I'm afraid you don't know me, Mr. Sutherland, notwithstanding I have sat on your knee and sometimes plucked at your beard in my infantile insistence upon attention."

"I am afraid I don't know you," he answered. "I feel that I know nobody now, not even my son."

He had hoped she would look up at this, but she did not.

"Will my little girl think me very curious and very impertinent if I ask her what my son Frederick was saying when I came into the room?"

She looked up now, and with visible candour answered him immediately and to the point:

"Frederick is in trouble, Mr. Sutherland. He has felt the need of a friend who could appreciate this, and he has asked me to be that friend. Besides, he brought me a packet of letters which he entreated me to keep for him. I took them, Mr. Sutherland, and I will keep them as he asked me to do, safe from everybody's inspection, even my own."

Oh! why had he questioned her? He did not want to know of these letters; he did not want to know that Frederick possessed anything which he was afraid to retain in his own possession.

"My son did wrong," said he, "to confide anything to your care which he did not desire to retain in his own home. I feel that I ought to see these letters, for if my son is in trouble, as you say, I, his father, ought to know it."

"I am not sure about that," she smiled. "His trouble may be of a different nature than you imagine. Frederick has led a life that he regrets. I think his chief source of suffering lies in the fact that it is so hard for him to make others believe that he means to do differently in the future."

"Does he mean to do differently?"

She flushed. "He says so, Mr. Sutherland. And I, for one, cannot help believing him. Don't you see that he begins to look like another man?"

Mr. Sutherland was taken aback. He had noticed this fact, and had found it a hard one to understand. To ascertain what her explanation of it might be, he replied at once:

"There is a change in him—a very evident change. What is the occasion of it? To what do you ascribe it, Agnes?"

How breathlessly he waited for her answer! Had she any suspicion of the awful doubts which were so deeply agitating himself that night? She did not appear to have.

"I hesitate," she faltered, "but not from any doubt of Frederick, to tell you just what I think lies at the bottom of the sudden change observable in him. Miss Page (you see, I can name her, if you cannot) has proved herself so unworthy of his regard that the shock he has received has opened his eyes to certain failings of his own which made his weakness in her regard possible. I do not know of any other explanation. Do you?"

At this direct question, breathed though it was by tender lips, and launched in ignorance of the barb which carried it to his heart, Mr. Sutherland recoiled and cast an anxious look upon the door. Then with forced composure he quietly said: "If you who are so much nearer his age, and, let me hope, his sympathy, do not feel sure of his real feelings, how should I, who am his father, but have never been his confidant?"

"Oh," she cried, holding out her hands, "such a good father! Some day he will appreciate that fact as well as others. Believe it, Mr. Sutherland, believe it." And then, ashamed of her glowing interest, which was a little more pronounced than became her simple attitude of friend toward a man professedly in love with another woman, she faltered and cast the shyest of looks upward at the face she had never seen turned toward her with anything but kindness. "I have confidence in Frederick's good heart," she added, with something like dignity.

"Would God that I could share it!" was the only answer she received. Before she could recover from the shock of these words, Mr. Sutherland was gone.

Agnes was more or less disconcerted by this interview. There was a lingering in her step that night, as she trod the little white-embowered chamber sacred to her girlish dreams, which bespake an overcharged heart; a heart that, before she slept, found relief in these few words whispered by her into the night air, laden with the sweetness of honeysuckles:

"Can it be that he is right? Did I need such a warning, —I, who have hated this man, and who thought that it was my hatred which made it impossible for me to think of anything or anybody else since we parted from each other last night? O me, if it is so! "

And from the great, wide world without, tremulous with moonlight, the echo seemed to come back:

"Woe to thee, Agnes Halliday, if this be so! "

XX

A SURPRISE FOR MR. SUTHERLAND

Meanwhile Mr. Sutherland and Frederick stood facing each other in the former's library. Nothing had been said during their walk down the hill, and nothing seemed likely to proceed from Frederick now, though his father waited with great and growing agitation for some explanation that would relieve the immense strain on his heart. At last he himself spoke, dryly, as we all speak when the heart is fullest and we fear to reveal the depth of our emotions.

"What papers were those you gave into Agnes Halliday's keeping? Anything which we could not have more safely, not to say discreetly, harboured in our own house? "

Frederick, taken aback, for he had not realised that his father had seen these papers, hesitated for a moment; then he boldly said:

"They were letters—old letters—which I felt to be better out of this house than in it. I could not destroy them, so I gave them into the guardianship of the most conscientious person I know. I hope you won't demand to see those letters. Indeed, sir, I hope you won't demand to see them. They were not written for your eye, and I would rather rest under your displeasure than have them in any way made public. "

Frederick showed such earnestness, rather than fear, that Mr. Sutherland was astonished.

"When were these letters written? " he asked. "Lately, or before— You say they are old; how old? "

Frederick's breath came easier.

"Some of them were written years ago—most of them, in fact. It is a personal matter—every man has such. I wish I could have destroyed them. You will leave them with Agnes, sir? "

"You astonish me, " said Mr. Sutherland, relieved that he could at least hope that these letters were in nowise connected with the subject of his own frightful suspicions. "A young girl, to whom you certainly were most indifferent a week ago, is a curious guardian of letters you decline to show your father."

"I know it," was Frederick's sole reply.

Somehow the humility with which this was uttered touched Mr. Sutherland and roused hopes he had supposed dead. He looked his son for the first time directly in the eye, and with a beating heart said:

"Your secrets, if you have such, might better be entrusted to your father. You have no better friend—" and there he stopped with a horrified, despairing feeling of inward weakness. If Frederick had committed a crime, anything would be better than knowing it. Turning partially aside, he fingered the papers on the desk before which he was standing. A large envelope, containing some legal document, lay before him. Taking it up mechanically, he opened it. Frederick as mechanically watched him.

"I know," said the latter, "that I have no better friend. You have been too good, too indulgent. What is it, father? You change colour, look ill, what is there in that paper?"

Mr. Sutherland straightened himself; there was a great reserve of strength in this broken-down man yet. Fixing Frederick with a gaze more penetrating than any he had yet bestowed upon him, he folded his hands behind him with the document held tightly between them, and remarked:

"When you borrowed that money from me you did it like a man who expected to repay it. Why? Whence did you expect to receive the money with which to repay me? Answer, Frederick; this is your hour for confession."

Frederick turned so pale his father dropped his eyes in mercy.

"Confess?" he repeated. "What should I confess? My sins? They are too many. As for that money, I hoped to return it as any son might hope to reimburse his father for money advanced to pay a gambler's debt. I said I meant to work. My first money earned shall be offered to you. I—"

"Well? Well? " His father was holding the document he had just read, opened out before his eyes.

"Didn't you expect THIS? " he asked. "Didn't you know that that poor woman, that wretchedly murdered, most unhappy woman, whose death the whole town mourns, had made you her heir? That by the terms of this document, seen by me here and now for the first time, I am made executor and you the inheritor of the one hundred thousand dollars or more left by Agatha Webb? "

"No! " cried Frederick, his eyes glued to the paper, his whole face and form expressing something more akin to terror than surprise. "Has she done this? Why should she? I hardly knew her. "

"No, you hardly knew her. And she? She hardly knew you; if she had she would have abhorred rather than enriched you. Frederick, I had rather see you dead than stand before me the inheritor of Philemon and Agatha Webb's hard-earned savings. "

"You are right; it would be better, " murmured Frederick, hardly heeding what he said. Then, as he encountered his father's eye resting upon him with implacable scrutiny, he added, in weak repetition: "Why should she give her money to me? What was I to her that she should will me her fortune? "

The father's finger trembled to a certain line in the document, which seemed to offer some explanation of this; but Frederick did not follow it. He had seen that his father was expecting a reply to the question he had previously put, and he was casting about in his mind how to answer it.

"When did you know of this will? " Mr. Sutherland now repeated. "For know of it you did before you came to me for money. "

Frederick summoned up his full courage and confronted his father resolutely.

"No, " said he, "I did not know of it. It is as much of a surprise to me as it is to you. "

He lied. Mr. Sutherland knew that he lied and Frederick knew that he knew it. A shadow fell between them, which the older, with that unspeakable fear upon him roused by Sweetwater's whispered suspicions, dared no longer attempt to lift.

After a few minutes in which Frederick seemed to see his father age before his eyes, Mr. Sutherland coldly remarked:

"Dr. Talbot must know of this will. It has been sent here to me from Boston by a lawyer who drew it up two years ago. The coroner may not as yet have heard of it. Will you accompany me to his office tomorrow? I should like to have him see that we wish to be open with him in an affair of such importance."

"I will accompany you gladly," said Frederick, and seeing that his father neither wished nor was able to say anything further, he bowed with distant ceremony as to a stranger and quietly withdrew. But when the door had closed between them and only the memory of his father's changed countenance remained to trouble him, he paused and laid his hand again on the knob, as if tempted to return. But he left without doing so, only to turn again at the end of the hall and gaze wistfully back. Yet he went on.

As he opened his own door and disappeared within, he said half audibly:

"Easy to destroy me now, Amabel. One word and I am lost!"

BOOK II

THE MAN OF NO REPUTATION

XXI

SWEETWATER REASONS

And what of Sweetwater, in whose thoughts and actions the interest now centres?

When he left Mr. Sutherland it was with feelings such as few who knew him supposed him capable of experiencing. Unattractive as he was in every way, ungainly in figure and unprepossessing of countenance, this butt of the more favoured youth in town had a heart whose secret fires were all the warmer for being so persistently covered, and this heart was wrung with trouble and heavy with a struggle that bade fair to leave him without rest that night, if not for many nights to come. Why? One word will explain. Unknown to the world at large and almost unknown to himself, his best affections were fixed upon the man whose happiness he thus unexpectedly saw himself destined to destroy. He loved Mr. Sutherland.

The suspicion which he now found transferred in his own mind from the young girl whose blood-stained slippers he had purloined during the excitement of the first alarm, to the unprincipled but only son of his one benefactor, had not been lightly embraced or thoughtlessly expressed. He had had time to think it out in all its bearings. During that long walk from Portchester churchyard to Mr. Halliday's door, he had been turning over in his mind everything that he had heard and seen in connection with this matter, till the dim vision of Frederick's figure going on before him was not more apparent to his sight than was the guilt he so deplored to his inward understanding.

He could not help but recognise him as the active party in the crime he had hitherto charged Amabel with. With the clew offered by Frederick's secret anguish at the grave of Agatha, he could read the whole story of this detestable crime as plainly as if it had been written in letters of fire on the circle of the surrounding darkness. Such anguish under such circumstances on the part of such a man could mean but one thing—remorse; and remorse in the breast of one so proverbially careless and corrupt, over the death of a woman who was neither relative nor friend, could have but one interpretation, and that was guilt.

No other explanation was possible. Could one be given, or if any evidence could be adduced in contradiction of this assumption, he would have dismissed his new suspicion with more heartiness even than he had embraced his former one. He did not wish to believe Frederick guilty. He would have purchased an inner conviction of his innocence almost at the price of his own life, not because of any latent interest in the young man himself, but because he was Charles Sutherland's son, and the dear, if unworthy, centre of all that noble man's hopes, aims, and happiness. But he could come upon no fact capable of shaking his present belief. Taking for truth Amabel's account of what she had seen and done on that fatal night—something which he had hesitated over the previous day, but which he now found himself forced to accept or do violence to his own secret convictions—and adding to it such facts as had come to his own knowledge in his self-imposed role of detective, he had but to test the events of that night by his present theory of Frederick's guilt, to find them hang together in a way too complete for mistake.

For what had been his reasons for charging Amabel herself with the guilt of a crime she only professed to have been a partial witness to?

They were many.

First—The forced nature of her explanations in regard to her motive for leaving a merry ball and betaking herself to the midnight road in her party dress and slippers. A woman of her well-known unsympathetic nature might use the misery of the Zabels as a pretext for slipping into town at night, but never would be influenced by it as a motive.

Second—The equally unsatisfactory nature of the reasons she gave for leaving the course she had marked out for herself and entering upon the pursuit of an unknown man into a house in which she had no personal interest and from which she had just seen a bloody dagger thrown out. The most callous of women would have shrunk from letting her curiosity carry her thus far.

Third—The poverty of her plea that, after having braved so much in her desire to identify this criminal, she was so frightened at his near approach as to fail to lift her head when the opportunity was given her to recognise him.

Fourth—Her professed inability to account for the presence of the orchid from her hair being found in the room with Batsy.

Fifth—Her evident attempt to throw the onus of the crime on an old man manifestly incapable from physical causes of committing it.

Sixth—The improbability, which she herself should have recognised, of this old man, in his extremely weak condition, ignoring the hiding-places offered by the woods back of his own house, for the sake of one not only involving a long walk, but situated close to a much-frequented road, and almost in view of the Sutherland mansion.

Seventh—The transparent excuse of sympathy for the old man and her desire to save him from the consequences of his crime, which she offered in extenuation of her own criminal avowal of having first found and then reburied the ill-gotten gains she had come upon in her persistent pursuit of the flying criminal. So impulsive an act might be consistent with the blind compassion of some weak-headed but warm-hearted woman, but not with her self- interested nature, incapable of performing any heroic deed save from personal motives or the most headlong passion.

Lastly—The weakness of her explanation in regard to the cause which led her to peer into the Zabel cottage through a hole made in the window-shade. Curiosity has its limits even in a woman's breast, and unless she hoped to see more than was indicated by her words, her action was but the precursor of a personal entrance into a room where we have every reason to believe the twenty- dollar bill was left.

A telling record and sufficient to favour the theory of her personal guilt if, after due thought, certain facts in contradiction to this assumption had not offered themselves to his mind even before he thought of Frederick as the unknown man she had followed down the hillside, as, for instance:

This crime, if committed by her, was done deliberately and with a premeditation antedating her departure from the ballroom. Yet she went upon this errand in slippers, white slippers at that, something which so cool and calculating a woman would have avoided, however careless she might have shown herself in other regards.

Again, guilt awakens cunning, even in the dullest breast; but she, keen beyond most men even, and so self-poised that the most searching examination could not shake her self-control, betrayed an utter carelessness as to what she did with these slippers on her return, thrusting them into a place easily accessible to the most casual search. Had she been conscious of guilt and thus amenable to law, the sight of blood and mud-stains on those slippers would have appalled her, and she would have made some attempt to destroy them, and not put them behind a picture and forgotten them.

Again, would she have been so careless with a flower she knew to be identified with herself? A woman who deliberately involves herself in crime has quick eyes; she would have seen that flower fall. At all events, if she had been immediately responsible for its being on the scene of crime she would, with her quick wit, have found some excuse or explanation for it, instead of defying her examiners with some such words as these: "It is a fact for you to explain. I only know that I did not carry this flower into that room of death."

Again, had she been actuated in her attempt to fix the crime on old James Zabel by a personal consciousness of guilt and a personal dread, she would not have stopped at suggestion in her allusions to the person she watched burying the treasure in the woods. Instead of speaking of him as a shadow whose flight she had followed at a distance, she would have described his figure as that of the same old man she had seen enter the Zabel cottage a few minutes before, there being no reason for indefiniteness on this point, her conscience being sufficiently elastic for any falsehood that would further her ends. And lastly, her manner, under the examination to which she had been subjected, was not that of one who felt herself under a personal attack. It was a strange, suggestive, hesitating manner, baffling alike to him who had more or less sounded her strange nature and to those who had no previous knowledge of her freaks and subtle intellectual power, and only reaching its height of hateful charm and mysterious daring when Frederick appeared on the scene and joined, or seemed to join, himself to the number of her examiners.

Now, let all suspicion of her as an active agent in this crime be dropped, assume Frederick to be the culprit and she the simple accessory after the fact, and see how inconsistencies vanish, and how much more natural the whole conduct of this mysterious woman appears.

Amabel Page left a merry dance at midnight and stole away into the Sutherland garden in her party dress and slippers—why? Not to fulfil an errand which anyone who knows her cold and unsympathetic nature can but regard as a pretext, but because she felt it imperative to see if her lover (with whose character, temptations, and necessities she was fully acquainted, and in whose excited and preoccupied manner she had probably discovered signs of a secretly growing purpose) meant indeed to elude his guests and slip away to town on the dangerous and unholy enterprise suggested by their mutual knowledge of the money to be obtained there by one daring enough to enter a certain house open like their own to midnight visitors.

She followed at such an hour and into such a place, not an unknown man casually come upon, but her lover, whom she had tracked from the garden of his father's house, where she had lain in wait for him. It took courage to do this, but a courage no longer beyond the limit of feminine daring, for her fate was bound up in his and she could not but feel the impulse to save him from the consequences of crime, if not from the crime itself.

As for the aforementioned flower, what more natural than that Frederick should have transferred it from her hair to his buttonhole during some of their interviews at the ball, and that it should have fallen from its place to the floor in the midst of his possible struggle with Batsy?

And with this assumption of her perfect knowledge as to who the man was who had entered Mrs. Webb's house, how much easier it is to understand why she did not lift her head when she heard him descend the stairs! No woman, even one so depraved as she, would wish to see the handsome face of her lover in the glare of a freshly committed crime, and besides she might very easily be afraid of him, for a man has but a blow for the suddenly detected witness of his crime unless that witness is his confidant, which from every indication Sweetwater felt bound to believe Amabel was not.

Her flight to the Zabel cottage, after an experience which would madden most women, can now be understood. She was still following her lover. The plan of making Agatha's old and wretched friend amenable for her death originated with Frederick and not with Amabel. It was he who first started for the Zabel cottage. It was he who left the bank bill there. This is all clear, and even the one contradictory fact of the dagger having been seen in the old man's hand was not a stumbling-block to Sweetwater. With the audacity of one confident of his own insight, he explained it to himself thus: The dagger thrown from the window by the assassin, possibly because he knew of Zabel's expected visit there that night, fell on the grass and was picked up by Amabel, only to be flung down again in the brightest part of the lawn. It was lying there then, when, a few minutes later and before either Frederick or Amabel had left the house, the old man entered the yard in a state of misery bordering on frenzy. He and his brother were starving, had been starving for days. He was too proud to own his want, and too loyal to his brother to leave him for the sake of the food prepared for them both at Agatha's house, and this was why he had hesitated over his duty till this late hour, when his own secret misery or, perhaps, the hope of relieving his brother drove him to enter the gate he had been accustomed to see open before him in glad hospitality. He finds the lights burning in the house above and below, and encouraged by the welcome they seem to hold out, he staggers up the path, ignorant of the tragedy which was at that very moment being enacted behind those lighted windows. But half-way toward the house he stops, the courage which has brought him so far suddenly fails, and in one of those quick visions which sometimes visit men in extremity, he foresees the astonishment which his emaciated figure is likely to cause in these two old friends, and burying his face in his hands he stops and bitterly communes with himself before venturing farther. Fatal stop! fatal communing! for as he stands there he sees a dagger, his own old dagger, how lost or how found he probably did not stop to ask, lying on the grass and offering in its dumb way suggestions as to how he might end this struggle without any further suffering. Dizzy with the new hope, preferring death to the humiliation he saw before him in Agatha's cottage, he dashes out of the yard, almost upsetting Mr. Crane, who was passing by on his homeward way from an errand of mercy. A little while later Amabel comes upon him lying across his own doorstep. He has made an effort to enter, but his long walk and the excitement of this last bitter hour have been too much for him. As she watches him he gains strength and struggles to his feet, while she, aghast at the sight of the dagger she had herself flung down in Agatha's yard, and dreading the encounter between this old man and the lover she had been following to this place, creeps around the house and looks into the first window she finds open. What does she expect to see? Frederick brought face to face with this desperate figure with its uplifted knife. But instead of that she beholds another old man seated at a table and—Amabel had paused when she reached that AND—and Sweetwater had not then seen how important this pause was, but now he understood it. Now he saw that if she had not had a subtle purpose in view, that if she had wished to tell the truth rather than produce false inferences in the minds of those about her calculated to save the criminal as she called him, she would have completed her sentence thus: "I saw an old man seated at a table and Frederick Sutherland standing over him. " For Sweetwater had no longer a doubt that Frederick was in that room at that moment. What further she saw, whether she was witness to an encounter between this intruder and James, or whether by some lingering on the latter's part Frederick was able to leave the house without running across him, was a matter of comparative unimportance. What is of importance is that he did leave it and that Amabel, knowing it was Frederick, strove to make her auditors believe it was Zabel, who carried the remainder of the money into the woods. Yet she did not say so, and if her words on this subject could be carefully recalled, one would see that it was still her lover she was following and no old man, tottering on the verge of the grave and only surviving because of the task he was bent on performing.

Amabel's excuse for handling the treasure, and for her reburial of the same, comes now within the bounds of possibility. She hoped to share this money some day, and her greed was too great for her to let such an amount lie there untouched, while her caution led her to bury it deeper, even at the risk of the discovery she was too inexperienced to fear.

That she should forget to feign surprise when the alarm of murder was raised was very natural, and so was the fact that a woman with a soul so blunted to all delicate instincts, and with a mind so intent upon perfecting the scheme entered into by the murderer of throwing the blame upon the man whose dagger had been made use of, should persist in visiting the scene of crime and calling attention to the spot where that dagger had fallen. And so with her manner before her examiners. Baffling as that manner was, it still showed streaks of consistency, when you thought of it as the cloak of a subtle, unprincipled woman, who sees amongst her interlocutors the guilty man whom by a word she can destroy, but whom she exerts herself to save, even at the cost of a series of bizarre explanations.

She was playing with a life, a life she loved, but not with sincerity sufficient to rob the game of a certain delicate, if inconceivable, intellectual enjoyment. [Footnote: That Sweetwater in his hate, and with no real clew to the real situation, should come so near the truth as in this last supposition, shows the keenness of his insight.]

And Frederick? Had there been anything in his former life or in his conduct since the murder to give the lie to these heavy doubts against him? On the contrary. Though Sweetwater knew little of the dark record which had made this young man the disgrace of his family, what he did know was so much against him that he could well see that the distance usually existing between simple dissipation and desperate crime might be easily bridged by some great necessity for money. Had there been such a necessity? Sweetwater found it easy to believe so. And Frederick's manner? Was it that of an honest man simply shocked by the suspicions which had fallen upon the woman he loved? Had he, Sweetwater, not observed certain telltale moments in his late behaviour that required a deeper explanation even than this?

The cry, for instance, with which he had rushed from the empty ballroom into the woods on the opposite side of the road! Was it a natural cry or an easily explainable one? "Thank God! this terrible night is over! " Strange language to be uttered by this man at such a time and in such a place, if he did not already know what was to make this night of nights memorable through all this region. He did know, and this cry which had struck Sweetwater strangely at the time and still more strangely when he regarded it simply as a coincidence, now took on all the force of a revelation and the irresistible bubbling up in Frederick's breast of that remorse which had just found its full expression on Agatha's grave.

To some that remorse and all his other signs of suffering might be explained by his passion for the real criminal. But to Sweetwater it was only too evident that an egotist like Frederick Sutherland cannot suffer for another to such an extent as this, and that a personal explanation must be given for so personal a grief, even if that explanation involves the dreadful charge of murder.

It was when Sweetwater reached this point in his reasoning that Frederick disappeared beneath Mr. Halliday's porch, and Mr. Sutherland came up behind him. After the short conversation in which Sweetwater saw his own doubts more than reflected in the uneasy consciousness of this stricken father, he went home and the struggle of his life began.

XXII

SWEETWATER ACTS

Sweetwater had promised Mr. Sutherland that he would keep counsel in regard to his present convictions concerning Frederick's guilt; but this he knew he could not do if he remained in Sutherlandtown and fell under the pitiless examination of Mr. Courtney, the shrewd and able prosecuting attorney of the district. He was too young, too honest, and had made himself too conspicuous in this affair to succeed in an undertaking requiring so much dissimulation, if not actual falsehood. Indeed, he was not sure that in his present state of mind he could hear Frederick's name mentioned without flushing, and slight as such a hint might be, it would be enough to direct attention to Frederick, which once done could but lead to discovery and permanent disgrace to all who bore the name of Sutherland.

What was he to do then? How avoid a consequence he found himself absolutely unable to face? It was a problem which this night must solve for him. But how? As I have said, he went down to his house to think.

Sweetwater was not a man of absolute rectitude. He was not so much high-minded as large-hearted. He had, besides, certain foibles. In the first place, he was vain, and vanity in a very plain man is all the more acute since it centres in his capabilities, rather than in his appearance. Had Sweetwater been handsome, or even passably attractive, he might have been satisfied with the approbation of demure maidens and a comradeship with his fellows. But being one who could hope for nothing of this kind, not even for a decent return to the unreasoning heart-worship he felt himself capable of paying, and which he had once paid for a few short days till warned of his presumption by the insolence of the recipient, he had fixed his hope and his ambition on doing something which would rouse the admiration of those about him and bring him into that prominence to which he felt himself entitled. That he, a skilful musician, should desire to be known as a brilliant detective, is only one of the anomalies of human nature which it would be folly and a waste of time on our part to endeavour to explain. That, having chosen to exercise his wits in this way, he should so well succeed that he dared not for his life continue in the work he had so publicly undertaken, occasioned in him a pang of disappointment almost as insufferable as that brought by the realisation of what his efforts were likely to bring upon the man to whose benevolence he owed his very life. Hence his struggle, which must be measured by the extent of his desires and the limitations which had been set to his nature by his surroundings and the circumstances of his life and daily history.

If we enter with him into the humble cottage where he was born and from which he had hardly strayed more than a dozen miles in the twenty-two years of his circumscribed life, we may be able to understand him better.

It was an unpainted house perched on an arid hillside, with nothing before it but the limitless sea. He had found his way to it mechanically, but as he approached the narrow doorway he paused and turned his face towards the stretch of heaving waters, whose low or loud booming had been first his cradle song and then the ceaseless accompaniment of his later thoughts and aspirations. It was heaving yet, ceaselessly heaving, and in its loud complaint there was a sound of moaning not always to be found there, or so it seemed to Sweetwater in his present troubled mood.

Sighing as this sound reached his ear, and shuddering as its meaning touched his heart, Sweetwater pushed open the door of his small house, and entered.

"It is I, mamsie!" he shouted, in what he meant to be his usual voice; but to a sensitive ear—and what ear is so sensitive as a mother's?—there was a tremble in it that was not wholly natural.

"Is anything the matter, dear?" called out that mother, in reply.

The question made him start, though he replied quickly enough, and in more guarded tones:

"No, mamsie. Go to sleep. I'm tired, that's all."

Would to God that was all! He recalled with envy the days when he dragged himself into the house at sundown, after twelve long hours of work on the docks. As he paused in the dark hallway and listened till he heard the breathing of her who had called him DEAR—the only one in the world who ever had or ever would call him DEAR—he had glimpses of that old self which made him question if his self-tutoring on the violin, and the restless ambition which had driven him out of the ways of his ancestors into strange attempts for which he was not prepared by any previous discipline, had brought him happiness or improved his manhood. He was forced to acknowledge that the sleep of those far-distant nights of his busy boyhood was sweeter than the wakefulness of these later days, and that it would have been better for him, and infinitely better for her, if he had remained at the carpenter's bench and been satisfied with a repetition of his father's existence.

His mother was the only person sharing that small house with him, and once assured that she was asleep, he lighted a lamp in the empty kitchen and sat down.

It was just twelve o'clock. This, to anyone accustomed to this peculiar young man's habits, had nothing unusual in it. He was accustomed to come home late and sit thus by himself for a short time before going up-stairs. But, to one capable of reading his sharp and none too mobile countenance, there was a change in the character of the brooding into which he now sank, which, had that mother been awake to watch him, would have made every turn of his eye and movement of his hand interesting and important.

In the first place, the careless attitude into which he had fallen was totally at variance with the restless glance which took in every object in that well-known room so associated with his mother and her daily work that he could not imagine her in any other surroundings, and wondered sometimes if she would seem any longer his mother if transplanted to other scenes and engaged in other tasks.

Little things, petty objects of household use or ornament, which he had seen all his life without specially noticing them, seemed under the stress of his present mood to acquire a sudden importance and fix themselves indelibly in his memory. There, on a nail driven long before he was born, hung the little round lid-holder he had pieced together in his earliest years and presented to his mother in a gush of pride greater than any he had since experienced. She had never used it, but it always hung upon the one nail in the one place, as a symbol of his love and of hers. And there, higher up on the end of the shelf barren enough of ornaments, God wot, were a broken toy and a much-defaced primer, mementos likewise of his childhood; and farther along the wall, on a sort of raised bench, a keg, the spigot of which he was once guilty of turning on in his infantile longing for sweets, only to find he could not turn it back again until all the floor was covered with molasses, and his appetite for the forbidden gratified to the full. And yonder, dangling from a peg, never devoted to any other use, hung his father's old hat, just where he had placed it on the fatal morning when he came in and lay down on the sitting-room lounge for the last time; and close to it, lovingly close to it, Sweetwater thought, his mother's apron, the apron he had seen her wear at supper, and which he would see her wear at breakfast, with all its suggestions of ceaseless work and patient every-day thrift.

Somehow, he could not bear the sight of that apron. With the expectation now forming in his mind, of leaving this home and leaving this mother, this symbol of humble toil became an intolerable grief to him. Jumping up, he turned in another direction; but now another group of objects equally eloquent came under his eye. It was his mother's work-basket he saw, with a piece of sewing in it intended for him, and as if this were not enough, the table set for two, and at his place a little covered dish which held the one sweetmeat he craved for breakfast. The spectacles lying beside her plate told him how old she was, and as he thought of her failing strength and enfeebled ways, he jumped up again and sought another corner. But here his glances fell on his violin, and a new series of emotions awakened within him. He loved the instrument and played as much from natural intuition as acquired knowledge, but in the plan of action he had laid out for himself his violin could have no part. He would have to leave it behind. Feeling that his regrets were fast becoming too much for him, he left the humble kitchen and went up-stairs. But not to sleep. Locking the door (something he never remembered doing before in all his life), he began to handle over his clothes and other trivial belongings. Choosing out a certain strong suit, he laid it out on the bed and then went to a bureau drawer and drew out an old-fashioned wallet. This he opened, but after he had counted the few bills it contained he shook his head and put them all back, only retaining a little silver, which he slipped into one of the pockets of the suit he had chosen. Then he searched for and found a little Bible which his mother had once given him. He was about to thrust that into another pocket, but he seemed to think better of this, too, for he ended by putting it back into the drawer and taking instead a bit from one of his mother's old aprons which he had chanced upon on the stairway. This he placed as carefully in his watch pocket as if it had been the picture of a girl he loved. Then he undressed and went to bed.

Mrs. Sweetwater said afterwards that she never knew Caleb to talk so much and eat so little as he did that next morning at breakfast. Such plans as he detailed for unmasking the murderer of Mrs. Webb! Such business for the day! So many people to see! It made her quite dizzy, she said. And, indeed, Sweetwater was more than usually voluble that morning, —perhaps because he could not bear his mother's satisfied smile; and when he went out of the house it was with a laugh and a cheery "Good-bye, mamsie" that was in spiking contrast to the irrepressible exclamation of grief which escaped him when the door was closed between them. Ah, when should he enter those four walls again, and when should he see the old mother?

He proceeded immediately to town. A ship was preparing to sail that morning for the Brazils, and the wharves were alive with bustle. He stopped a moment to contemplate the great hulk rising and falling at her moorings, then he passed on and entered the building where he had every reason to expect to find Dr. Talbot and Knapp in discussion. It was very important to him that morning to learn just how they felt concerning the great matter absorbing him, for if suspicion was taking the direction of Frederick, or if he saw it was at all likely to do so, then would his struggle be cut short and all necessity for leaving town be at an end. It was to save Frederick from this danger that he was prepared to cut all the ties binding him to this place, and nothing short of the prospect of accomplishing this would make him willing to undergo such a sacrifice.

"Well, Sweetwater, any news, eh? " was the half-jeering, half-condescending greeting he received from the coroner.

Sweetwater, who had regained entire control over his feelings as soon as he found himself under the eye of this man and the supercilious detective he had attempted to rival, gave a careless shrug and passed the question on to Knapp. "Have you any news? " he asked.

Knapp, who would probably not have acknowledged it if he had, smiled the indulgent smile of a self-satisfied superior and uttered a few equivocal sentences. This was gall and wormwood to Sweetwater, but he kept his temper admirably and, with an air of bravado entirely assumed for the occasion, said to Dr. Talbot:

"I think I shall have something to tell you soon which will materially aid you in your search for witnesses. By to-morrow, at least, I shall know whether I am right or wrong in thinking I have discovered an important witness in quite an unexpected quarter. "

Sweetwater knew of no new witness, but it was necessary for him not only to have a pretext for the move he contemplated, but to so impress these men with an idea of his extreme interest in the approaching proceedings, that no suspicion should ever arise of his having premeditated an escape from them. He wished to appear the victim of accident; and this is why he took nothing from his home which would betray any intention of leaving it.

"Ha! indeed! " ejaculated the coroner with growing interest. "And may I ask——"

"Please, " urged Sweetwater, with a side look at Knapp, "do not ask me anything just yet. This afternoon, say, after I have had a certain interview with—What, are they setting sails on the Hesper already? " he burst out, with a quick glance from the window at the great ship riding at anchor a little distance from them in the harbour. "There is a man on her I must see. Excuse me—Oh, Mr. Sutherland! "

He fell back in confusion. That gentleman had just entered the room in company with Frederick.

XXIII

A SINISTER PAIR

"I beg your pardon, " stammered Sweetwater, starting aside and losing on the instant all further disposition to leave the room.

Indeed, he had not the courage to do so, even if he had had the will. The joint appearance of these two men in this place, and at an hour so far in advance of that which usually saw Mr. Sutherland enter the town, was far too significant in his eyes for him to ignore it. Had any explanation taken place between them, and had Mr. Sutherland's integrity triumphed over personal considerations to the point of his bringing Frederick here to confess?

Meanwhile Dr. Talbot had risen with a full and hearty greeting which proved to Sweetwater's uneasy mind that notwithstanding Knapp's disquieting reticence no direct suspicion had as yet fallen on the unhappy Frederick. Then he waited for what Mr. Sutherland had to say, for it was evident he had come there to say something. Sweetwater waited, too, frozen almost into immobility by the fear that it would be something injudicious, for never had he seen any man so changed as Mr. Sutherland in these last twelve hours, nor did it need a highly penetrating eye to detect that the relations between him and Frederick were strained to a point that made it almost impossible for them to more than assume their old confidential attitude. Knapp, knowing them but superficially, did not perceive this, but Dr. Talbot was not blind to it, as was shown by the inquiring look he directed towards them both while waiting.

Mr. Sutherland spoke at last.

"Pardon me for interrupting you so early, " said he, with a certain tremble in his voice which Sweetwater quaked to hear. "For certain reasons, I should be very glad to know, WE should be very glad to know, if during your investigations into the cause and manner of Agatha Webb's death, you have come upon a copy of her will. "

"No. "

Talbot was at once interested, so was Knapp, while Sweetwater withdrew further into his corner in anxious endeavour to hide his blanching cheek. "We have found nothing. We do not even know that she has made a will. "

"I ask, " pursued Mr. Sutherland, with a slight glance toward Frederick, who seemed, at least in Sweetwater's judgment, to have braced himself up to bear this interview unmoved, "because I have not only received intimation that she made such a will, but have even been entrusted with a copy of it as chief executor of the same. It came to me in a letter from Boston yesterday. Its contents were a surprise to me. Frederick, hand me a chair. These accumulated misfortunes—for we all suffer under the afflictions which have beset this town—have made me feel my years. "

Sweetwater drew his breath more freely. He thought he might understand by this last sentence that Mr. Sutherland had come here for a different cause than he had at first feared. Frederick, on the contrary, betrayed a failing ability to hide his emotion. He brought his father a chair, placed it, and was drawing back out of sight when Mr. Sutherland prevented him by a mild command to hand the paper he had brought to the coroner.

There was something in his manner that made Sweetwater lean forward and Frederick look up, so that the father's and son's eyes met under that young man's scrutiny. But while he saw meaning in both their regards, there was nothing like collusion, and, baffled by these appearances, which, while interesting, told him little or nothing, he transferred his attention to Dr. Talbot and Knapp, who had drawn together to see what this paper contained.

"As I have said, the contents of this will are a surprise to me, " faltered Mr. Sutherland. "They are equally so to my son. He can hardly be said to have been a friend even of the extraordinary woman who thus leaves him her whole fortune. "

"I never spoke with her but twice, " exclaimed Frederick with a studied coldness, which was so evidently the cloak of inner agitation that Sweetwater trembled for its effect, notwithstanding the state of his own thoughts, which were in a ferment. Frederick, the inheritor of Agatha Webb's fortune! Frederick, concerning whom his father had said on the previous night that he possessed no motive for wishing this good woman's death! Was it the discovery that such a motive existed which had so aged this man in the last twelve hours?

Sweetwater dared not turn again to see. His own face might convey too much of his own fears, doubts, and struggle.

But the coroner, for whose next words Sweetwater listened with acute expectancy, seemed to be moved simply by the unexpectedness of the occurrence. Glancing at Frederick with more interest than he had ever before shown him, he cried with a certain show of enthusiasm:

"A pretty fortune! A very pretty fortune! " Then with a deprecatory air natural to him in addressing Mr. Sutherland, "Would it be indiscreet for me to ask to what our dear friend Agatha alludes in her reference to your late lamented wife? " His finger was on a clause of the will and his lips next minute mechanically repeated what he was pointing at:

"'In remembrance of services rendered me in early life by Marietta Sutherland, wife of Charles Sutherland of Sutherlandtown, I bequeath to Frederick, sole child of her affection, all the property, real and personal, of which I die possessed. ' Services rendered! They must have been very important ones, " suggested Dr. Talbot.

Mr. Sutherland's expression was one of entire perplexity and doubt.

"I do not remember my wife ever speaking of any special act of kindness she was enabled to show Agatha Webb. They were always friends, but never intimate ones. However, Agatha could be trusted to make no mistake. She doubtless knew to what she referred. Mrs. Sutherland was fully capable of doing an extremely kind act in secret. "

For all his respect for the speaker, Dr. Talbot did not seem quite satisfied. He glanced at Frederick and fumbled the paper uneasily.

"Perhaps you were acquainted with the reason for this legacy—this large legacy, " he emphasised.

Frederick, thus called upon, nay, forced to speak, raised his head, and without perhaps bestowing so much as a thought on the young man behind him who was inwardly quivering in anxious expectancy of some betrayal on his part which would precipitate disgrace and lifelong sorrow on all who bore the name of Sutherland, met Dr.

Talbot's inquiring glance with a simple earnestness surprising to them all, and said:

"My record is so much against me that I am not surprised that you wonder at my being left with Mrs. Webb's fortune. Perhaps she did not fully realise the lack of estimation in which I am deservedly held in this place, or perhaps, and this would be much more like her, she hoped that the responsibility of owing my independence to so good and so unfortunate a woman might make a man of me."

There was a manliness in Frederick's words and bearing that took them all by surprise. Mr. Sutherland's dejection visibly lightened, while Sweetwater, conscious of the more than vital interests hanging upon the impression which might be made by this event upon the minds of the men present, turned slightly so as to bring their faces into the line of his vision.

The result was a conviction that as yet no real suspicion of Frederick had seized upon either of their minds. Knapp's face was perfectly calm and almost indifferent, while the good coroner, who saw this and every other circumstance connected with this affair through the one medium of his belief in Amabel's guilt, was surveying Frederick with something like sympathy.

"I fear," said he, "that others were not as ignorant of your prospective good fortune as you were yourself," at which Frederick's cheek turned a dark red, though he said nothing, and Sweetwater, with a sudden involuntary gesture indicative of resolve, gazed for a moment breathlessly at the ship, and then with an unexpected and highly impetuous movement dashed from the room crying loudly:

"I've seen him! I've seen him! he's just going on board the ship. Wait for me, Dr. Talbot. I'll be back in fifteen minutes with such a witness—"

Here the door slammed. But they could hear his hurrying footsteps as he plunged down the stairs and rushed away from the building.

It was an unexpected termination to an interview fast becoming unbearable to the two Sutherlands, but no one, not even the old gentleman himself, took in its full significance.

He was, however, more than agitated by the occurrence and could hardly prevent himself from repeating aloud Sweetwater's final word, which after their interview at Mr. Halliday's gate, the night before, seemed to convey to him at once a warning and a threat. To keep himself from what he feared might prove a self-betrayal, he faltered out in very evident dismay:

"What is the matter? What has come over the lad?"

"Oh!" cried Dr. Talbot, "he's been watching that ship for an hour. He is after some man he has just seen go aboard her. Says he's a new and important witness in this case. Perhaps he is. Sweetwater is no man's fool, for all his small eyes and retreating chin. If you want proof of it, wait till he comes back. He'll be sure to have something to say."

Meanwhile they had all pressed forward to the window. Frederick, who carefully kept his face out of his father's view, bent half-way over the sill in his anxiety to watch the flying figure of Sweetwater, who was making straight for the dock, while Knapp, roused at last, leaned over his shoulder and pointed to the sailors on the deck, who were pulling in the last ropes, preparatory to sailing.

"He's too late: they won't let him aboard now. What a fool to hang around here till he saw his man, instead of being at the dock to nab him! That comes of trusting a country bumpkin. I knew he'd fail us at the pinch. They lack training, these would-be detectives. See, now! He's run up against the mate, and the mate pushes him back. His cake is all dough, unless he's got a warrant. Has he a warrant, Dr. Talbot?"

"No," said the coroner, "he didn't ask for one. He didn't even tell me whom he wanted. Can it be one of those two passengers you see on the forward deck, there?"

It might well be. Even from a distance these two men presented a sinister appearance that made them quite marked figures among the crowd of hurrying sailors and belated passengers.

"One of them is peering over the rail with a very evident air of anxiety. His eye is on Sweetwater, who is dancing with impatience. See, he is gesticulating like a monkey, and—By the powers, they are going to let him go aboard!"

Mr. Sutherland, who had been leaning heavily against the window-jamb in the agitation of doubt and suspense which Sweetwater's unaccountable conduct had evoked, here crossed to the other side and stole a determined look at Frederick. Was his son personally interested in this attempt of the amateur detective? Did he know whom Sweetwater sought, and was he suffering as much or more than himself from the uncertainty and fearful possibilities of the moment? He thought he knew Frederick's face, and that he read dread there, but Frederick had changed so completely since the commission of this crime that even his father could no longer be sure of the correct meaning either of his words or expression.

The torture of the moment continued.

"He climbs like a squirrel, " remarked Dr. Talbot, with a touch of enthusiasm. "Look at him now—he's on the quarterdeck and will be down in the cabins before you can say Jack Robinson. I warrant they have told him to hurry. Captain Dunlap isn't the man to wait five minutes after the ropes are pulled in. "

"Those two men have shrunk away behind some mast or other, " cried Knapp. "They are the fellows he's after. But what can they have to do with the murder? Have you ever seen them here about town, Dr. Talbot? "

"Not that I remember; they have a foreign air about them. Look like South Americans. "

"Well, they're going to South America. Sweetwater can't stop them. He has barely time to get off the ship himself. There goes the last rope! Have they forgotten him? They're drawing up the ladder. "

"No: the mate stops them; see, he's calling the fellow. I can hear his voice, can't you? Sweetwater's game is up. He'll have to leave in a hurry. What's the rumpus now? "

"Nothing, only they've scattered to look for him; the fox is down in the cabins and won't come up, laughing in his sleeve, no doubt, at keeping the vessel waiting while he hunts up his witness. "

"If it's one of those two men he's laying a trap for he won't snare him in a hurry. They're sneaks, those two, and—Why, the sailors are coming back shaking their heads. I can almost hear from here the captain's oaths. "

"And such a favourable wind for getting out of the harbour! Sweetwater, my boy, you are distinguishing yourself. If your witness don't pan out well you won't hear the last of this in a hurry. "

"It looks as if they meant to sail without waiting to put him ashore, " observed Frederick in a low tone, too carefully modulated not to strike his father as unnatural.

"By jingoes, so it does! " ejaculated Knapp. "There go the sails! The pilot's hand is on the wheel, and Dr. Talbot, are you going to let your cunning amateur detective and his important witness slip away from you like this? "

"I cannot help myself, " said the coroner, a little dazed himself at this unexpected chance. "My voice wouldn't reach them from this place; besides they wouldn't heed me if it did. The ship is already under way and we won't see Sweetwater again till the pilot's boat comes back. "

Mr. Sutherland moved from the window and crossed to the door like a man in a dream. Frederick, instantly conscious of his departure, turned to follow him, but presently stopped and addressing Knapp for the first time, observed quietly:

"This is all very exciting, but I think your estimate of this fellow Sweetwater is just. He's a busybody and craves notoriety above everything. He had no witness on board, or, if he had, it was an imaginary one. You will see him return quite crestfallen before night, with some trumped-up excuse of mistaken identity. "

The shrug which Knapp gave dismissed Sweetwater as completely from the affair as if he had never been in it.

"I think I may now regard myself as having this matter in my sole charge, " was his curt remark, as he turned away, while Frederick, with a respectful bow to Dr. Talbot, remarked in leaving:

"I am at your service, Dr. Talbot, if you require me to testify at the inquest in regard to this will. My testimony can all be concentrated into the one sentence, 'I did not expect this bequest, and have no theories to advance in explanation of it. ' But it has made me feel myself Mrs. Webb's debtor, and given me a justifiable interest in the inquiry which, I am told, you open to- morrow into the cause and manner of her death. If there is a guilty person in this case, I shall raise no barrier in the way of his conviction."

And while the coroner's face still showed the embarrassment which this last sentence called up, his mind being now, as ever, fixed on Amabel, Frederick offered his arm to his father, whose condition was not improved by the excitements of the last half- hour, and proceeded to lead him from the building.

Whatever they thought, or however each strove to hide their conclusions from the other, no words passed between them till they came in full sight of the sea, on a distant billow of which the noble-ship bound for the Brazils rode triumphantly on its outward course. Then Mr. Sutherland remarked, with a suggestive glance at the vessel:

"The young man who has found an unexpected passage on that vessel will not come back with the pilot."

Was the sigh which was Frederick's only answer one of relief? It certainly seemed so.

XXIV

IN THE SHADOW OF THE MAST

Mr. Sutherland was right. Sweetwater did not return with the pilot. According to the latter there was no Sweetwater on board the ship to return. At all events the minutest search had not succeeded in finding him in the cabins, though no one had seen him leave the vessel, or, indeed, seen him at all after his hasty dash below decks. It was thought on board that he had succeeded in reaching shore before the ship set sail, and the pilot was suitably surprised at learning this was not so. So were Sweetwater's friends and associates with the exception of a certain old gentleman living on the hill, and Knapp the detective. He, that is the latter, had his explanation at his tongue's end:

"Sweetwater is a fakir. He thought he could carry off the honours from the regular force, and when he found he couldn't he quietly disappeared. We shall hear of him again in the Brazils."

An opinion that speedily gained ground, so that in a few hours Sweetwater was all but forgotten, save by his mother, whose heart was filled with suspense, and by Mr. Sutherland, whose breast was burdened by gratitude. The amazing fact of Frederick, the village scapegrace and Amabel's reckless, if aristocratic, lover, having been made the legatee of the upright Mrs. Webb's secret savings had something to do with this. With such a topic at hand, not only the gossips, but those who had the matter of Agatha's murder in hand, found ample material to occupy their thoughts and tongues, without wasting time over a presumptuous busybody, who had not wits enough to know that five minutes before sailing-time is an unfortunate moment in which to enter a ship.

And where was Sweetwater, that he could not be found on the shore or on the ship? We will follow him and see. Accustomed from his youth to ramble over the vessels while in port, he knew this one as well as he did his mother's house. It was, therefore, a surprise to the sailors when, shortly after the departure of the pilot, they came upon him lying in the hold, half buried under a box which had partially fallen upon him. He was unconscious, or appeared to be so, and when brought into open light showed marks of physical distress and injury; but his eye was clear and his expression hardly as rueful as one would expect in a man who finds himself en route for the Brazils with barely a couple of dollars in his pocket and every prospect of being obliged to work before the mast to earn his passage. Even the captain noticed this and eyed him with suspicion. But Sweetwater, rousing to the necessities of the occasion, forthwith showed such a mixture of discouragement and perplexity that the honest sailor was deceived and abated half at least of his oaths. He gave Sweetwater a hammock and admitted him to the mess, but told him that as soon as his bruises allowed him to work he should show himself on deck or expect the rough treatment commonly bestowed on stowaways.

It was a prospect to daunt some men, but not Sweetwater. Indeed it was no more than he had calculated upon when he left his savings behind with his old mother and entered upon this enterprise with only a little change in his pocket. He had undertaken out of love and gratitude to Mr. Sutherland to rid Frederick of a dangerous witness and he felt able to complete the sacrifice. More than that, he was even strangely happy for a time. The elation of the willing victim was his, that is for a few short hours, then he began to think of his mother. How had she borne his sudden departure? What would she think had befallen him, and how long would he have to wait before he could send her word of his safety? If he was to be of real service to the man he venerated, he must be lost long enough for the public mind to have become settled in regard to the mysteries of the Webb murder and for his own boastful connection with it to be forgotten. This might mean years of exile. He rather thought it did; meanwhile his mother! Of himself he thought little.

By sundown he felt himself sufficiently recovered from his bruises to go up on deck. It was a mild night, and the sea was running in smooth long waves that as yet but faintly presaged the storm brewing on the distant horizon. As he inhaled the fresh air, the joy of renewed health began to infuse its life into his veins and lift the oppression from his heart, and, glad of a few minutes of quiet enjoyment, he withdrew to a solitary portion of the deck and allowed himself to forget his troubles in contemplation of the rapidly deepening sky and boundless stretch of waters.

But such griefs and anxieties as weighed upon this man's breast are not so easily shaken off. Before he realised it his thoughts had recurred to the old theme, and he was wondering if he was really of sufficient insignificance in the eyes of his fellow- townsmen not to be sought for and found in that distant country to which he was bound.

Would they, in spite of his precautions, suspect that he had planned this evasion and insist on his return, or would he be allowed to slip away and drop out of sight like the white froth he was watching on the top of the ever-shifting waves? He had boasted of possessing a witness. Would they believe that boast and send a detective in search of him, or would they take his words for the bombast they really were and proceed with their investigations in happy relief at the loss of his intrusive assistance?

As this was a question impossible for him to answer, he turned to other thoughts and fretted himself for a while with memories of Amabel's disdain and Frederick's careless acceptance of a sacrifice he could never know the cost of, mixed strangely with relief at being free of it all and on the verge of another life. As the dark settled, his head fell farther and farther forward on the rail he was leaning against, till he became to any passing eye but a blurred shadow mixing with other shadows equally immovable.

Unlike them, however, his shadow suddenly shifted. Two men had drawn near him, one speaking pure Spanish and the other English. The English was all that Sweetwater could understand, and this half of the conversation was certainly startling enough. Though he could not, of coarse, know to what or whom it referred, and though it certainly had nothing to do with him, or any interest he represented or understood, he could not help listening and remembering every word. The English-speaking man uttered the first sentence he comprehended. It was this:

"Shall it be to-night? "

The answer was in Spanish.

Again the English voice:

"He has come up. I saw him distinctly as he passed the second mast. "

More Spanish; then English:

"You may if you want to, but I'll never breathe easy while he's on the ship. Are you sure he's the fellow we fear? "

A rapid flow of words from which Sweetwater got nothing. Then slowly and distinctly in the sinister tones he had already begun to shiver at:

"Very good. The R. F. A. should pay well for this, " with the quick addition following a hurried whisper: "All right! I'd send a dozen men to the bottom for half that money. But 'ware there! Here's a fellow watching us! If he has heard—"

Sweetwater turned, saw two desperate faces projected toward him, realised that something awful, unheard of, was about to happen, and would have uttered a yell of dismay, but that the very intensity of his fright took away his breath. The next minute he felt himself launched into space and enveloped in the darkness of the chilling waters. He had been lifted bodily and flung headlong into the sea.

XXV

IN EXTREMITY

Sweetwater's one thought as he sank was, "Now Mr. Sutherland need fear me no longer."

But the instinct of life is strong in every heart, and when he found himself breathing the air again he threw out his arms wildly and grasped a spar.

It was life to him, hope, reconnection with his kind. He clutched, clung, and, feeling himself floating, uttered a shout of mingled joy and appeal that unhappily was smothered in the noise of the waters and the now rapidly rising wind.

Whence had come this spar in his desperate need? He never knew, but somewhere in his remote consciousness an impression remained of a shock to the waves following his own plunge into the water, which might mean that this spar had been thrown out after him, perhaps by the already repentant hands of the wretches who had tossed him to his death. However it came, or from whatever source, it had at least given him an opportunity to measure his doom and realise the agonies of hope when it alternates with despair.

The darkness was impenetrable. It was no longer that of heaven, but of the nether world, or so it seemed to this dazed soul, plunged suddenly from dreams of exile into the valley of the shadow of death. And such a death! As he realised its horrors, as he felt the chill of night and the oncoming storm strike its piercing fangs into his marrow, and knew that his existence and the hope of ever again seeing the dear old face at the fireside rested upon the strength of his will and the tenacity of his life- clutch, he felt his heart fail, and the breath that was his life cease in a gurgle of terror. But he clung on, and, though no comfort came, still clung, while vague memories of long-ago shipwrecks, and stories told in his youth of men, women, and children tossing for hours on a drifting plank, flashed through his benumbed brain, and lent their horror to his own sensations of apprehension and despair.

He wanted to live. Now that the dread spectre had risen out of the water and had its clutch on his hair, he realised that the world held much for him, and that even in exile he might work and love and enjoy God's heaven and earth, the green fields and the blue sky. Not such skies as were above him now. No, this was not sky that overarched him, but a horrible vault in which the clouds, rushing in torn masses, had the aspect of demons stooping to contend for him with those other demons that with long arms and irresistible grip were dragging at him from below. He was alone on a whirling spar in the midst of a midnight ocean, but horror and a pitiless imagination made this conflict more than that of the elements, and his position an isolation beyond that of man removed from his fellows. He was almost mad. Yet he clung.

Suddenly a better frame of mind prevailed. The sky was no lighter, save as the lightning came to relieve the overwhelming darkness by a still more overwhelming glare, nor were the waves less importunate or his hold on the spar more secure; but the horror seemed to have lifted, and the practical nature of the man reasserted itself. Other men had gone through worse dangers than these and survived to tell the tale, as he might survive to tell his. The will was all—will and an indomitable courage; and he had will and he had courage, or why had he left his home to dare a hard and threatening future purely from a sentiment of gratitude? Could he hold on long enough, daylight would come; and if, as he now thought possible, he had been thrown into the sea within twenty hours after leaving Sutherlandtown, then he must be not far from Cape Cod, and in the direct line of travel from New York to Boston. Rescue would come, and if the storm which was breaking over his head more and more furiously made it difficult for him to retain his hold, it certainly would not wreck his spar or drench him more than he was already drenched, while every blast would drive him shoreward. The clinging was all, and filial love would make him do that, even in the semi-unconsciousness which now and then swept over him. Only, would it not be better for Mr. Sutherland if he should fail and drop away into the yawning chasms of the unknown world beneath? There were moments when he thought so, and then his clutch perceptibly weakened; but only once did he come near losing his hold altogether. And that was when he thought he heard a laugh. A laugh, here in the midst of ocean! in the midst of storm! a laugh! Were demons a reality, then? Yes; but the demon he had heard was of his own imagination; it had a face of Medusa sweetness and the laugh—Only Amabel's rang out so thrillingly false, and with such diabolic triumph. Amabel, who might be laughing in her dreams at this very moment of his supreme misery, and who assuredly would laugh if conscious of his suffering and aware of the doom to which his self-sacrifice had brought him. Amabel! the thought of her made the night more dark, the waters more threatening, the future less promising. Yet he would hold on if only to spite her who hated him and whom he hated almost as much as he loved Mr. Sutherland.

It was his last conscious thought for hours. When morning broke he was but a nerveless figure, with sense enough to cling, and that was all.

XXVI

THE ADVENTURE OF THE PARCEL

"A man! Haul him in! Don't leave a poor fellow drifting about like that."

The speaker, a bluff, hearty skipper, whose sturdy craft had outridden one of the worst storms of the season, pointed to our poor friend Sweetwater, whose head could just be seen above the broken spar he clung to. In another moment a half-dozen hands were stretched for him, and the insensible form was drawn in and laid on a deck which still showed the results of the night's fierce conflict with the waters.

"Damn it! how ugly he is!" cried one of the sailors, with a leer at the half-drowned man's face. "I'd like to see the lass we'd please in saving him. He's only fit to poison a devil-fish!"

But though more than one laugh rang out, they gave him good care, and when Sweetwater came to life and realised that his blood was pulsing warmly again through his veins, and that a grey sky had taken the place of darkness, and a sound board supported limbs which for hours had yielded helplessly to the rocking billows, he saw a ring of hard but good-natured faces about him and realised quite well what had been done for him when one of them said:

"There! he'll do now; all hands on deck! We can get into New Bedford in two days if this wind holds. Nor' west!" shouted the skipper to the man at the tiller. "We'll sup with our old women in forty-eight hours!"

New Bedford! It was the only word Sweetwater heard. So, he was no farther away from Sutherlandtown than that. Evidently Providence had not meant him to escape. Or was it his fortitude that was being tried? A man as humble as he might easily be lost even in a place as small as New Bedford. It was his identity he must suppress. With that unrecognised he might remain in the next village to Sutherlandtown without fear of being called up as a witness against Frederick. But could he suppress it? He thought he could. At all events he meant to try.

"What's your name? " were the words he now heard shouted in his ear.

"Jonathan Briggs, " was his mumbled reply. "I was blown off a ship's deck in the gale last night. "

"What ship? "

"The Proserpine. " It was the first name that suggested itself to him.

"Oh, I thought it might have been the Hesper; she foundered off here last night. "

"Foundered? The Hesper? " The hot blood was shooting now through his veins.

"Yes, we just picked up her name-board. That was before we got a hold on you. "

Foundered! The ship from which he had been so mercilessly thrown! And all on board lost, perhaps. He began to realise the hand of Providence in his fate.

"It was the Hesper I sailed on. I'm not just clear yet in my head. My first voyage was made on the Proserpine. Well, bless the gale that blew me from that deck! "

He seemed incoherent, and they left him again for a little while. When they came back he had his story all ready, which imposed upon them just so far as it was for their interest. Their business on this coast was not precisely legitimate, and when they found he simply wanted to be set on shore, they were quite willing to do thus much for him. Only they regretted that he had barely two dollars and his own soaked clothing to give in exchange for the motley garments they trumped up among them for his present comfort. But he, as well as they, made the best of a bad bargain, he especially, as his clothes, which would be soon scattered among half a dozen families, were the only remaining clew connecting him with his native town. He could now be Jonathan Briggs indeed. Only who was Jonathan Briggs, and how was he to earn a living under these unexpected conditions?

At the end of a couple of days he was dexterously landed on the end of a long pier, which they passed without stopping, on their way to their own obscure anchorage. As he jumped from the rail to the pier and felt again the touch of terra firma he drew a long breath of uncontrollable elation. Yet he had not a cent in the world, no friends, and certainly no prospects. He did not even know whether to turn to the right or the left as he stepped out upon the docks, and when he had decided to turn to the right as being on the whole more lucky, he did not know whether to risk his fortune in the streets of the town or to plunge into one of the low-browed drinking houses whose signs confronted him on this water-lane.

He decided that his prospects for a dinner were slim in any case, and that his only hope of breaking fast that day lay in the use he might make of one of his three talents. Either he must find a fiddle to play on, a carpenter's bench to work at, or a piece of detective shadowing to do. The last would bring him before the notice of the police, which was just the thing he must avoid; so it was fiddling or carpentry he must seek, either of which would be difficult to obtain in his present garb. But of difficulties Sweetwater was not a man to take note. He had undertaken out of pure love for a good man to lose himself. He had accomplished this, and now was he to complain because in doing so he was likely to go hungry for a day or two? No; Amabel might laugh at him, or he might fancy she did, while struggling in the midst of rapidly engulfing waters, but would she laugh at him now? He did not think she would. She was of the kind who sometimes go hungry themselves in old age. Some premonition of this might give her a fellow feeling.

He came to a stand before a little child sitting on an ill-kept doorstep. Smiling at her kindly, he waited for her first expression to see how he appeared in the eyes of innocence. Not so bad a man, it seemed, though his naturally plain countenance was not relieved by the seaman's cap and knitted shirt he wore. For she laughed as she looked at him, and only ran away because there wasn't room for him to pass beside her.

Comforted a little, he sauntered on, glancing here and there with that sharp eye of his for a piece of work to be done. Suddenly he came to a halt. A market-woman had got into an altercation with an oysterman, and her stall had been upset in the contention, and her vegetables were rolling here and there. He righted her stall, picked up her vegetables, and in return got two apples and a red herring he would not have given to a dog at home. Yet it was the sweetest morsel he had ever tasted, and the apples might have been grown in the garden of the Hesperides from the satisfaction and pleasure they gave this hungry man. Then, refreshed, he dashed into the town. It should now go hard but he would earn a night's lodging.

The day was windy and he was going along a narrow street, when something floated down from a window above past his head. It was a woman's veil, and as he looked up to see where it came from he met the eyes of its owner looking down from an open casement above him. She was gesticulating, and seemed to point to someone up the street. Glad to seize at anything which promised emolument or adventure, he shouted up and asked her what she wanted.

"That man down there! " she cried; "the one in a long black coat going up the street. Keep after him and stop him; tell him the telegram has come. Quick, quick, before he gets around the corner! He will pay you; run! "

Sweetwater, with joy in his heart, —for five cents was a boon to him in the present condition of his affairs, —rushed after the man she had pointed out and hastily stopped him.

"Someone, " he added, "a woman in a window back there, bade me run after you and say the telegram has come. She told me you would pay me, " he added, for he saw the man was turning hastily back, without thinking of the messenger. "I need the money, and the run was a sharp one. "

With a preoccupied air, the man thrust his hand into his pocket, pulled out a coin, and handed it to him. Then he walked hurriedly off. Evidently the news was welcome to him. But Sweetwater stood rooted to the ground. The man had given him a five-dollar gold piece instead of the nickel he had evidently intended.

How hungrily Sweetwater eyed that coin! In it was lodging, food, perhaps a new article or so of clothing. But after a moment of indecision which might well be forgiven him, he followed speedily after the man and overtook him just as he reached the house from which the woman's veil had floated.

"Sir, pardon me; but you gave me five dollars instead of five cents. It was a mistake; I cannot keep the money. "

The man, who was not just the sort from whom kindness would be expected, looked at the money in Sweetwater's palm, then at the miserable, mud-bespattered clothes he wore (he had got that mud helping the poor market-woman), and stared hard at the face of the man who looked so needy and yet returned him five dollars.

"You're an honest fellow, " he declared, not offering to take back the gold piece. Then, with a quick glance up at the window, "Would you like to earn that money? "

Sweetwater broke out into a smile, which changed his whole countenance.

"Wouldn't I, sir? "

The man eyed him for another minute with scrutinising intensity. Then he said shortly:

"Come up-stairs with me. "

They entered the house, went up a flight or two, and stopped at a door which was slightly ajar.

"We are going into the presence of a lady, " remarked the man. "Wait here until I call you. "

Sweetwater waited, the many thoughts going through his mind not preventing him from observing all that passed.

The man, who had left the door wide open, approached the lady who was awaiting him, and who was apparently the same one who had sent Sweetwater on his errand, and entered into a low but animated conversation. She held a telegram in her hand which she showed him, and then after a little earnest parley and a number of pleading looks from them both toward the waiting Sweetwater, she disappeared into another room, from which she brought a parcel neatly done up, which she handed to the man with a strange gesture. Another hurried exchange of words and a meaning look which did not escape the sharp eye of the watchful messenger, and the man turned and gave the parcel into Sweetwater's hands.

"You are to carry this, " said he, "to the town hall. In the second room to the right on entering you will see a table surrounded by chairs, which at this hour ought to be empty. At the head of the table you will find an arm-chair. On the table directly in front of this you will lay this packet. Mark you, directly before the chair and not too far from the edge of the table. Then you are to come out. If you see anyone, say you came to leave some papers for Mr. Gifford. Do this and you may keep the five dollars and welcome. "

Sweetwater hesitated. There was something in the errand or in the manner of the man and woman that he did not like.

"Don't potter! " spoke up the latter, with an impatient look at her watch. "Mr. Gifford will expect those papers. "

Sweetwater's sensitive fingers closed on the package he held. It did not feel like papers.

"Are you going? " asked the man.

Sweetwater looked up with a smile. "Large pay for so slight a commission, " he ventured, turning the packet over and over in his hand.

"But then you will execute it at once, and according to the instructions I have given you, " retorted the man. "It is your trustworthiness I pay for. Now go. "

Sweetwater turned to go. After all it was probably all right, and five dollars easily earned is doubly five dollars. As he reached the staircase he stumbled. The shoes he wore did not fit him.

"Be careful, there! " shouted the woman, in a shrill, almost frightened voice, while the man stumbled back into the room in a haste which seemed wholly uncalled for. "If you let the packet fall you will do injury to its contents. Go softly, man, go softly! "

Yet they had said it held papers!

Troubled, yet hardly knowing what his duty was, Sweetwater hastened down the stairs, and took his way up the street. The town hall should be easy to find; indeed, he thought he saw it in the distance. As he went, he asked himself two questions: Could he fail to deliver the package according to instructions, and yet earn his money? And was there any way of so delivering it without risk to the recipient or dereliction of duty to the man who had intrusted it to him and whose money he wished to earn? To the first question his conscience at once answered no; to the second the reply came more slowly, and before fixing his mind determinedly upon it he asked himself why he felt that this was no ordinary commission. He could answer readily enough. First, the pay was too large, arguing that either the packet or the placing of the packet in a certain position on Mr. Gifford's table was of uncommon importance to this man or this woman. Secondly, the woman, though plainly and inconspicuously clad, had the face of a more than ordinarily unscrupulous adventuress, while her companion was one of those saturnine-faced men we sometimes meet, whose first look puts us on our guard and whom, if we hope nothing from him, we instinctively shun. Third, they did not look like inhabitants of the house and rooms in which he found them. Nothing beyond the necessary articles of furniture was to be seen there; not a trunk, not an article of clothing, nor any of the little things that mark a woman's presence in a spot where she expects to spend a day or even an hour. Consequently they were transients and perhaps already in the act of flight. Then he was being followed. Of this he felt sure. He had followed people himself, and something in his own sensations assured him that his movements were under surveillance. It would, therefore, not do to show any consciousness of this, and he went on directly and as straight to his goal as his rather limited knowledge of the streets would allow. He was determined to earn this money and to earn it without disadvantage to anyone. And he thought he saw his way.

At the entrance of the town hall he hesitated an instant. An officer was standing in the doorway, it would be easy to call his attention to the packet he held and ask him to keep his eye on it. But this might involve him with the police, and this was something, as we know, which he was more than anxious to avoid. He reverted to his first idea.

Mixing with the crowd just now hurrying to and fro through the long corridors, he reached the room designated and found it, as he had been warned he should, empty.

Approaching the table, he laid down the packet just as he had been directed, in front of the big arm chair, and then, casting a hurried look towards the door and failing to find anyone watching him, he took up a pencil lying near-by and scrawled hastily across the top of the packet the word "Suspicious. " This he calculated would act as a warning to Mr. Gifford in case there was anything wrong about the package, and pass as a joke with him, and even the sender, if there was not. And satisfied that he had both earned his money and done justice to his own apprehensions, he turned to retrace his steps. As before, the corridors were alive with hurrying men of various ages and appearance, but only two attracted his notice. One of these was a large, intellectual- looking man, who turned into the room from which he had just emerged, and the other a short, fair man, with a countenance he had known from boyhood. Mr. Stone of Sutherlandtown was within ten paces of him, and he was as well known to the good postmaster as the postmaster was to him. Could anyone have foreseen such a chance!

Turning his back with a slow slouch, he made for a rear door he saw swinging in and out before him. As he passed through he cast a quick look behind him. He had not been recognised. In great relief he rushed on, knocking against a man standing against one of the outside pillars.

"Halloo! " shouted this man.

Sweetwater stopped. There was a tone of authority in the voice which he could not resist.

XXVII

THE ADVENTURE OF THE SCRAP OF PAPER AND THE THREE WORDS

"What are you trying to do? Why do you fall over a man like that? Are you drunk?"

Sweetwater drew himself up, made a sheepish bow, and muttered pantingly:

"Excuse me, sir. I'm in a hurry; I'm a messenger."

The man who was not in a hurry seemed disposed to keep him for a moment. He had caught sight of Sweetwater's eye, which was his one remarkable feature, and he had also been impressed by that word messenger, for he repeated it with some emphasis.

"A messenger, eh? Are you going on a message now?"

Sweetwater, who was anxious to get away from the vicinity of Mr. Stone, shrugged his shoulders in careless denial, and was pushing on when the gentleman again detained him.

"Do you know," said he, "that I like your looks? You are not a beauty, but you look like a fellow who, if he promised to do a thing, would do it and do it mighty well too."

Sweetwater could not restrain a certain movement of pride. He was honest, and he knew it, but the fact had not always been so openly recognised.

"I have just earned five dollars by doing a commission for a man," said he, with a straightforward look. "See, sir. It was honestly earned."

The man, who was young and had a rather dashing but inscrutable physiognomy, glanced at the coin Sweetwater showed him and betrayed a certain disappointment.

"So you're flush," said he. "Don't want another job?"

"Oh, as to that, " said Sweetwater, edging slowly down the street, "I'm always ready for business. Five dollars won't last forever, and, besides, I'm in need of new togs. "

"Well, rather, " retorted the other, carelessly following him. "Do you mind going up to Boston? "

Boston! Another jump toward home.

"No, " said Sweetwater, hesitatingly, "not if it's made worth my while. Do you want your message delivered to-day? "

"At once. That is, this evening. It's a task involving patience and more or less shrewd judgment. Have you these qualities, my friend? One would not judge it from your clothes. "

"My clothes! " laughed Sweetwater. Life was growing very interesting all at once. "I know it takes patience to WEAR them, and as for any lack of judgment I may show in their choice, I should just like to say I did not choose them myself, sir; they fell to me promiscuous-like as a sort of legacy from friends. You'll see what I'll do in that way if you give me the chance to earn an extra ten. "

"Ah, it's ten dollars you want. Well, come in here and have a drink and then we'll see. "

They were before a saloon house of less than humble pretensions, and as he followed the young gentleman in it struck him that it was himself rather than his well-dressed and airy companion who would be expected to drink here. But he made no remark, though he intended to surprise the man by his temperance.

"Now, look here, " said the young gentleman, suddenly seating himself at a dingy table in a very dark corner and motioning Sweetwater to do the same; "I've been looking for a man all day to go up to Boston for me, and I think you'll do. You know Boston? "

Sweetwater had great command over himself, but he flushed slightly at this question, though it was so dark where he sat with this man that it made very little difference.

"I have been there, " said he.

"Very well, then, you will go again to-night. You will arrive there about seven, you will go the rounds of some half-dozen places whose names I will give you, and when you come across a certain gentleman whom I will describe to you, you will give him—"

"Not a package?" Sweetwater broke out with a certain sort of dread of a repetition of his late experience.

"No, this slip on which two words are written. He will want one more word, but before you give it to him you must ask for your ten dollars. You'll get them," he answered in response to a glance of suspicion from Sweetwater. Sweetwater was convinced that he had got hold of another suspicious job. It made him a little serious. "Do I look like a go-between for crooks?" he asked himself. "I'm afraid I'm not so much of a success as I thought myself." But he said to the man before him: "Ten dollars is small pay for such business. Twenty-five would be nearer the mark."

"Very well, he will give you twenty-five dollars. I forgot that ten dollars was but little in advance of your expenses."

"Twenty-five if I find him, and he is in funds. What if I don't?"

"Nothing."

"Nothing?"

"Except your ticket; that I'll give you."

Sweetwater did not know what to say. Like the preceding job it might be innocent and it might not. And then, he did not like going to Boston, where he was liable to meet more than one who knew him.

"There is no harm in the business," observed the other, carelessly, pushing a glass of whiskey which had just been served him toward Sweetwater. "I would even be willing to do it myself, if I could leave New Bedford to-night, but I can't. Come! It's as easy as crooking your elbow."

"Just now you said it wasn't," growled Sweetwater, drinking from his glass. "But no matter about that, go ahead, I'll do it. Shall I have to buy other clothes?"

"I'd buy a new pair of trousers, " suggested the other. "The rest you can get in Boston. You don't want to be too much in evidence, you know. "

Sweetwater agreed with. him. To attract attention was what he most dreaded. "When does the train start? " he asked.

The young man told him.

"Well, that will give me time to buy what I want. Now, what are your instructions? "

The young man gave him a memorandum, containing four addresses. "You will find him at one of these places, " said he. "And now to know your man when you see him. He is a large, handsome fellow, with red hair and a moustache like the devil. He has been hurt, and wears his left hand in a sling, but he can play cards, and will be found playing cards, and in very good company too. You will have to use your discretion in approaching him. When once he sees this bit of paper, all will be easy. He knows what these two words mean well enough, and the third one, the one that is worth twenty-five dollars to you, is FREDERICK. "

Sweetwater, who had drunk half his glass, started so at this word, which was always humming in his brain, that he knocked over his tumbler and spilled what was left in it.

"I hope I won't forget that word, " he remarked, in a careless tone, intended to carry off his momentary show of feeling.

"If you do, then don't expect the twenty-five dollars, " retorted the other, finishing his own glass, but not offering to renew Sweetwater's.

Sweetwater laughed, said he thought he could trust his memory, and rose. In a half-hour he was at the depot, and in another fifteen minutes speeding out of New Bedford on his way to Boston.

He had had but one anxiety—that Mr. Stone might be going up to Boston too. But, once relieved of this apprehension, he settled back, and for the first time in twelve hours had a minute in which to ask himself who he was, and what he was about. Adventure had followed so fast upon adventure that he was in a more or less dazed condition, and felt as little capable of connecting event with event as if he had been asked to recall the changing pictures of a kaleidoscope. That affair of the packet, now, was it or was it not serious, and would he ever know what it meant or how it turned out?

Like a child who had been given a pebble, and told to throw it over the wall, he had thrown and run, giving a shout of warning, it is true, but not knowing, nor ever likely to know, where the stone had fallen, or what it was meant to do. Then this new commission on which he was bent—was it in any way connected with the other, or merely the odd result of his being in the right place at the right moment? He was inclined to think the latter. And yet how odd it was that one doubtful errand should be followed by another, in a town no larger than New Bedford, forcing him from scene to scene, till he found himself speeding toward the city he least desired to enter, and from which he had the most to fear!

But brooding over a case like this brings small comfort. He felt that he had been juggled with, but he neither knew by whose hand nor in what cause. If the hand was that of Providence, why he had only to go on following the beck of the moment, while if it was that of Fate, the very uselessness of struggling with it was apparent at once. Poor reasoning, perhaps, but no other offered, and satisfied that whatever came his intentions were above question, he settled himself at last for a nap, of which he certainly stood in good need. When he awoke he was in Boston.

The first thing he did was to show his list of addresses and inquire into what quarter they would lead him. To his surprise he found it to be the fashionable quarter. Two of them were names of well-known club-houses, a third that of a first-class restaurant, and the fourth that of a private house on Commonwealth Avenue. Heigho! and he was dressed like a tramp, or nearly so!

"Queer messenger, I, for such kind of work, " thought he. "I wonder why he lighted on such a rough-looking customer. He must have had his reasons. I wonder if he wished the errand to fail. He bore himself very nonchalantly at the depot. When I last saw him his face and attitude were those of a totally unconcerned man. Have I been sent on a fool's chase after all? "

The absurdity of this conclusion struck him, however, as he reasoned: "Why, then, should he have paid my fare? Not as a benefit to me, of course, but for his own ends, whatever they might be. Let us see, then, what those ends are. So now for the gentleman of the red hair who plays cards with one arm in a sling. "

He thought that he might get entrance into the club-houses easily enough. He possessed a certain amount of insinuation when necessity required, and, if hard-featured, had a good expression which in unprejudiced minds defied criticism. Of porters and doorkeepers he was not afraid, and these were the men he must first encounter.

At the first club-house he succeeded easily enough in getting word with the man waiting in the large hall, and before many minutes learned that the object of his search was not to be found there that evening. He also learned his name, which was a great step towards the success of his embassy. It was Wattles, Captain Wattles, a marked man evidently, even in this exclusive and aristocratic club.

Armed with this new knowledge, be made his way to the second building of the kind and boldly demanded speech with Captain Wattles. But Captain Wattles had not yet arrived and he went out again this time to look him up at the restaurant.

He was not there. As Sweetwater was going out two gentlemen came in, one of whom said to the other in passing:

"Sick, do you say? I thought Wattles was made of iron. "

"So he was, " returned the other, "before that accident to his arm. Now the least thing upsets him. He's down at Haberstow's. "

That was all; the door was swung to between them. Sweetwater had received his clew, but what a clew! Haberstow's? Where was that?

Thinking the bold course the best one, he re-entered the restaurant and approached the gentlemen he had just seen enter.

"I heard you speak the name of Captain Wattles, " said he. "I am hunting for Captain Wattles. Can you tell me where he is? "

He soon saw that he had struck the wrong men for information. They not only refused to answer him, but treated him with open disdain. Unwilling to lose time, he left them, and having no other resource, hastened to the last place mentioned on his list.

It was now late, too late to enter a private house under ordinary circumstances, but this house was lighted up, and a carriage stood in front of it; so he had the courage to run up the steps and consult the large door-plate visible from the sidewalk. It read thus:

HABERSTOW.

Fortune had favoured him better than he expected.

He hesitated a moment, then decided to ring the bell. But before he had done so, the door opened and an old gentleman appeared seeing a younger man out. The latter had his arm in a sling, and bore himself with a fierceness that made his appearance somewhat alarming; the other seemed to be in an irate state of mind.

"No apologies! " the former was saying. "I don't mind the night air; I'm not so ill as that. When I'm myself again we'll have a little more talk. My compliments to your daughter, sir. I wish you a very good evening, or rather night. "

The old gentleman bowed, and as he did so Sweetwater caught a glimpse (it was the shortest glimpse in the world) of a sweet face beaming from a doorway far down the hall. There was pain in it and a yearning anxiety that made it very beautiful; then it vanished, and the old gentleman, uttering some few sarcastic words, closed the door, and Sweetwater found himself alone and in darkness.

The kaleidoscope had been given another turn.

Dashing down the stoop, he came upon the gentleman who had preceded him, just as he was seating himself in the carriage.

"Pardon me, " he gasped, as the driver caught up the reins; "you have forgotten something. " Then, as Captain Wattles looked hastily out, "You have forgotten me. "

The oath that rang out from under that twitching red moustache was something to startle even him. But he clung to the carriage window and presently managed to say:

"A messenger, sir, from New Bedford. I have been on the hunt for you for two hours. It won't keep, sir, for more than a half-hour longer. Where shall I find you during that time? "

Captain Wattles, on whom the name New Bedford seemed to have made some impression, pointed up at the coachman's box with a growl, in which command mingled strangely with menace. Then he threw himself back. Evidently the captain was not in very good humour.

Sweetwater, taking this as an order to seat himself beside the driver, did so, and the carriage drove off. It went at a rapid pace, and before he had time to propound more than a question or two to the coachman, it stopped before a large apartment-house in a brilliantly lighted street.

Captain Wattles got out, and Sweetwater followed him. The former, who seemed to have forgotten Sweetwater, walked past him and entered the building with a stride and swing that made the plain, lean, insignificant-looking messenger behind him feel smaller than ever. Indeed, he had never felt so small, for not only was the captain a man of superb proportions and conspicuous bearing, but he possessed, in spite of his fiery hair and fierce moustache, that beaute de diable which is at once threatening and imposing. Added to this, he was angry and so absorbed in his own thoughts that he would be very apt to visit punishment of no light character upon anyone who interfered with him. A pleasing prospect for Sweetwater, who, however, kept on with the dogged determination of his character up the first flight of stairs and then up another till they stopped, Captain Wattles first and afterwards his humble follower, before a small door into which the captain endeavoured to fit a key. The oaths which followed his failure to do this were not very encouraging to the man behind, nor was the kick which he gave the door after the second more successful attempt calculated to act in a very reassuring way upon anyone whose future pay for a doubtful task rested upon this man's good nature.

The darkness which met them both on the threshold of this now open room was speedily relieved by a burst of electric light, that

Agatha Webb

flooded the whole apartment and brought out the captain's swaggering form and threatening features with startling distinctness. He had thrown off his hat and was relieving himself of a cloak in a furious way that caused Sweetwater to shrink back, and, as the French say, efface himself as much as possible behind a clothes-tree standing near the door. That the captain had entirely forgotten him was evident, and for the present moment that gentleman was too angry to care or even notice if a dozen men stood at the door. As he was talking all this time, or rather jerking out sharp sentences, as men do when in a towering rage, Sweetwater was glad to be left unnoticed, for much can be gathered from scattered sentences, especially when a man is in too reckless a frame of mind to weigh them. He, therefore, made but little movement and listened; and these are some of the ejaculations and scraps of talk he heard:

"The old purse-proud fool! Honoured by my friendship, but not ready to accept me as his daughter's suitor! As if I would lounge away hours that mean dollars to me in his stiff old drawing-room, just to hear his everlasting drone about stocks up and stocks down, and politics gone all wrong. He has heard that I play cards, and — How pretty she looked! I believe I half like that girl, and when I think she has a million in her own right — Damn it, if I cannot win her openly and with papa's consent, I will carry her off with only her own. She's worth the effort, doubly worth it, and when I have her and her money — Eh! Who are you?"

He had seen Sweetwater at last, which was not strange, seeing that he had turned his way, and was within two feet of him.

"What are you doing here, and who let you in? Get out, or —"

"A message, Captain Wattles! A message from New Bedford. You have forgotten, sir; you bade me follow you."

It was curious to see the menace slowly die out of the face of this flushed and angry man as he met Sweetwater's calm eye and unabashed front, and noticed, as he had not done at first, the slip of paper which the latter resolutely held out.

"New Bedford; ah, from Campbell, I take it. Let me see!" And the hand which had shook with rage now trembled with a very different sort of emotion as he took the slip, cast his eyes over it, and then looked back at Sweetwater.

Now, Sweetwater knew the two words written on that paper. He could see out of the back of his head at times, and he had been able to make out these words when the man in New Bedford was writing them.

"Happenings; Afghanistan, " with the figures 2000 after the latter.

Not much sense in them singly or in conjunction, but the captain, muttering them over to himself, consulted a little book which he took from his breast pocket and found, or seemed to, a clew to their meaning. It could only have been a partial one, however, for in another instant he turned on Sweetwater with a sour look and a thundering oath.

"Is this all? " he shouted. "Does he call this a complete message? "

"There is another word, " returned Sweetwater, "which he bade me give you by word of mouth; but that word don't go for nothing. It's worth just twenty-five dollars. I've earned it, sir. I came up from New Bedford on purpose to deliver it to you. "

Sweetwater expected a blow, but he only got a stare.

"Twenty-five dollars, " muttered the captain. "Well, it's fortunate that I have them. And who are you? " he asked. "Not one of Campbell's pick-ups, surely? "

"I am a confidential messenger, " smiled Sweetwater, amused against his will at finding a name for himself. "I carry messages and execute commissions that require more or less discretion in the handling. I am paid well. Twenty-five dollars is the price of this job."

"So you have had the honour of informing me before, " blustered the other with an attempt to hide some serious emotion. "Why, man, what do you fear? Don't you see I'm hurt? You could knock me over with a feather if you touched my game arm. "

"Twenty-five dollars, " repeated Sweetwater.

The captain grew angrier. "Dash it! aren't you going to have them? What's the word? "

But Sweetwater wasn't going to be caught by chaff.

"C. O. D., " he insisted firmly, standing his ground, though certain that the blow would now fall. But no, the captain laughed, and tugging away with his one free hand at his pocket, he brought out a pocketbook, from which he managed deftly enough to draw out three bills. "There, " said he, laying them on the table, but keeping one long vigorous finger on them. "Now, the word. "

Sweetwater laid his own hand on the bills.

"Frederick, " said he.

"Ah! " said the other thoughtfully, lifting his finger and proceeding to stride up and down the room. "He's a stiff one. What he says, he will do. Two thousand dollars! and soon, too, I warrant. Well, I'm in a devil of a fix at last. " He had again forgotten the presence of Sweetwater.

Suddenly he turned or rather stopped. His eye was on the messenger, but he did not even see him. "One Frederick must offset the other, " he cried. "It's the only loophole out, " and he threw himself into a chair from which he immediately sprang up again with a yell. He had hurt his wounded arm.

Pandemonium reigned in that small room for a minute, then his eye fell again on Sweetwater, who, under the fascination of the spectacle offered him, had only just succeeded in finding the knob of the door. This time there was recognition in his look.

"Wait! " he cried. "I may have use for you too. Confidential messengers are hard to come by, and one that Campbell would employ must be all right. Sit down there! I'll talk to you when I'm ready. "

Sweetwater was not slow in obeying this command. Business was booming with him. Besides, the name of Frederick acted like a charm upon him. There seemed to be so many Fredericks in the world, and one of them lay in such a curious way near his heart.

Meanwhile the captain reseated himself, but more carefully. He had a plan or method of procedure to think out, or so it seemed, for he sat a long time in rigid immobility, with only the scowl of perplexity or ill-temper on his brow to show the nature of his thoughts. Then he drew a sheet of paper toward him, and began to write a letter. He was so absorbed over this letter and the manipulation of it, having but one hand to work with, that Sweetwater determined upon a hazardous stroke. The little book which the captain had consulted, and which had undoubtedly furnished him with a key to those two incongruous words, lay on the floor not far from him, having been flung from its owner's hand during the moments of passion and suffering I have above mentioned. To reach this book with his foot, to draw it toward him, and, finally, to get hold of it with his hand, was not difficult for one who aspired to be a detective, and had already done some good work in that direction. But it was harder to turn the leaves and find the words he sought without attracting the attention of his fierce companion. He, however, succeeded in doing this at last, the long list of words he found on every page being arranged alphabetically. It was a private code for telegraphic or cable messages, and he soon found that "Happenings" meant: "Our little game discovered; play straight until I give you the wink. " And that "Afghanistan" stood for: "Hush money. " As the latter was followed by the figures I have mentioned, the purport of the message needed no explanation, but the word "Frederick" did. So he searched for that, only to find that it was not in the book. There was but one conclusion to draw. This name was perfectly well known between them, and was that of the person, no doubt, who laid claim to the two thousand dollars.

Satisfied at holding this clew to the riddle, he dropped the book again at his side and skilfully kicked it far out into the room. Captain Wattles had seen nothing. He was a man who took in only one thing at a time.

The penning of that letter went on laboriously. It took so long that Sweetwater dozed, or pretended to, and when it was at last done, the clock on the mantelpiece had struck two.

"Halloo there, now! " suddenly shouted the captain, turning on the messenger. "Are you ready for another journey? "

"That depends, " smiled Sweetwater, rising sleepily and advancing. "Haven't got over the last one yet, and would rather sleep than start out again. "

"Oh, you want pay? Well, you'll get that fast enough if you succeed in your mission. This letter" he shook it with an impatient hand— "should be worth two thousand five hundred dollars to me. If you bring me back that money or its equivalent within twenty-four hours, I will give you a clean hundred of it. Good enough pay, I take it, for five hours' journey. Better than sleep, eh? Besides, you can doze on the cars."

Sweetwater agreed with him in all these assertions. Putting on his cap, he reached for the letter. He didn't like being made an instrument for blackmail, but he was curious to see to whom he was about to be sent. But the captain had grown suddenly wary.

"This is not a letter to be dropped in the mailbox," said he. "You brought me a line here whose prompt delivery has prevented me from making a fool of myself to-night. You must do as much with this one. It is to be carried to its destination by yourself, given to the person whose name you will find written on it, and the answer brought back before you sleep, mind you, unless you snatch a wink or so on the cars. That it is night need not disturb you. It will be daylight before you arrive at the place to which this is addressed, and if you cannot get into the house at so early an hour, whistle three times like this—listen and one of the windows will presently fly up. You have had no trouble finding me; you'll have no trouble finding him. When you return, hunt me up as you did to-night. Only you need not trouble yourself to look for me at Haberstow's," he added under his breath in a tone that was no doubt highly satisfactory to himself. "I shall not be there. And now, off with you!" he shouted. "You've your hundred dollars to make before daylight, and it's already after two."

Sweetwater, who had stolen a glimpse at the superscription on the letter he held, stumbled as he went out of the door. It was directed, as he had expected, to a Frederick, probably to the second one of whom Captain Wattles had spoken, but not, as he had expected, to a stranger. The name on the letter was Frederick Sutherland, and the place of his destination was Sutherlandtown.

XXVIII

"WHO ARE YOU?"

The round had come full circle. By various chances and a train of circumstances for which he could not account, he had been turned from his first intention and was being brought back stage by stage to the very spot he had thought it his duty to fly from. Was this fate? He began to think so, and no longer so much as dreamed of struggling against it. But he felt very much dazed, and walked away through the now partially deserted streets with an odd sense of failure that was only compensated by the hope he now cherished of seeing his mother again, and being once more Caleb Sweetwater of Sutherlandtown.

He was clearer, however, after a few blocks of rapid walking, and then he began to wonder over the contents of the letter he held, and how they would affect its recipient. Was it a new danger he was bringing him? Instead of aiding Mr. Sutherland in keeping his dangerous secret, was he destined to bring disgrace upon him, not only by his testimony before the coroner, but by means of this letter, which, whatever it contained, certainly could not bode good to the man from whom it was designed to wrest two thousand five hundred dollars?

The fear that he was destined to do so grew upon him rapidly, and the temptation to open the letter and make himself master of its contents before leaving town at last became so strong that his sense of honour paled before it, and he made up his mind that before he ventured into the precincts of Sutherlandtown he would know just what sort of a bombshell he was carrying into the Sutherland family. To do this he stopped at the first respectable lodging-house he encountered and hired a room. Calling for hot water "piping hot, " he told them—he subjected the letter to the effects of steam and presently had it open. He was not disappointed in its contents, save that they were even more dangerous than he had anticipated. Captain Wattles was an old crony of Frederick's and knew his record better than anyone else in the world. From this fact and the added one that Frederick had stood in special need of money at the time of Agatha Webb's murder, the writer had no hesitation in believing him guilty of the crime which opened his way to a fortune, and though under ordinary circumstances he would, as his friend

Frederick already knew, be perfectly willing to keep his opinions to himself, he was just now under the same necessity for money that Frederick had been at that fatal time, and must therefore see the colour of two thousand five hundred dollars before the day was out if Frederick desired to have his name kept out of the Boston papers. That it had been kept out up to this time argued that the crime had been well enough hidden to make the alternative thus offered an important one.

There was no signature.

Sweetwater, affected to an extent he little expected, resealed the letter, made his excuses to the landlord, and left the house. Now he could see why he had not been allowed to make his useless sacrifice. Another man than himself suspected Frederick, and by a word could precipitate the doom he already saw hung too low above the devoted head of Mr. Sutherland's son to be averted.

"Yet I'll attempt that too, " burst impetuously from his lips. "If I fail, I can but go back with a knowledge of this added danger. If I succeed, why I must still go back. From some persons and from some complications it is useless to attempt flight. "

Returning to the club-house he had first entered in his search for Captain Wattles, he asked if that gentleman had yet come in. This time he was answered by an affirmative, though he might almost as well have not been, for the captain was playing cards in a private room and would not submit to any interruption.

"He will submit to mine, " retorted Sweetwater to the man who had told him this. "Or wait; hand him back this letter and say that the messenger refuses to deliver it. "

This brought the captain out, as he had fully expected it would.

"Why, what—" began that gentleman in a furious rage.

But Sweetwater, laying his hand on the arm he knew to be so sensitive, rose on tiptoe and managed to whisper in the angry man's ear:

"You are a card-sharp, and it will be easy enough to ruin you. Threaten Frederick Sutherland and in two weeks you will be boycotted by every club in this city. Twenty-five hundred dollars won't pay you for that."

This from a nondescript fellow with no grains of a gentleman about him in form, feature, or apparel! The captain stared nonplussed, too much taken aback to be even angry.

Suddenly he cried:

"How do you know all this? How do you know what is or is not in the letter I gave you?"

Sweetwater, with a shrug that in its quiet significance seemed to make him at once the equal of his interrogator, quietly pressed the quivering limb under his hand and calmly replied:

"I know because I have read it. Before putting my head in the lion's mouth, I make it a point to count his teeth," and lifting his hand, he drew back, leaving the captain reeling.

"What is your name? Who are you?" shouted out Wattles as Sweetwater was drawing off.

It was the third time he had been asked that question within twenty-four hours, but not before with this telling emphasis. "Who are you, I say, and what can you do to me—?"

"I am—But that is an insignificant detail unworthy of your curiosity. As to what I can do, wait and see. But first burn that letter."

And turning his back he fled out of the building, followed by oaths which, if not loud, were certainly deep and very far-reaching.

It was the first time Captain Wattles had met his match in audacity.

XXIX

HOME AGAIN

On his way to the depot, Sweetwater went into the Herald office and bought a morning paper. At the station he opened it. There was one column devoted to the wreck of the Hesper, and a whole half-page to the proceedings of the third day's inquiry into the cause and manner of Agatha Webb's death. Merely noting that his name was mentioned among the lost, in the first article, he began to read the latter with justifiable eagerness. The assurance given in Captain Wattles's letter was true. No direct suspicion had as yet fallen on Frederick. As the lover of Amabel Page, his name was necessarily mentioned, but neither in the account of the inquest nor in the editorials on the subject could he find any proof that either the public or police had got hold of the great idea that he was the man who had preceded Amabel to Agatha's cottage. Relieved on this score, Sweetwater entered more fully into the particulars, and found that though the jury had sat three days, very little more had come to light than was known on the morning he made that bold dash into the Hesper. Most of the witnesses had given in their testimony, Amabel's being the chief, and though no open accusation had been made, it was evident from the trend of the questions put to the latter that Amabel's connection with the affair was looked upon as criminal and as placing her in a very suspicious light. Her replies, however, as once before, under a similar but less formal examination, failed to convey any recognition on her part either of this suspicion or of her own position; yet they were not exactly frank, and Sweetwater saw, or thought he saw (naturally failing to have a key to the situation), that she was still working upon her old plan of saving both herself and Frederick, by throwing whatever suspicion her words might raise upon the deceased Zabel. He did not know, and perhaps it was just as well that he did not at this especial juncture, that she was only biding her time—now very nearly at hand—and that instead of loving Frederick, she hated him, and was determined upon his destruction. Reading, as a final clause, that Mr. Sutherland was expected to testify soon in explanation of his position as executor of Mrs. Webb's will, Sweetwater grew very serious, and, while no change took place in his mind as to his present duty, he decided that his return must be as unobtrusive as possible, and his only too timely reappearance on the scene of the inquiry kept secret till Mr. Sutherland had given his evidence and retired from under the eyes of his excited fellow-citizens.

"The sight of me might unnerve him, " was Sweetwater's thought, "precipitating the very catastrophe we dread. One look, one word on his part indicative of his inner apprehensions that his son had a hand in the crime which has so benefited him, and nothing can save Frederick from the charge of murder. Not Knapp's skill, my silence, or Amabel's finesse. The young man will be lost. "

He did not know, as we do, that Amabel's finesse was devoted to winning a husband for herself, and that, in the event of failure, the action she threatened against her quondam lover would be precipitated that very day at the moment when the clock struck twelve.

. . . . . .

Sweetwater arrived home by the way of Portchester. He had seen one or two persons he knew, but, so far, had himself escaped recognition. The morning light was dimly breaking when he strode into the outskirts of Sutherlandtown and began to descend the hill. As he passed Mr. Halliday's house he looked up, and was astonished to see a light burning in one deeply embowered window. Alas! he did not know how early one anxious heart woke during those troublous days. The Sutherland house was dark, but as he crept very close under its overhanging eaves he heard a deep sigh uttered over his head, and knew that someone was up here also in anxious expectation of a day that was destined to hold more than even he anticipated.

Meanwhile, the sea grew rosy, and the mother's cottage was as yet far off. Hurrying on, he came at last under the eye of more than one of the early risers of Sutherlandtown.

"What, Sweetwater! Alive and well! "

"Hey, Sweetwater, we thought you were lost on the Hesper! "

"Halloo! Home in time to see the pretty Amabel arrested? " Phrases like these met him at more than one corner; but he eluded them all, stopping only to put one hesitating question. Was his mother well?

Home fears had made themselves felt with his near approach to that humble cottage door.

BOOK III

HAD BATSY LIVED!

XXX

WHAT FOLLOWED THE STEIKING OF THE CLOCK

It was the last day of the inquest, and to many it bade fair to be the least interesting. All the witnesses who had anything to say had long ago given in their testimony, and when at or near noon Sweetwater slid into the inconspicuous seat he had succeeded in obtaining near the coroner, it was to find in two faces only any signs of the eagerness and expectancy which filled his own breast to suffocation. But as these faces were those of Agnes Halliday and Amabel Page, he soon recognised that his own judgment was not at fault, and that notwithstanding outward appearances and the languid interest shown in the now lagging proceedings, the moment presaged an event full of unseen but vital consequence.

Frederick was not visible in the great hall; but that he was near at hand soon became evident from the change Sweetwater now saw in Amabel. For while she had hitherto sat under the universal gaze with only the faint smile of conscious beauty on her inscrutable features, she roused as the hands of the clock moved toward noon, and glanced at the great door of entrance with an evil expectancy that startled even Sweetwater, so little had he really understood the nature of the passions labouring in that venomous breast.

Next moment the door opened, and Frederick and his father came in. The air of triumphant satisfaction with which Amabel sank back into her seat was as marked in its character as her previous suspense. What did it mean? Sweetwater, noting it, and the vivid contrast it offered to Frederick's air of depression, felt that his return had been well timed.

Mr. Sutherland was looking very feeble. As he took the chair offered him, the change in his appearance was apparent to all who knew him, and there were few there who did not know him. And, startled by these evidences of suffering which they could not understand and feared to interpret even to themselves, more than one devoted friend stole uneasy glances at Frederick to see if he too were under the cloud which seemed to envelop his father almost beyond recognition.

But Frederick was looking at Amabel, and his erect head and determined aspect made him a conspicuous figure in the room. She who had called up this expression, and alone comprehended it fully, smiled as she met his eye, with that curious slow dipping of her dimples which had more than once confounded the coroner, and rendered her at once the admiration and abhorrence of the crowd who for so long a time had had the opportunity of watching her.

Frederick, to whom this smile conveyed a last hope as well as a last threat, looked away as soon as possible, but not before her eyes had fallen in their old inquiring way to his hands, from which he had removed the ring which up to this hour he had invariably worn on his third finger. In this glance of hers and this action of his began the struggle that was to make that day memorable in many hearts.

After the first stir occasioned by the entrance of two such important persons the crowd settled back into its old quietude under the coroner's hand. A tedious witness was having his slow say, and to him a full attention was being given in the hope that some real enlightenment would come at last to settle the questions which had been raised by Amabel's incomplete and unsatisfactory testimony. But no man can furnish what he does not possess, and the few final minutes before noon passed by without any addition being made to the facts which had already been presented for general consideration.

As the witness sat down the clock began to strike. As the slow, hesitating strokes rang out, Sweetwater saw Frederick yield to a sudden but most profound emotion. The old fear, which we understand, if Sweetwater did not, had again seized the victim of Amabel's ambition, and under her eye, which was blazing full upon him now with a fell and steady purpose, he found his right hand stealing toward the left in the significant action she expected. Better to yield than fall headlong into the pit one word of hers would open. He had not meant to yield, but now that the moment had come, now that he must at once and forever choose between a course that led simply to personal unhappiness and one that involved not only himself, but those dearest to him, in disgrace and sorrow, he felt himself weaken to the point of clutching at whatever would save him from the consequences of confession. Moral strength and that tenacity of purpose which only comes from years of self-control were too lately awakened in his breast to sustain him now. As stroke after stroke fell on the ear, he felt himself yielding beyond recovery, and had almost touched his finger in the significant action of assent which Amabel awaited with breathless expectation, when—was it miracle or only the suggestion of his better nature? —the memory of a face full of holy pleading rose from the past before his eyes and with an inner cry of "Mother! " he flung his hand out and clutched his father's arm in a way to break the charm of his own dread and end forever the effects of the intolerable fascination that was working upon him. Next minute the last stroke of noon rang out, and the hour was up which Amabel had set as the limit of her silence.

A pause, which to their two hearts if to no others seemed strangely appropriate, followed the cessation of these sounds, then the witness was dismissed, and Amabel, taking advantage of the movement, was about to lean toward Mr. Courtney, when Frederick, leaping with a bound to his feet, drew all eyes towards himself with the cry:

"Let me be put on my oath. I have testimony to give of the utmost importance in this case. "

The coroner was astounded; everyone was astounded. No one had expected anything from him, and instinctively every eye turned towards Amabel to see how she was affected by his action.

Strangely, evidently, for the look with which she settled back in her seat was one which no one who saw it ever forgot, though it conveyed no hint of her real feelings, which were somewhat chaotic.

Frederick, who had forgotten her now that he had made up his mind to speak, waited for the coroner's reply.

"If you have testimony, " said that gentleman after exchanging a few hurried words with Mr. Courtney and the surprised Knapp, "you can do no better than give it to us at once. Mr. Frederick Sutherland, will you take the stand? "

With a noble air from which all hesitation had vanished, Frederick started towards the place indicated, but stopped before he had taken a half-dozen steps and glanced back at his father, who was visibly succumbing under this last shock.

"Go! " he whispered, but in so thrilling a tone it was heard to the remotest corner of the room. "Spare me the anguish of saying what I have to say in your presence. I could not bear it. You could not bear it. Later, if you will wait for me in one of these rooms, I will repeat my tale in your ears, but go now. It is my last entreaty. "

There was a silence; no one ventured a dissent, no one so much as made a gesture of disapproval. Then Mr. Sutherland struggled to his feet, cast one last look around him, and disappeared through a door which had opened like magic before him. Then and not till then did Frederick move forward.

The moment was intense. The coroner seemed to share the universal excitement, for his first question was a leading one and brought out this startling admission:

"I have obtruded myself into this inquiry and now ask to be heard by this jury, because no man knows more than I do of the manner and cause of Agatha Webb's death. This you will believe when I tell you that *I* was the person Miss Page followed into Mrs. Webb's house and whom she heard descend the stairs during the moment she crouched behind the figure of the sleeping Philemon. "

It was more, infinitely more, than anyone there had expected. It was not only an acknowledgment but a confession, and the shock, the surprise, the alarm, which it occasioned even to those who had never had much confidence in this young man's virtue, was almost appalling in its intensity. Had it not been for the consciousness of Mr. Sutherland's near presence the feeling would have risen to outbreak; and many voices were held in subjection by the remembrance of this venerated man's last look, that otherwise would have made themselves heard in despite of the restrictions of the place and the authority of the police.

To Frederick it was a moment of immeasurable grief and humiliation. On every face, in every shrinking form, in subdued murmurs and open cries, he read instant and complete condemnation, and yet in all his life from boyhood up to this hour, never had he been so worthy of their esteem and consideration. But though he felt the iron enter his soul, he did not lose his determined attitude. He had observed a change in Amabel and a change in Agnes, and if only to disappoint the vile triumph of the one and raise again the drooping courage of the other, he withstood the clamour and began speaking again, before the coroner had been able to fully restore quiet.

"I know, " said he, "what this acknowledgment must convey to the minds of the jury and people here assembled. But if anyone who listens to me thinks me guilty of the death I was so unfortunate as to have witnessed, he will be doing me a wrong which Agatha Webb would be the first to condemn. Dr. Talbot, and you, gentlemen of the jury, in the face of God and man, I here declare that Mrs. Webb, in my presence and before my eyes, gave to herself the blow which has robbed us all of a most valuable life. She was not murdered. "

It was a solemn assertion, but it failed to convince the crowd before him. As by one impulse men and women broke into a tumult. Mr. Sutherland was forgotten and cries of "Never! She was too good! It's all calumny! A wretched lie! " broke in unrestrained excitement from every part of the large room. In vain the coroner smote with his gavel, in vain the local police endeavoured to restore order; the tide was up and over-swept everything for an instant till silence was suddenly restored by the sight of Amabel smoothing out the folds of her crisp white frock with an incredulous, almost insulting, smile that at once fixed attention again on Frederick. He seized the occasion and spoke up in a tone of great resolve.

"I have made an assertion, " said he, "before God and before this jury. To make it seem a credible one I shall have to tell my own story from the beginning. Am I allowed to do so, Mr. Coroner? "

"You are, " was the firm response.

"Then, gentlemen, " continued Frederick, still without looking at Amabel, whose smile had acquired a mockery that drew the eyes of the jury toward her more than once during the following recital, "you know, and the public generally now know, that Mrs. Webb has left me the greater portion of the money of which she died possessed. I have never before acknowledged to anyone, not even to the good man who awaits this jury's verdict on the other side of that door yonder, that she had reasons for this, good reasons, reasons of which up to the very evening of her death I was myself ignorant, as I was ignorant of her intentions in my regard, or that I was the special object of her attention, or that we were under any mutual obligations in any way. Why, then, I should have thought of going to her in the great strait in which I found myself on that day, I cannot say. I knew she had money in her house; this I had unhappily been made acquainted with in an accidental way, and I knew she was of kindly disposition and quite capable of doing a very unselfish act. Still, this would not seem to be reason enough for me to intrude upon her late at night with a plea for a large loan of money, had I not been in a desperate condition of mind, which made any attempt seem reasonable that promised relief from the unendurable burden of a pressing and disreputable debt. I was obliged to have money, a great deal of money, and I had to have it at once; and while I know that this will not serve to lighten the suspicion I have brought upon myself by my late admissions, it is the only explanation I can give you for leaving the ball at my father's house and hurrying down secretly and alone into town to the little cottage where, as I had been told early in the evening, a small entertainment was being given, which would insure its being open even at so late an hour as midnight. Miss Page, who will, I am sure, pardon the introduction of her name into this narrative, has taken pains to declare to you that in the expedition she herself made into town that evening, she followed some person's steps down-hill. This is very likely true, and those steps were probably mine, for after leaving the house by the garden door, I came directly down the main road to the corner of the lane running past Mrs. Webb's cottage. Having already seen from the hillside the light burning in her upper windows, I felt encouraged to proceed, and so hastened on till I came to the gate on High Street. Here I had a moment of hesitation, and thoughts bitter enough for me to recall them at this moment came into my mind, making that instant, perhaps, the very worst in my life; but they passed, thank God, and with no more desperate feeling than a sullen intention of having my own way about this money, I lifted the latch of the front door and stepped in.

"I had expected to find a jovial group of friends in her little ground parlour, or at least to hear the sound of merry voices and laughter in the rooms above; but no sounds of any sort awaited me; indeed the house seemed strangely silent for one so fully lighted, and, astonished at this, I pushed the door ajar at my left and looked in. An unexpected and pitiful sight awaited me. Seated at a table set with abundance of untasted food, I saw the master of the house with his head sunk forward on his arms, asleep. The expected guests had failed to arrive, and he, tired out with waiting, had fallen into a doze at the board.

"This was a condition of things for which I was not prepared. Mrs. Webb, whom I wished to see, was probably upstairs, and while I might summon her by a sturdy rap on the door beside which I stood, I had so little desire to wake her husband, of whose mental condition I was well aware, that I could not bring myself to make any loud noise within his hearing. Yet I had not the courage to retreat. All my hope of relief from the many difficulties that menaced me lay in the generosity of this great-hearted woman, and if out of pusillanimity I let this hour go by without making my appeal, nothing but shame and disaster awaited me. Yet how could I hope to lure her downstairs without noise? I could not, and so, yielding to the impulse of the moment, without any realisation, I here swear, of the effect which my unexpected presence would have on the noble woman overhead, I slipped up the narrow staircase, and catching at that moment the sound of her voice calling out to Batsy, I stepped up to the door I saw standing open before me and confronted her before she could move from the table before which she was sitting, counting over a large roll of money.

"My look (and it was doubtless not a common look, for the sight of a mass of money at that moment, when money was everything to me, roused every lurking demon in my breast) seemed to appall, if it did not frighten her, for she rose, and meeting my eye with a gaze in which shock and some strange and poignant agony totally incomprehensible to me were strangely blended, she cried out:

"'No, no, Frederick! You don't know what you are doing. If you want my money, take it; if you want my life, I will give it to you with my own hand. Don't stain yours—don't—'

"I did not understand her. I did not know until I thought it over afterward that my hand was thrust convulsively into my breast in a way which, taken with my wild mien, made me look as if I had come to murder her for the money over which she was hovering. I was blind, deaf to everything but that money, and bending madly forward in a state of mental intoxication awful enough for me to remember now, I answered her frenzied words by some such broken exclamations as these:

"'Give, then! I want hundreds—thousands—now, now, to save myself! Disgrace, shame, prison await me if I don't have them. Give, give!' And my hand went out toward it, not toward her; but she mistook the action, mistook my purpose, and, with a heart- broken cry, to save me, ME, from crime, the worst crime of which humanity is capable, she caught up a dagger lying only too near her hand in the open drawer against which she leaned, and in a moment of fathomless anguish which we who can never know more than the outward seeming of her life can hardly measure, plunged against it and—I can tell you no more. Her blood and Batsy's shriek from the adjoining room swam through my consciousness, and then she fell, as I supposed, dead upon the floor, and I, in scarcely better case, fell also.

"This, as God lives, is the truth concerning the wound found in the breast of this never-to-be-forgotten woman."

The feeling, the pathos, the anguish even, to be found in his tone made this story, strange and incredible as it seemed, appear for the moment plausible.

"And Batsy?" asked the coroner.

"Must have fallen when we did, for I never heard her voice after the first scream. But I shall speak of her again. What I must now explain is how the money in Mrs. Webb's drawer came into my possession, and how the dagger she had planted in her breast came to be found on the lawn outside. When I came to myself, and that must have been very soon, I found that the blow of which I had been such a horrified witness had not yet proved fatal. The eyes I had seen close, as I had supposed, forever, were now open, and she was looking at me with a smile that has never left my memory, and never will.

"'There is no blood on you,' she murmured. 'You did not strike the blow. Was it money only that you wanted, Frederick? If so, you could have had it without crime. There are five hundred dollars on that table. Take them and let them pave your way to a better life. My death will help you to remember.' Do these words, this action of hers, seem incredible to you, sirs? Alas! alas! they will not when I tell you"—and here he cast one anxious, deeply anxious, glance at the room in which Mr. Sutherland was hidden—"that unknown to me, unknown to anyone living but herself, unknown to that good man from whom it can no longer be kept hidden, Agatha Webb was my mother. I am Philemon's son and not the offspring of Charles and Marietta Sutherland!"

XXXI

A WITNESS LOST

Impossible! Incredible!

Like a wave suddenly lifted the whole assemblage rose in surprise if not in protest. But there was no outburst. The very depth of the feelings evoked made all ebullition impossible, and as one sees the billow pause ere it breaks, and gradually subside, so this crowd yielded to its awe, and man by man sank back into his seat till quiet was again restored, and only a circle of listening faces confronted the man who had just stirred a whole roomful to its depths. Seeing this, and realising his opportunity, Frederick at once entered into the explanations for which each heart there panted.

"This will be overwhelming news to him who has cared for me since infancy. You have heard him call me son; with what words shall I overthrow his confidence in the truth and rectitude of his long-buried wife and make him know in his old age that he has wasted years of patience upon one who was not of his blood or lineage? The wonder, the incredulity you manifest are my best excuse for my long delay in revealing the secret entrusted to me by this dying woman."

An awed silence greeted these words. Never was the interest of a crowd more intense or its passions held in greater restraint. Yet Agnes's tears flowed freely, and Amabel's smiles—well, their expression had changed; and to Sweetwater, who alone had eyes for her now, they were surcharged with a tragic meaning, strange to see in one of her callous nature.

Frederick's voice broke as he proceeded in his self-imposed task.

"The astounding fact which I have just communicated to you was made known by my mother, with the dagger still plunged in her breast. She would not let me draw it out. She knew that death would follow that act, and she prized every moment remaining to her because of the bliss she enjoyed of seeing and having near her her only living child. The love, the passion, the boundless devotion she showed in those last few minutes transformed me in an instant from a selfish brute into a deeply repentant man. I knelt before her in anguish. I made her feel that, wicked as I had been, I was not the conscienceless wretch she had imagined, and that she was mistaken as to the motives which led me into her presence. And when I saw, by her clearing brow and peaceful look, that I had fully persuaded her of this, I let her speak what words she would, and tell, as she was able, the secret tragedy of her life.

"It is a sacred story to me, and if you must know it, let it be from her own words in the letters she left behind her. She only told me that to save me from the fate of the children who had preceded me, the five little girls and boys who had perished almost at birth in her arms, she had parted from me in early infancy to Mrs. Sutherland, then mourning the sudden death of her only child; that this had been done secretly and under circumstances calculated to deceive Mr. Sutherland, consequently he had never known I was not his own child, and in terror of the effect which the truth might have upon him she enjoined me not to enlighten him now, if by any sacrifice on my part I could rightfully avoid it; that she was happy in having me hear the truth before she died; that the joy which this gave her was so great she did not regret her fatal act, violent and uncalled for as it was, for it had showed her my heart and allowed me to read hers. Then she talked of my father, by whom I mean him whom you call Philemon; and she made me promise I would care for him to the last with tenderness, saying that I would be able to do this without seeming impropriety, since she had willed me all her fortune under this proviso. Finally, she gave me a key, and pointing out where the money lay hidden, bade me carry it away as her last gift, together with the package of letters I would find with it. And when I had taken these and given her back the key, she told me that but for one thing she would die happy. And though her strength and breath were fast failing her, she made me understand that she was worried about the Zabels, who had not come according to a sacred custom between them, to celebrate the anniversary of her wedding, and prayed me to see the two old gentlemen before I slept, since nothing but death or dire distress would have kept them from gratifying the one whim of my father's failing mind. I promised, and with perfect peace in her face, she pointed to the dagger in her breast.

"But before I could lay my hand upon it she called for Batsy. 'I want her to hear me declare before I go, ' said she, 'that this stroke was delivered by myself upon myself. ' But when I rose to look for Batsy I found that the shock of her mistress's fatal act had killed her and that only her dead body was lying across the window-sill of the adjoining room. It was a chance that robbed me of the only witness who could testify to my innocence, in case my presence in this house of death should become known, and realising all the danger in which it threw me, I did not dare to tell my mother, for fear it would make her last moments miserable. So I told her that the poor woman had understood what she wished, but was too terrified to move or speak; and this satisfied my mother and made her last breath one of trust and contented love. She died as I drew the dagger from her breast, and seeing this, I was seized with horror of the instrument which had cost me such a dear and valuable life and flung it wildly from the window. Then I lifted her and laid her where you found her, on the sofa. I did not know that the dagger was an old-time gift of her former lover, James Zabel, much less that it bore his initials on the handle."

He paused, and the awe occasioned by the scene he had described was so deep and the silence so prolonged that a shudder passed over the whole assemblage when from some unknown quarter a single cutting voice arose in this one short, mocking comment:

"Oh, the fairy tale!"

Was it Amabel who spoke? Some thought so and looked her way, but they only beheld a sweet, tear-stained face turned with an air of moving appeal upon Frederick as if begging pardon for the wicked doubts which had driven him to this defence.

Frederick met that look with one so severe it partook of harshness; then, resuming his testimony, he said:

"It is of the Zabel brothers I must now speak, and of how one of them, James by name, came to be involved in this affair.

"When I left my dead mother's side I was in such a state of mind that I passed with scarcely so much as a glance the room where my new-found father sat sleeping. But as I hastened on toward the quarter where the Zabels lived, I was seized by such compunction for his desolate state that I faltered in my rapid flight and did not arrive at the place of my destination as quickly as I intended. When I did I found the house dark and the silence sepulchral. But I did not turn away. Remembering my mother's anxiety, an anxiety so extreme it disturbed her final moments, I approached the front door and was about to knock when I found it open. Greatly astonished, I at once passed in, and, seeing my way perfectly in the moonlight, entered the room on the left, the door of which also stood open. It was the second house I had entered unannounced that night, and in this as in the other I encountered a man sitting asleep by the table.

"It was John, the elder of the two, and, perceiving that he was suffering for food and in a condition of extreme misery, I took out the first bill my hand encountered in my overfull pockets and laid it on the table by his side. As I did so he gave a sigh, but did not wake; and satisfied that I had done all that was wise and all that even my mother would expect of me under the circumstances, and fearing to encounter the other brother if I lingered, I hastened away and took the shortest path home. Had I been more of a man, or if my visit to Mrs. Webb had been actuated by a more communicable motive, I would have gone at once to the good man who believed me to be of his own flesh and blood, and told him of the strange and heart-rending adventure which had changed the whole tenor of my thoughts and life, and begged his advice as to what I had better do under the difficult circumstances in which I found myself placed. But the memory of a thousand past ingratitudes, together with the knowledge of the shock which he could not fail to receive on learning at this late day, and under conditions at once so tragic and full of menace, that the child which his long-buried wife had once placed in his arms as his own was neither of her blood nor his, rose up between us and caused me not only to attempt silence, but to secrete in the adjoining woods the money I had received, in the vain hope that all visible connection between myself and my mother's tragic death would thus be lost. You see I had not calculated on Miss Amabel Page."

The flash he here received from that lady's eyes startled the crowd, and gave Sweetwater, already suffering under shock after shock of mingled surprise and wonder, his first definite idea that he had never rightly understood the relations between these two, and that something besides justice had actuated Amabel in her treatment of this young man. This feeling was shared by others, and a reaction set in in Frederick's favour, which even affected the officials who were conducting the inquiry. This was shown by the difference of manner now assumed by the coroner and by the more easily impressed Sweetwater, who had not yet learned the indispensable art of hiding his feelings. Frederick himself felt the change and showed it by the look of relief and growing confidence he cast at Agnes.

Of the questions and answers which now passed between him and the various members of the jury I need give no account. They but emphasised facts already known, and produced but little change in the general feeling, which was now one of suppressed pity for all who had been drawn into the meshes of this tragic mystery. When he was allowed to resume his seat, the name of Miss Amabel Page was again called.

She rose with a bound. Nought that she had anticipated had occurred; facts of which she could know nothing had changed the aspect of affairs and made the position of Frederick something so remote from any she could have imagined, that she was still in the maze of the numberless conflicting emotions which these revelations were calculated to call out in one who had risked all on the hazard of a die and lost. She did not even know at this moment whether she was glad or sorry he could explain so cleverly his anomalous position. She had caught the look he had cast at Agnes, and while this angered her, it did not greatly modify her opinion that he was destined for herself. For, however other people might feel, she did not for a moment believe his story. She had not a pure enough heart to do so. To her all self-sacrifice was an anomaly. No woman of the mental or physical strength of Agatha Webb would plant a dagger in her own breast just to prevent another person from committing a crime, were he lover, husband, or son. So Amabel believed and so would these others believe also when once relieved of the magnetic personality of this extraordinary witness. Yet how thrilling it had been to hear him plead his cause so well! It was almost worth the loss of her revenge to meet his look of hate, and dream of the possibility of turning it later into the old look of love. Yes, yes, she loved him now; not for his position, for that was gone; not even for his money, for she could contemplate its loss; but for himself, who had so boldly shown that he was stronger than she and could triumph over her by the sheer force of his masculine daring.

With such feelings, what should she say to these men; how conduct herself under questions which would be much more searching now than before? She could not even decide in her own mind. She must let impulse have its way.

Happily, she took the right stand at first. She did not endeavour to make any corrections in her former testimony, only acknowledging that the flower whose presence on the scene of death had been such a mystery, had fallen from her hair at the ball and that she had seen

Frederick pick it up and put it in his buttonhole. Beyond this, and the inferences it afterward awakened in her mind, she would not go, though many present, and among them Frederick, felt confident that her attitude had been one of suspicion from the first, and that it was to follow him rather than to supply the wants of the old man, Zabel, she had left the ball and found her way to Agatha Webb's cottage.

XXXII

WHY AGATHA WEBB WILL NEVER BE FORGOTTEN IN SUTHERLANDTOWN

Meanwhile Sweetwater had been witness to a series of pantomimic actions that interested him more than Amabel's conduct under this final examination. Frederick, who had evidently some request to make or direction to give, had sent a written line to the coroner, who, on reading it, had passed it over to Knapp, who a few minutes later was to be seen in conference with Agnes Halliday. As a result, the latter rose and left the room, followed by the detective. She was gone a half-hour, then simultaneously with her reappearance, Sweetwater saw Knapp hand a bundle of letters to the coroner, who, upon opening them, chose out several which he proceeded to read to the jury. They were the letters referred to by Frederick as having been given to him by his mother. The first was dated thirty-five years previously and was in the handwriting of Agatha herself. It was directed to James Zabel, and was read amid a profound hush.

DEAR JAMES:

You are too presumptuous. When I let you carry me away from John in that maddening reel last night, I did not mean you to draw the inference you did. That you did draw it argues a touch of vanity in a man who is not alone in the field where he imagines himself victor. John, who is humbler, sees some merit in—well, in Frederick Snow, let us say. So do I, but merit does not always win, any more than presumption. When we meet, let it be as friends, but as friends only. A girl cannot be driven into love. To ride on your big mare, Judith, is bliss enough for my twenty years. Why don't you find it so too? I think I hear you say you do, but only when she stops at a certain gate on Portchester highway. Folly! there are other roads and other gates, though if I should see you enter one—There! my pen is galloping away with me faster than Judith ever did, and it is time I drew rein. Present my regards to John—But no; then he would know I had written you a letter, and that might hurt him. How could he guess it was only a scolding letter, such as it would grieve him to receive, and that it does not count for anything! Were it to Frederick Snow, now— There! some horses are so hard to pull up—and so are some pens. I will come to a standstill, but not before your door.

Respectfully your neighbour,

AGATHA GILCHRIST.

DEAR JAMES:

I know I have a temper, a wicked temper, and now you know it too. When it is roused, I forget love, gratitude, and everything else that should restrain me, and utter words I am myself astonished at. But I do not get roused often, and when all is over I am not averse to apologising or even to begging forgiveness. My father says my temper will undo me, but I am much more afraid of my heart than I am of my temper. For instance, here I am writing to you again just because I raised my riding-whip and said—But you know what I said, and I am not fond of recalling the words, for I cannot do so without seeing your look of surprise and contrasting it with that of Philemon's. Yours had judgment in it, while Philemon's held only indulgence. Yet I liked yours best, or should have liked it best if it were not for the insufferable pride which is a part of my being. Temper such as mine OUGHT to surprise you, yet would I be Agatha Gilchrist without it? I very much fear not. And not being Agatha Gilchrist, should I have your love? Again I fear not. James, forgive me. When I am happier, when I know my own heart, I will have less provocation. Then, if that heart turns your way, you will find a great and bountiful serenity where now there are lowering and thunderous tempests. Philemon said last night that he would be content to have my fierce word o' mornings, if only I would give him one drop out of the honey of my better nature when the sun went down and twilight brought reflection and love. But I did not like him any the better for saying this. YOU would not halve the day so. The cup with which you would refresh yourself must hold no bitterness. Will it not have to be proffered, then, by other hands than those of

AGATHA GILCHRIST?

MR. PHILEMON WEBB.

Respected Sir:

You are persistent. I am willing to tell YOU, though I shall never confide so much to another, that it will take a stronger nature than yours, and one that loves me less, to hold me faithful and make me the happy, devoted wife which I must be if I would not be a demon.

I cannot, I dare not, marry where I am not held in a passionate, self-forgetful subjection. I am too proud, too sensitive, too little mistress of myself when angry or aroused. If, like some strong women, I loved what was weaker than myself, and could be controlled by goodness and unlimited kindness, I might venture to risk living at the side of the most indulgent and upright man I know. But I am not of that kind. Strength only can command my admiration or subdue my pride. I must fear where I love, and own for husband him who has first shown himself my master.

So do not fret any more for me, for you, less than any man I know, will ever claim my obedience or command my love. Not that I will not yield my heart to you, but that I cannot; and, knowing that I cannot, feel it honest to say so before any more of your fine, young manhood is wasted. Go your ways, then, Philemon, and leave me to the rougher paths my feet were made to tread. I like you now and feel something like a tender regard for your goodness, but if you persist in a courtship which only my father is inclined to smile upon, you will call up an antagonism that can lead to nothing but evil, for the serpent that lies coiled in my breast has deadly fangs, and is to be feared, as you should know who have more than once seen me angry.

Do not blame John or James Zabel, or Frederick Snow, or even Samuel Barton for this. It would be the same if none of these men existed. I was not made to triumph over a kindly nature, but to yield the haughtiest heart in all this county to the gentle but firm control of its natural master. Do you want to know who that master is? I cannot tell you, for I have not yet named him to myself.

DEAR JAMES:

I am going away. I am going to leave Portchester for several months. I am going to see the world. I did not tell you this last night for fear of weakening under your entreaties, or should I say commands? Lately I have felt myself weakening more than once, and I want to know what it means. Absence will teach me, absence and the sight of new faces. Do you quarrel with this necessity? Do you think I should know my mind without any such test? Alas! James, it is not a simple mind and it baffles me at times. Let us then give it a chance. If the glow and glamour of elegant city life can make me forget certain snatches of talk at our old gate, or that night when you drew my hand through your arm and softly kissed my fingertips, then I am no mate for you, whose love, however critical, has never wavered, but has made itself felt, even in rebuke, as the strongest, sweetest thing that has entered my turbulent life. Because I would be worthy of you, I submit to a separation which will either be a permanent one or the last that will ever take place between you and me. John will not bear this as well as you, yet he does not love me as well, possibly because to him I am simply a superior being, while to you I am a loving but imperfect woman who wishes to do right but can only do so under the highest guidance.

DEAR JOHN:

I feel that I owe you a letter because you have been so patient. You may show it to James if you like, but I mean it for you as an old and dear friend who will one day dance at my wedding.

I am living in a whirl of enjoyment. I am seeing and tasting of pleasures I have only dreamed about till now. From a farmhouse kitchen to Mrs. Andrews's drawing-room is a lively change for a girl who loves dress and show only less than daily intercourse with famous men and brilliant women. But I am bearing it nobly and have developed tastes I did not know I possessed; expensive tastes, John, which I fear may unfit me for the humble life of a Portchester matron. Can you imagine me dressed in rich brocade, sitting in the midst of Washington's choicest citizens and exchanging sallies with senators and judges? You may find it hard, yet so it is, and no one seems to think I am out of place, nor do I feel so, only—do not tell James—there are movements in my heart at times which make me shut my eyes when the lights are brightest, and dream, if but for an instant, of home and the tumble-down gateway where I have so often leaned when someone (you know who it is now, John, and I shall not hurt you too deeply by mentioning him) was saying good-night and calling down the blessings of Heaven upon a head not worthy to receive them.

Does this argue my speedy return? Perhaps. Yet I do not know. There are fond hearts here also, and a life in this country's centre would be a great life for me if only I could forget the touch of a certain restraining hand which has great power over me even as a memory. For the sake of that touch shall I give up the grandeur and charm of this broad life? Answer, John. You know him and me well enough now to say.

DEAR JOHN:

I do not understand your letter. You speak in affectionate terms of everybody, yet you beg me to wait and not be in a hurry to return. Why? Do you not realise that such words only make me the more anxious to see old Portchester again? If there is anything amiss at home, or if James is learning to do without me—but you do not say that; you only intimate that perhaps I will be better able to make up my mind later than now, and hint of great things to come if I will only hold my affections in check a little longer. This is all very ambiguous and demands a fuller explanation. So write to me once more, John, or I shall sever every engagement I have made here and return.

DEAR JOHN:

Your letter is plain enough this time. James read the letter I wrote you about my pleasure in the life here and was displeased at it. He thinks I am growing worldly and losing that simplicity which he has always looked upon as my most attractive characteristic. So! so! Well, James is right; I am becoming less the country girl and more the woman of the world every day I remain here. That means I am becoming less worthy of him. So—But whatever else I have to say on this topic must be said to him. For this you will pardon me like the good brother you are. I cannot help my preference. He is nearer my own age; besides, we were made for each other.

DEAR JAMES:

I am not worldly; I am not carried away by the pleasures and satisfactions of this place, —at least not to the point of forgetting what is dearer and better. I have seen Washington, I have seen gay life; I like it, but I LOVE Portchester. Consequently I am going to return to Portchester, and that very soon. Indeed I cannot stay away much longer, and if you are glad of this, and if you wish to be convinced that a girl who has been wearing brocade and jewels can content herself quite gaily again with calico, come up to the dear old gate a week from now and you will have the opportunity. Do you object to flowers? I may wear a flower in my hair.

Your wayward but ever-constant

AGATHA.

DEAR JAMES:

Why must I write? Why am I not content with the memory of last night? When one's cup is quite full, a cup that has been so long in filling, —must some few drops escape just to show that a great joy like mine is not satisfied to be simply quiescent? I have suffered so long from uncertainty, have tried you and tried myself with so tedious an indecision, that, now I know no other man can ever move my heart as you have done, the ecstasy of it makes me over-demonstrative. I want to tell you that I love you; that I do not simply accept your love, but give you back in fullest measure all the devotion you have heaped upon me in spite of my many faults and failings. You took me to your heart last night, and seemed satisfied; but it does not satisfy me that I just let you do it without telling you that I am proud and happy to be the chosen one of your heart, and that as I saw your smile and the proud passion which lit up your face, I felt how much sweeter was the dear domestic bliss you promised me than the more brilliant but colder life of a statesman's wife in Washington.

I missed the flower from my hair when I went back to my room last night. Did you take it, dear? If so, do not cherish it. I hate to think of anything withering on your breast. My love is deathless, James, and owns no such symbol as that. But perhaps you are not thinking of my love, but of my faults. If so, let the flower remain where you have put it; and when you gaze on it say, "Thus is it with the defects of my darling; once in full bloom, now a withered remembrance. When I gathered her they began to fade. " O James, I feel as if I never could feel anger again.

DEAR JAMES:

I do not, I cannot, believe it. Though you said to me on going out, "Your father will explain, " I cannot content myself with his explanations and will never believe what he said of you except you confirm his accusations by your own act. If, after I have told you exactly what passed between us, you return me this and other letters, then I shall know that I have leaned my weight on a hollow staff, and that henceforth I am to be without protector or comforter in this world.

O James, were we not happy! I believed in you and felt that you believed in me. When we stood heart to heart under the elm tree (was it only last night?) and you swore that if it lay in the power of earthly man to make me happy, I should taste every sweet that a woman's heart naturally craved, I thought my heaven had already come and that now it only remained for me to create yours. Yet that very minute my father was approaching us, and in another instant we heard these words:

"James, I must talk with you before you make my daughter forget herself any further. " Forget herself! What had happened? This was not the way my father had been accustomed to talk, much as he had always favoured the suit of Philemon Webb, and pleased as he would have been had my choice fallen on him. Forget herself! I looked at you to see how these insulting words would affect you. But while you turned pale, or seemed to do so in the fading moonlight, you were not quite so unprepared for them as I was myself, and instead of showing anger, followed my father into the house, leaving me shivering in a spot which had held no chill for me a moment before. You were gone—how long? To me it seemed an hour, and perhaps it was. It would seem to take that long for a man's face to show such change as yours did when you confronted me again in the moonlight. Yet a lightning stroke makes quick work, and perhaps my countenance in that one minute showed as great a change as yours. Else why did you shudder away from me, and to my passionate appeal reply with this one short phrase: "Your father will explain"? Did you think any other words than yours would satisfy me, or that I could believe even him when he accused you of a base and dishonest act? Much as I have always loved and revered my father, I find it impossible not to hope that in his wish to see me united to Philemon he has resorted to an unworthy subterfuge to separate us; therefore I give you our interview word for word. May it shock you as much as it shocked me. Here is what he said first:

"Agatha, you cannot marry James Zabel. He is not an honest man. He has defrauded me, ME, your father, of several thousand dollars. In a clever way, too, showing him to be as subtle as he is unprincipled. Shall I tell you the wretched story, my girl? He has left me to do so. He sees as plainly as I do that any communication between you two after the discovery I have this day made would be but an added offence. He is at least a gentleman, which is something, considering how near he came to being my son- in-law. "

I may have answered. People do cry out when they are stabbed, sometimes, but I rather think I did not say a word, only looked a disdain which at that minute was as measureless as my belief in you. YOU dishonest? YOU—Or perhaps I laughed; that would have been truer to my feeling; yes, I must have laughed.

My father's next words indicated that I did something.

"You do not believe in his guilt, " he went on, and there was a kindness in his tone which gave me my first feeling of real terror. "I can readily comprehend that, Agatha. He has been in my office and acted under my eye for several years now, and I had almost as much confidence in him as you had, notwithstanding the fact that I liked him much better as my confidential clerk than as your probable or prospective husband. He has never held the key to my heart; would God he never had to yours! But he was a good and reliable man in the office, or so I thought, and I gave into his hand much of the work I ought to have done myself, especially since my health has more or less failed me. My trust he abused. A month ago—it was during that ill turn you remember I received a letter from a man I had never expected to hear from again. He was in my debt some ten thousand dollars, and wrote that he had brought with him as much of this sum as he had been able to save in the last five years, to Sutherlandtown, where he was now laid up with a dangerous illness from which he had small hope of recovering. Would I come there and get it? He was a stranger and wished to take no one into his confidence, but he had the money and would be glad to place it in my hands. He added that as he was a lone man, without friends or relatives to inherit from him, he felt a decided pleasure at the prospect of satisfying his only creditor, and devoutly hoped he would be well enough to realise the transaction and receive my receipt. But if his fever increased and he should be delirious or unconscious when I reached him, then I was to lift up the left-hand corner of the mattress on which he lay and take from underneath his head a black wallet in which I would find the money promised me. He had elsewhere enough to pay all his expenses, so that the full contents of the wallet were mine.

"I remembered the man and I wanted the money; so, not being able to go for it myself, I authorised James Zabel to collect it for me. He started at once for Sutherlandtown, and in a few hours returned with the wallet alluded to. Though I was suffering intensely at the time, I remember distinctly the air with which he laid it down and the words with which he endeavoured to carry off a certain secret excitement visible in him. 'Mr. Orr was alive, sir, and fully conscious; but he will not outlive the night. He seemed quite satisfied with the messenger and gave up the wallet without any hesitation. ' I roused up and looked at him. 'What has shaken you up so? ' I asked. He was silent a moment before replying. 'I have ridden fast, ' said he; then more slowly, 'One feels sorry for a man dying alone and amongst strangers. ' I thought he showed an unnecessary emotion, but paid no further heed to it at the time.

"The wallet held two thousand and more dollars, which was less than I expected, but yet a goodly sum and very welcome. As I was counting it over I glanced at the paper accompanying it. It was an acknowledgment of debt and mentioned the exact sum I should find in the wallet—$2753.67. Pointing them out to James, I remarked, 'The figures are in different ink from the words. How do you account for that? ' I thought his answer rather long in coming, though when it did come it was calm, if not studied. 'I presume, ' said he, 'that the sum was inserted at Sutherlandtown, after Mr. Orr was quite sure just how much he could spare for the liquidation of this old debt. ' 'Very likely, ' I assented, not bestowing another thought upon the matter.

"But to-day it has been forced back upon my attention in a curious if not providential way. I was over in Sutherlandtown for the first time since my illness, and having some curiosity about my unfortunate but honest debtor, went to the hotel and asked to see the room in which he died. It being empty they at once showed it to me; and satisfied that he had been made comfortable in his last hours, I was turning away, when I espied on a table in one corner an inkstand and what seemed to be an old copy-book. Why I stopped and approached this table I do not know, but once in front of it I remembered what Zabel had said about the figures, and taking up the pen I saw there, I dipped it in the ink-pot and attempted to scribble a number or two on a piece of loose paper I found in the copy-book. The ink was thick and the pen corroded, so that it was not till after several ineffectual efforts that I succeeded in making any strokes that were at all legible. But when I did, they were so exactly similar in colour to the numbers inserted in Mr. Orr's memorandum (which I had fortunately brought with me) that I was instantly satisfied this especial portion of the writing had been done, as James had said, in this room, and with the very pen I was then handling. As there was nothing extraordinary in this, I was turning away, when a gust of wind from the open window lifted the loose sheet of paper I had been scribbling on and landed it, the other side up, on the carpet. As I stooped for it I saw figures on it, and feeling sure that they had been scrawled there by Mr. Orr in his attempt to make the pen write, I pulled out the memorandum again and compared the two minutely. They were the work of the same hand, but the figures on the stray leaf differed from those in the memorandum in a very important particular. Those in the memorandum began with a 2, while those on the stray sheet began with a 7—a striking difference. Look, Agatha, here is the piece of paper just as I found it. You see here, there, and everywhere the one set of figures, 7753.67. Here it is hardly legible, here it is blotted with too much ink, here it is faint but sufficiently distinct, and here—well, there can be no mistake about these figures, 7753.67; yet the memorandum reads, $2753.67, and the money returned to me amounts to $2753.67—a clean five thousand dollars' difference."

Here, James, my father paused, perhaps to give me a commiserating look, though I did not need it; perhaps to give himself a moment in which to regain courage for what he still had to say. I did not break the silence; I was too sure of your integrity; besides, my tongue could not have moved if it would; all my faculties seemed frozen except that instinct which cried out continually within me: "No! there is no fault in James. He has done no wrong. No one but himself shall ever convince me that he has robbed anyone of anything except poor me of my poor heart. " But inner cries of this kind are inaudible and after a moment's interval my father went on:

"Five thousand dollars is no petty sum, and the discrepancy in the two sets of figures which seemed to involve me in so considerable a loss set me thinking. Convinced that Mr. Orr would not be likely to scribble one number over so many times if it was not the one then in his mind, I went to Mr. Forsyth's office and borrowed a magnifying-glass, through which I again subjected the figures in the memorandum to a rigid scrutiny. The result was a positive conviction that they had been tampered with after their first writing, either by Mr. Orr himself or by another whom I need not name. The 2 had originally been a 7, and I could even see where the top line of the 7 had been given a curl and where a horizontal stroke had been added at the bottom.

"Agatha, I came home as troubled a man as there was in all these parts. I remembered the suppressed excitement which had been in James Zabel's face when he handed me over the money, and I remembered also that you loved him, or thought you did, and that, love or no love, you were pledged to marry him. If I had not recalled all this I might have proceeded more warily. As it was, I took the bold and open course and gave James Zabel an opportunity to explain himself. Agatha, he did not embrace it. He listened to my accusations and followed my finger when I pointed out the discrepancy between the two sets of figures, but he made no protestations of innocence, nor did he show me the front of an honest man when I asked if he expected me to believe that the wallet had held only two thousand and over when Mr. Orr handed it over to him. On the contrary he seemed to shrink into himself like a person whose life has been suddenly blasted, and replying that he would expect me to believe nothing except his extreme contrition at the abuse of confidence of which he had been guilty, begged me to wait till to-morrow before taking any active steps in the matter. I replied that I would show him that much consideration if he would immediately drop all pretensions to your hand. This put him in a bad way; but he left, as you see, with just a simple injunction to you to seek from me an explanation of his strange departure. Does that look like innocence or does it look like guilt?"

I found my tongue at this and passionately cried: "James Zabel's life, as I have known it, shows him to be an honest man. If he has done what you suggest, given you but a portion of the money entrusted to him and altered the figures in the memorandum to suit the amount he brought you, then there is a discrepancy between this act and all the other acts of his life which I find it more difficult to reconcile than you did the two sets of figures in Mr. Orr's handwriting. Father, I must hear from his own lips a confirmation of your suspicions before I will credit them."

And this is why I write you so minute an account of what passed between my father and myself last night. If his account of the matter is a correct one, and you have nothing to add to it in way of explanation, then the return of this letter will be token enough that my father has been just in his accusations and that the bond between us must be broken. But if—O James, if you are the true man I consider you, and all that I have heard is a fabrication or mistake, then come to me at once; do not delay, but come at once, and the sight of your face at the gate will be enough to establish your innocence in my eyes.

AGATHA. The letter that followed this was very short:

DEAR JAMES:

The package of letters has been received. God help me to bear this shock to all my hopes and the death of all my girlish beliefs. I am not angry. Only those who have something left to hold on to in life can be angry.

My father tells me he has received a packet too. It contained five thousand dollars in ten five-hundred-dollar notes. James! James! was not my love enough, that you should want my father's money too?

I have begged my father, and he has promised me, to keep the cause of this rupture secret. No one shall know from either of us that James Zabel has any flaw in his nature.

The next letter was dated some months later. It is to Philemon:

DEAR PHILEMON:

The gloves are too small; besides, I never wear gloves. I hate their restraint and do not feel there is any good reason for hiding my hands, in this little country town where everyone knows me. Why not give them to Hattie Weller? She likes such things, while I have had my fill of finery. A girl whose one duty is to care for a dying father has no room left in her heart for vanities.

DEAR PHILEMON:

It is impossible. I have had my day of love and my heart is quite dead. Show your magnanimity by ceasing to urge me any longer to forget the past. It is all you can do for

AGATHA.

DEAR PHILEMON:

You WILL have my hand though I have told you that my heart does not go with it. It is hard to understand such persistence, but if you are satisfied to take a woman of my strength against her will, then God have mercy upon you, for I will be your wife.

But do not ask me to go to Sutherlandtown. I will live here. And do not expect to keep up your intimacy with the Zabels. There is no tie of affection remaining between James and myself, but if I am to shed that half-light over your home which is all I can promise and all that you can hope to receive, then keep me from all influence but your own. That this in time may grow sweet and dear to me is my earnest prayer to-day, for you are worthy of a true wife.

AGATHA.

DEAR JOHN:

I am going to be married. My father exacts it and there is no good reason why I should not give him this final satisfaction. At least I do not think there is; but if you or your brother differ from me—

Say good-bye to James from me. I pray that his life may be peaceful. I know that it will be honest.

AGATHA.

DEAR PHILEMON:

My father is worse. He fears that if we wait till Tuesday he will not be able to see us married. Decide, then, what our duty is; I am ready to abide by your pleasure.

AGATHA.

The following is from John Zabel to his brother James, and is dated one day after the above:

DEAR JAMES:

When you read this I will be far away, never to look in your face again, unless you bid me. Brother, brother, I meant it for the best, but God was not with me and I have made four hearts miserable without giving help to anyone.

When I read Agatha's letter—the last for more reasons than one that I shall ever receive from her—I seemed to feel as never before what I had done to blast your two lives. For the first time I realised to the full that but for me she might have been happy and you the respected husband of the one grand woman to be found in Portchester. That I had loved her so fiercely myself came back to me in reproach, and the thought that she perhaps suspected that the blame had fallen where it was not deserved roused me to such a pitch that I took the sudden and desperate resolution of telling her the truth before she gave her hand to Philemon. Why the daily sight of your misery should not have driven me before to this act, I cannot tell. Some remnants of the old jealousy may have been still festering in my heart; or the sense of the great distance between your self-sacrificing spirit and the selfishness of my weaker nature risen like a barrier between me and the only noble act left for a man in my position. Whatever the cause, it was not till to-day the full determination came to brave the obloquy of a full confession; but when it did come I did not pause till I reached Mr. Gilchrist's house and was ushered into his presence.

He was lying on the sitting-room lounge, looking very weak and exhausted, while on one side of him stood Agatha and on the other Philemon, both contemplating him with ill-concealed anxiety. I had not expected to find Philemon there, and for a moment I suffered the extreme agony of a man who has not measured the depth of the plunge he is about to take; but the sight of Agatha trembling under the shock of my unexpected presence restored me to myself and gave me firmness to proceed. Advancing with a bow, I spoke quickly the one word I had come there to say.

"Agatha, I have done you a great wrong and I am here to undo it. For months I have felt driven to confession, but not till to-day have I possessed the necessary courage. NOW, nothing shall hinder me."

I said this because I saw in both Mr. Gilchrist and Philemon a disposition to stop me where I was. Indeed Mr. Gilchrist had risen on his elbow and Philemon was making that pleading gesture of his which we know so well.

Agatha alone looked eager. "What is it?" she cried. "I have a right to know." I went to the door, shut it, and stood with my back against it, a figure of shame and despair; suddenly the confession burst from me. "Agatha," said I, "why did you break with my brother James? Because you thought him guilty of theft; because you believed he took the five thousand dollars out of the sum entrusted to him by Mr. Orr for your father. Agatha, it was not James who did this it was I; and James knew it, and bore the blame of my misdoing because he was always a loyal soul and took account of my weakness and knew, alas! too well, that open shame would kill me."

It was a weak plea and merited no reply. But the silence was so dreadful and lasted so long that I felt first crushed and then terrified. Raising my head, for I had not dared to look any of them in the face, I cast one glance at the group before me and dropped my head again, startled. Only one of the three was looking at me, and that was Agatha. The others had their heads turned aside, and I thought, or rather the passing fancy took me, that they shrank from meeting her gaze with something of the same shame and dread I myself felt. But she! Can I ever hope to make you realise her look, or comprehend the pang of utter self-abasement with which I succumbed before it? It was so terrible that I seemed to hear her utter words, though I am sure she did not speak; and with some wild idea of stemming the torrent of her reproaches, I made an effort at explanation, and impetuously cried: "It was not for my own good, Agatha, not for self altogether, I did this. I too loved you, madly, despairingly, and, good brother as I seemed, I was jealous of James and hoped to take his place in your regard if I could show a greater prosperity and get for you those things his limited prospects denied him. You enjoy money, beauty, ease; I could see that by your letters, and if James could not give them to you and I could—Oh, do not look at me like that! I see now that millions could not have bought you."

"Despicable!" was all that came from her lips. At which I shuddered and groped about for the handle of the door. But she would not let me go. Subduing with an unexpected grand self-restraint the emotions which had hitherto swelled too high in her breast for either speech or action, she thrust out one arm to stay me and said in short, commanding tones: "How was this thing done? You say you took the money, yet it was James who was sent to collect it—or so my father says." Here she tore her looks from me and cast one glance at her father. What she saw I cannot say, but her manner changed and henceforth she glanced his way as much as mine and with nearly as much emotion. "I am waiting to hear what you have to say," she exclaimed, laying her hand on the door over my head so as to leave me no opportunity for escape. I bowed and attempted an explanation.

"Agatha," said I, "the commission was given to James and he rode to Sutherlandtown to perform it. But it was on the day when he was accustomed to write to you, and he was not easy in his mind, for he feared he would miss sending you his usual letter. When, therefore, he came to the hotel and saw me in Philemon's room—I was often there in those days, often without Philemon's knowing it—he saw, or thought he did, a way out of his difficulties. Entering where I was, he explained to me his errand, and we being then—though never, alas! since—one in everything but the secret hopes he enjoyed, he asked me if I would go in his stead to Mr. Orr's room, present my credentials, and obtain the money while he wrote the letter with which his mind was full. Though my jealousy was aroused and I hated the letter he was about to write, I did not see how I could refuse him; so after receiving such credentials as he himself carried, and getting full instructions how to proceed, I left him writing at Philemon's table and hastened down the hall to the door he had pointed out. If Providence had been on the side of guilt, the circumstances could not have been more favourable for the deception I afterwards played. No one was in the hall, no one was with Mr. Orr to note that it was I instead of James who executed Mr. Gilchrist's commission. But I was thinking of no deception then. I proceeded quite innocently on my errand, and when the feeble voice of the invalid bade me enter, I experienced nothing but a feeling of compassion for a man dying in this desolate way, alone. Of course Mr. Orr was surprised to see a stranger, but after reading Mr. Gilchrist's letter which I handed him, he seemed quite satisfied and himself drew out the wallet at the head of his bed and handed it over. 'You will find, ' said he, 'a memorandum inside of the full amount, $7758.67. I should like to have returned Mr. Gilchrist the full ten thousand which I owe him, but this is all I possess, barring a hundred dollars which I have kept for my final expenses. ' 'Mr. Gilchrist will be satisfied, ' I assured him. 'Shall I make you out a receipt? ' He shook his head with a sad smile. 'I shall be dead in twenty-four hours. What good will a receipt do me? ' But it seemed unbusinesslike not to give it, so I went over to the table, where I saw a pen and paper, and recognising the necessity of counting the money before writing a receipt, I ran my eye over the bills, which were large, and found the wallet contained just the amount he had named. Then I glanced at the memorandum. It had evidently been made out by him at some previous time, for the body of the writing was in firm characters and the ink blue, while the figures were faintly inscribed in muddy black. The 7 especially was little more than a straight line, and as I looked at it the devil that is in every man's nature whispered at first carelessly, then with deeper and deeper insistence: 'How easy it would be to change that 7 to a 2! Only a little mark at the top and the least additional stroke at the bottom and these figures would stand for five thousand less. It might be a temptation to some men. ' It presently became a temptation to me; for, glancing furtively up, I discovered that Mr. Orr had fallen either into a sleep or into a condition of insensibility which made him oblivious to my movements. Five thousand dollars! just the sum of the ten five-hundred-dollar bills that made the bulk of the amount I had counted. In this village and at my age this sum would raise me at once to comparative independence. The temptation was too strong for resistance. I succumbed to it, and seizing the pen before me, I made the fatal marks. When I went back to James the wallet was in my hand, and the ten five-hundred-dollar bills in my breast pocket. "

Agatha had begun to shudder. She shook so she rattled the door against which I leaned.

"And when you found that Providence was not so much upon your side as you thought, when you saw that the fraud was known and that your brother was suspected of it—"

"Don't! " I pleaded, "don't make me recall that hour! "

But she was inexorable. "Recall that and every hour, " she commanded. "Tell me why he sacrificed himself, why he sacrificed me, to a cur—"

She feared her own tongue, she feared her own anger, and stopped. "Speak, " she whispered, and it was the most ghastly whisper that ever left mortal lips. I was but a foot from her and she held me as by a strong enchantment. I could not help obeying her.

"To make it all clear, " I pursued, "I must go back to the time I rejoined James in Philemon's room. He had finished his letter when I entered and was standing with it, sealed, in his hand. I may have cast it a disdainful glance. I may have shown that I was no longer the same man I had been when I left him a half-hour before, for he looked curiously at me for a moment previous to saying:

"'Is that the wallet you have there? Was Mr. Orr conscious, and did he give it to you himself? ' 'Mr. Orr was conscious, ' I returned, — and I didn't like the sound of my own voice, careful as I was to speak naturally, —' but he fainted just before I came out, and I think you had better ask the clerk as you go down to send someone up to him.'

"James was weighing the pocket-book in his hand. 'How much do you think there is in here? The debt was ten thousand. ' I had turned carelessly away and was looking out of the window. 'The memorandum inside gives the figures as two thousand, ' I declared. 'He apologises for not sending the full amount. He hasn't it. ' Again I felt James looking at me. Why? Could he see that guilty wad of bills lying on my breast? 'How came you to read the memorandum? ' he asked. 'Mr. Orr wished me to. I looked at it to please him. ' This was a lie—the first I had ever uttered. James's eyes had not moved. 'John, ' said he, 'this little bit of business seems to have disturbed you. I ought to have attended to it myself. I am quite sure I ought to have attended to it myself. ' 'The man is dying, ' I muttered. 'You escaped a sad sight. Be satisfied that you have got the money. Shall I post that letter for you? ' He put it jealously in his pocket, and again I saw him look at me, but he said nothing more except that he repeated that same phrase, 'I ought to have attended to it myself. Agatha might better have waited. ' Then he went out; but I remained till Philemon came home. My brother and myself were no longer companions; a crime divided us, —a crime he could not suspect, yet which made itself felt in both our hearts and prepared him for the revelation made to him by Mr. Gilchrist some weeks after. That night he came to Sutherlandtown, where I was, and entered my bedroom—not in the fraternal way of the old days, but as an elder enters the presence of a younger. 'John, ' he said, without any preamble or preparation, 'where are the five thousand dollars you kept back from Mr. Gilchrist? The memorandum said seven and you delivered to me only two. ' There are death-knells sounded in every life; those words sounded mine, or would have if he had not immediately added: 'There! I knew you had no stamina. I have taken your crime on myself, who am really to blame for it, since I delegated my duty to another, and you will only have to bear the disgrace of having James Zabel for a brother. In exchange, give me the money; it shall be returned to-morrow. You cannot have disposed of it already. After which, you, or rather I, will be in the eyes of the world only a thief in intent, not in fact. ' Had he only stopped there! —but he went on: 'Agatha is lost to me, John. In return, be to me the brother I always thought you up to the unhappy day the sin of Achan came between us. '

"YOU were lost to him! It was all I heard. YOU were lost to him! Then, if I acknowledged the crime I should not only take up my own burden of disgrace, but see him restored to his rights over the only woman I had ever loved. The sacrifice was great and my virtue was not equal to it. I gave him back the money, but I did not offer to assume the responsibility of my own crime. "

"And since?"

In what a hard tone she spoke!

"I have had to see Philemon gradually assume the rights James once enjoyed."

"John," she asked, —she was under violent self-restraint, —"why do you come now?"

I cast my eyes at Philemon. He was standing, as before, with his eyes turned away. There was discouragement in his attitude, mingled with a certain grand patience. Seeing that he was better able to bear her loss than either you or myself, I said to her very low, "I thought you ought to know the truth before you gave your final word. I am late, but I would have been TOO LATE a week from now."

Her hand fell from the door, but her eyes remained fixed on my face. Never have I sustained such a look; never will I encounter such another.

"It is too late NOW," she murmured. "The clergyman has just gone who united me to Philemon."

The next minute her back was towards me; she had faced her father and her new-made husband.

"Father, you knew this thing!" Keen, sharp, incisive, the words rang out. "I saw it in your face when he began to speak."

Mr. Gilchrist drooped slightly; lie was a very sick man and the scene had been a trying one.

"If I did," was his low response, "it was but lately. You were engaged then to Philemon. Why break up this second match?"

She eyed him as if she found it difficult to credit her ears. Such indifference to the claims of innocence was incredible to her. I saw her grand profile quiver, then the slow ebbing from her cheek of every drop of blood indignation had summoned there.

"And you, Philemon?" she suggested, with a somewhat softened aspect. "You committed this wrong ignorantly. Never having heard of this crime, you could not know on what false grounds I had been separated from James. "

I had started to escape, but stopped just beyond the threshold of the door as she uttered these words. Philemon was not as ignorant as she supposed. This was evident from his attitude and expression.

"Agatha, " he began, but at this first word, and before he could clasp the hands held helplessly out before her, she gave a great cry, and staggering back, eyed both her father and himself in a frenzy of indignation that was all the more uncontrollable from the superhuman effort which she had hitherto made to suppress it.

"You too! " she shrieked. "You too! and I have just sworn to love, honour, and obey you! Love YOU! Honour YOU! the unconscionable wretch who—"

But here Mr. Gilchrist rose. Weak, tottering, quivering with something more than anger, he approached his daughter and laid his finger on her lips.

"Be quiet! " he said. "Philemon is not to blame. A month ago he came to me and prayed that as a relief to his mind I would tell him why you had separated yourself from James. He had always thought the match, had fallen through on account of some foolish quarrel or incompatibility, but lately he had feared there was something more than he suspected in this break, something that he should know. So I told him why you had dismissed James; and whether he knew James better than we did, or whether he had seen something in his long acquaintance with these brothers which influenced his judgment, he said at once: 'This cannot be true of James. It is not in his nature to defraud any man; but John—I might believe it of John. Isn't there some complication here? ' I had never thought of John, and did not see how John could be mixed up with an affair I had supposed to be a secret between James and myself, but when we came to locate the day, Philemon remembered that on returning to his room that night, he had found John awaiting him. As his room was not five doors from that occupied by Mr. Orr, he was convinced that there was more to this matter than I had suspected. But when he laid the matter before James, he did not deny that John was guilty, but was peremptory in wishing you not to be told before your marriage. He knew that you were engaged to a good man, a man that your father approved, a man that could and would make you happy. He did not want to be the means of a second break, and besides, and this, I think, was at the bottom of the stand he took, for James Zabel was always the proudest man I ever knew, —he never could bear, he said, to give to one like Agatha a name which he knew and she knew was not entirely free from reproach. It would stand in the way of his happiness and ultimately of hers; his brother's dishonour was his. So while he still loved you, his only prayer was that after you were safely married and Philemon was sure of your affection, he should tell you that the man you once regarded so favourably was not unworthy of that regard. To obey him, Philemon has kept silent, while I— Agatha, what are you doing? Are you mad, my child?"

She looked so for the moment. Tearing off the ring which she had worn but an hour, she flung it on the floor. Then she threw her arms high up over her head and burst out in an awful voice:

"Curses on the father, curses on the husband, who have combined to make me rue the day I was born! The father I cannot disown, but the husband—"

"Hush!"

It was Mr. Gilchrist who dared her fury. Philemon said nothing.

"Hush! he may be the father of your children. Don't curse—"

But she only towered the higher and her beauty, from being simply majestic, became appalling.

"Children!" she cried. "If ever I bear children to this man, may the blight of Heaven strike them as it has struck me this day. May they die as my hopes have died, or, if they live, may they bruise his heart as mine is bruised, and curse their father as—"

Here I fled the house. I was shaking as if this awful denunciation had fallen on my own head. But before the door closed behind me, a different cry called me back. Mr. Gilchrist was lying lifeless on the floor, and Philemon, the patient, tender Philemon, had taken Agatha to his breast and was soothing her there as if the words she had showered upon him had been blessings instead of the most fearful curses which had ever left the lips of mortal woman.

The next letter was in Agatha's handwriting. It was dated some months later and was stained and crumpled more than any other in the whole packet. Could Philemon once have told why? Were these blotted lines the result of his tears falling fast upon them, tears of forty years ago, when he and she were young and love had been, doubtful? Was the sheet so yellowed and so seamed because it had been worn on his breast and folded and unfolded so often? Philemon, thou art in thy grave, sleeping sweetly at last by thy deeply idolised one, but these marks of feeling still remain indissolubly connected with the words that gave them birth.

DEAR PHILEMON:

You are gone for a day and a night only, but it seems a lengthened absence to me, meriting a little letter. You have been so good to me, Philemon, ever since that dreadful hour following our marriage, that sometimes—I hardly dare yet to say always—I feel that I am beginning to love you and that God did not deal with me so harshly when He cast me into your arms. Yesterday I tried to tell you this when you almost kissed me at parting. But I was afraid it was a momentary sentimentality and so kept still. But to-day such a warm well-spring of joy rises in my heart when I think that to-morrow the house will be bright again, and that in place of the empty wall opposite me at table I shall see your kindly and forbearing face, I know that the heart I had thought impregnable has begun to yield, and that daily gentleness, and a boundless consideration from one who had excuse for bitter thoughts and recrimination, are doing what all of us thought impossible a few short months ago.

Oh, I am so happy, Philemon, so happy to love where it is now my duty to love; and if it were not for that dreadful memory of a father dying with harsh words in his ears, and the knowledge that you, my husband, yet not my husband, are bearing ever about with you echoes of words that in another nature would have turned tenderness into gall, I could be merry also and sing as I go about the house making it pleasant and comfortable against your speedy return. As it is I can but lay my hand softly on my heart as its beatings grow too impetuous and say, "God bless my absent Philemon and help him to forgive me! I forgive him and love him as I never thought I could."

That you may see that these are not the weak outpourings of a lonely woman, I will here write that I heard to-day that John and James

Zabel have gone into partnership in the ship-building business, John's uncle having left him a legacy of several thousand dollars. I hope they will do well. James, they say, is full of business and is, to all appearance, perfectly cheerful. This relieves me from too much worry in his regard. God certainly knew what kind of a husband I needed. May you find yourself equally blessed in your wife.

Another letter to Philemon, a year later:

DEAR PHILEMON:

Hasten home, Philemon; I do not like these absences. I am just now too weak and fearful. Since we knew the great hope before us, I have looked often in your face for a sign that you remembered what this hope cannot but recall to my shuddering memory. Philemon, Philemon, was I mad? When I think what I said in my rage, and then feel the little life stirring about my heart, I wonder that God did not strike me dead rather than bestow upon me the greatest blessing that can come to woman. Philemon, Philemon, if anything should happen to the child! I think of it by day, I think of it by night. I know you think of it too, though you show me such a cheerful countenance and make such great plans for the future. "Will God remember my words, or will He forget? It seems as if my reason hung upon this question."

A note this time in answer to one from John Zabel:

DEAR JOHN:

Thank you for words which could have come from nobody else. My child is dead. Could I expect anything different? If I did, God has rebuked me.

Philemon thinks only of me. We understand each other so perfectly now that our greatest suffering comes in seeing each other's pain. My load I can bear, but HIS—Come and see me, John; and tell James our house is open to him. We have all done wrong, and are caught in one net of misfortune. Let it make us friends again.

Below this in Philemon's hand:

My wife is superstitious. Strong and capable as she is, she has regarded this sudden taking off of our first-born as a sign that certain words uttered by her on her marriage day, unhappily known to you and, as I take it, to James also, have been remembered by the righteous God above us. This is a weakness which I cannot combat. Can you, who alone of all the world beside know both it and its cause, help me by a renewed friendship, whose cheerful and natural character may gradually make her forget? If so, come like old neighbours, and dine with us on our wedding day. If God sees that we have buried the past and are ready to forgive each other the faults of our youth, perhaps He will further spare this good woman. I think she will be able to bear it. She has great strength except where a little child is concerned. That alone can henceforth stir the deepest recesses of her heart.

After this, a gap of years. One, two, three, four, five children were laid away to rest in Portchester churchyard, then Philemon and she came to Sutherlandtown; but not till after a certain event had occurred, best made known by this last letter to Philemon:

DEAREST HUSBAND:

Our babe is born, our sixth and our dearest, and the reproach of its first look had to be met by me alone. Oh, why did I leave you and come to this great Boston where I have no friend but Mrs. Sutherland? Did I think I could break the spell of fate or providence by giving birth to my last darling among strangers? I shall have to do something more than that if I would save this child to our old age. It is borne in upon me like fate that never will a child prosper at my breast or survive the clasp of my arms. If it is to live it must be reared by others. Some woman who has not brought down the curse of Heaven upon her by her own blasphemies must nourish the tender frame and receive the blessing of its growing love. Neither I nor you can hope to see recognition in our babe's eye. Before it can turn upon us with love, it will close in its last sleep and we will be left desolate. What shall we do, then, with this little son? To whose guardianship can we entrust it? Do you know a man good enough or a woman sufficiently tender? I do not, but if God wills that our little Frederick should live, He will raise up someone. By the pang of possible separation already tearing my heart, I believe that He WILL raise up someone. Meanwhile I do not dare to kiss the child, lest I should blight it. He is so sturdy, Philemon, so different from all the other five.

I open this to add that Mrs. Sutherland has just been in—with her five-weeks-old infant. His father is away, too, and has not yet seen his boy; and this is their first after ten years of marriage. Oh, that my future opened before me as brightly as hers!

The next letter opens with a cry:

Philemon! Come to me, Philemon! I have done what I threatened. I have made the sacrifice. Our child is no longer ours, and now, perhaps, he may live. But oh, my breaking heart! my empty arms! Help me to bear my desolation, for it is for life. We will never have another child.

And where is it? Ah, that is the wonder of it. Near you, Philemon, yet not too near. Mrs. Sutherland has it, and you may have seen its little face through the car window if you were in the station last night when the express passed through to Sutherlandtown. Ah! but she has her burden to bear too. An awful, secret burden like my own, only she will have the child—for, Philemon, she has taken it in lieu of her own, which died last night in my sight; and Mr. Sutherland does not know what she has done, and never will, if you keep the secret as I shall, for the sake of the life our little innocent has thus won.

What do I mean and how was it all? Philemon, it was God's work, all but the deception, and that is for the good of all, and to save four broken hearts. Listen. Yesterday, only yesterday, —it seems a month ago, —Mrs. Sutherland came again to see me with her baby in her arms. Mr. Sutherland is expected home, as you know, this week, and she was about to start out for Sutherlandtown so as to be in her own house when he came. The baby was looking well and she was the happiest of women; for the one wish of his heart and hers had been fulfilled and she was soon going to have the bliss of showing the child to his father. My own babe was on the bed asleep, and I, who am feeling wonderfully strong, was sitting up in a little chair as far away from him as possible, not out of hatred or indifference—oh, no! —but because he seemed to rest better when left entirely by himself and not under the hungry look of my eye. Mrs. Sutherland went over to look at it. "Oh, he is fair like my baby, " she said, "and almost as sturdy, though mine is a month older. " And she stooped down and kissed him. Philemon, he smiled for her, though he never had for me. I saw it with a greedy longing that almost made me cry out. Then I turned to her and we talked.

Of what? I cannot remember now. At home we had never been intimate friends. She is from Sutherlandtown and I am from Portchester, and the distance of nine miles is enough to estrange people. But here, each with a husband absent and a darling infant lying asleep under our eyes, interests we have never thought identical drew us to one another and we chatted with ever-increasing pleasure—when suddenly Mrs. Sutherland jumped up in a terrible fright. The infant she had been rocking on her breast was blue; the next minute it shuddered; the next—it lay in her arms DEAD!

I hear the shriek yet with which she fell with it still in her arms to the floor. Fortunately no other ears were open to her cry. I alone saw her misery. I alone heard her tale. The child had been poisoned, Philemon, poisoned by her. She had mistaken a cup of medicine for a cup of water and had given the child a few drops in a spoon just before setting out from her hotel. She had not known at the time what she had done, but now she remembered that the fatal cup was just like the other and that the two stood very near together. Oh, her innocent child, and oh, her husband!

It seemed as if the latter thought would drive her wild. "He has so wished for a child, " she moaned. "We have been married ten years and this baby seemed to have been sent from heaven. He will curse me, he will hate me, he will never be able after this to bear me in his sight. " This was not true of Mr. Sutherland, but it was useless to argue with her. Instead of attempting it, I took another way to stop her ravings. Lifting the child out of her hands, I first listened at its heart, and then, finding it was really dead, —Philemon, I have seen too many lifeless children not to know, —I began slowly to undress it. "What are you doing? " she cried. "Mrs. Webb, Mrs. Webb, what are you doing? " For reply I pointed to the bed, where two little arms could be seen feebly fluttering. "You shall have my child, " I whispered. "I have carried too many babies to the tomb to dare risk bringing up another. " And catching her poor wandering spirit with my eye, I held her while I told her my story.

Philemon, I saved that woman. Before I had finished speaking I saw the reason return to her eye and the dawning of a pitiful hope in her passion-drawn face. She looked at the child in my arms and then she looked at the one in the bed, and the long-drawn sigh with which she finally bent down and wept over our darling told me that my cause was won. The rest was easy. When the clothes of the two children had been exchanged, she took our baby in her arms and prepared to leave. Then I stopped her. "Swear, " I cried, holding her by the arm and lifting my other hand to heaven, "swear you will be a mother to this child! Swear you will love it as your own and rear it in the paths of truth and righteousness! " The convulsive clasp with which she drew the baby to her breast assured me more than her shuddering "I swear! " that her heart had already opened to it. I dropped her arm and covered my face with my hands. I could not see my darling go; it was worse than death for the moment it was worse than death. "O God, save him! " I groaned. "God, make him an honour—" But here she caught me by the arm. Her clutch was frenzied, her teeth were chattering. "Swear in your turn! " she gasped. "Swear that if I do a mother's duty by this boy, you will keep my secret and never, never reveal to my husband, to the boy, or to the world that you have any claims upon him! " It was like tearing the heart from my breast with my own hand, but I swore, Philemon, and she in her turn drew back. But suddenly she faced me again, terror and doubt in all her looks. "Your husband! " she whispered. "Can you keep such a secret from him? You will breathe it in your dreams. " "I shall tell him, " I answered. "Tell him! " The hair seemed to rise on her forehead and she shook so that I feared she would drop the babe. "Be careful! " I cried. "See! you frighten the babe. My husband has but one heart with me. What I do he will subscribe to. Do not fear Philemon. " So I promised in your name. Gradually she grew calmer. When I saw she was steady again, I motioned her to go. Even my more than mortal strength was failing, and the baby—Philemon, I had never kissed it and I did not kiss it then. I heard her feet draw slowly towards the door, I heard her hand fall on the knob, heard it turn, uttered one cry, and then—-

They found me an hour after, lying along the floor, clasping the dead infant in my arms. I was in a swoon, and they all think I fell with the child, as perhaps I did, and that its little life went out during my insensibility. Of its features, like and yet unlike our boy's, no one seems to take heed. The nurse who cared for it is gone, and who else would know that little face but me? They are very good to me, and are full of self-reproaches for leaving me so long in my part of the building alone. But though they watch me now, I have contrived to write this letter, which you will get with the one telling of the baby's death and my own dangerous condition. Destroy it, Philemon, and then COME. Nothing in all the world will give me comfort but your hand laid under my head and your true eyes looking into mine. Ah, we must love each other now, and live humbly! All our woe has come from my early girlish delight in gay and elegant things. From this day on I eschew all vanities and find in your affection alone the solace which Heaven will not deny to our bewildered hearts. Perhaps in this way the blessing that has been denied us will be visited on our child, who will live. I am now sure, to be the delight of our hearts and the pride of our eyes, even though we are denied the bliss of his presence and affection.

Mrs. Sutherland was not seen to enter or go out of my rooms. Being on her way to the depot, she kept on her way, and must be now in her own home. Her secret is safe, but ours—oh, you will help me to preserve it! Help me not to betray—tell them I have lost five babies before this one—delirious—there may be an inquest—she must not be mentioned—let all the blame fall on me if there is blame—I fell—there is a bruise on the baby's forehead—and—and- -I am growing incoherent—I will try and direct this and then love—love—O God!

[A scrawl for the name.]

Under it these words:

Though bidden to destroy this, I have never dared to do so. Some day it may be of inestimable value to us or our boy. PHILEMON WEBB.

This was the last letter found in the first packet. As it was laid down, sobs were heard all over the room, and Frederick, who for some time now had been sitting with his head in his hands, ventured to look up and say: "Do you wonder that I endeavoured to keep this secret, bought at such a price and sealed by the death of her I thought my mother and of her who really was? Gentlemen, Mr. Sutherland loved his wife and honoured her memory. To tell him, as I shall have to within the hour, that the child she placed in his arms twenty-five years ago was an alien, and that all his love, his care, his disappointment, and his sufferings had been lavished on the son of a neighbour, required greater courage than to face doubt on the faces of my fellow-townsmen, or anything, in short, but absolute arraignment on the charge of murder. Hence my silence, hence my indecision, till this woman"—here he pointed a scornful finger at Amabel, now shrinking in her chair—"drove me to it by secretly threatening me with a testimony which would have made me the murderer of my mother and the lasting disgrace of a good man who alone has been without blame from the beginning to the end of this desperate affair. She was about to speak when I forestalled her. My punishment, if I deserve such, will be to sit and hear in your presence the reading of the letters still remaining in the coroner's hands. "

These letters were certain ones written by Agatha to her unacknowledged son. They had never been sent. The first one dated from his earliest infancy, and its simple and touching hopefulness sent a thrill through every heart. It read as follows:

Three years old, my darling! and the health flush has not faded from your cheek nor the bright gold from your hair.

Oh, how I bless Mrs. Sutherland that she did not rebuke me when your father and I came to Sutherlandtown and set up our home where I could at least see your merry form toddling through the streets, holding on to the hand of her who now claims your love. My darling, my pride, my angel, so near and yet so far removed, will you ever know, even in the heaven to which we all look for joy after our weary pilgrimage is over, how often in this troublous world, and in these days of your early infancy, I have crept out of my warm bed, dressed myself, and, without a word to your father, whose heart it would break, gone out and climbed the steep hillside just to look at the window of your room to see if it were light or dark and you awake or sleeping? To breathe the scent of the eglantine which climbs up to your nursery window, I have braved the night-damps and the watching eyes of Heaven; but you have a child's blissful ignorance of all this; you only grow and grow and live, my darling, LIVE! —which is the only boon I crave, the only recompense I ask.

Have I but added another sin to my account and brought a worse vengeance on myself than that of seeing you die in your early infancy? Frederick, my son, my son, I heard you swear to-day! Not lightly, thoughtlessly, as boys sometimes will in imitation of their elders, but bitterly, revengefully, as if the seeds of evil passions were already pushing to life in the boyish breast I thought so innocent. Did you wonder at the strange woman who stopped you? Did you realise the awful woe from which my commonplace words sprang? No, no, what grown mind could take that in, least of all a child's? To have forsworn the bliss of motherhood and entered upon a life of deception for THIS! Truly Heaven is implacable and my last sin is to be punished more inexorably than my first.

There are worse evils than death. This I have always heard, but now I know it. God was merciful when He slew my babes, and I, presumptous in my rebellion, and the efforts with which I tried to prevent His work. Frederick, you are weak, dissipated, and without conscience. The darling babe, the beautiful child, has grown into a reckless youth whose impulses Mr. Sutherland will find it hard to restrain, and over whom his mother—do *I* call her your mother? — has little influence, though she tries hard to do a mother's part and save herself and myself from boundless regret. My boy, my boy, do you feel the lack of your own mother's vigour? Might you have lived under my care and owned a better restraint and learned to work and live a respectable life in circumstances less provocative of self-indulgence? Such questions, when they rise, are maddening. When I see them form themselves in Philemon's eyes I drive them out with all the force of my influence, which is still strong over him. But when they make way in my own breast, I can find no relief, not even in prayer. Frederick, were I to tell you the truth about your parentage, would the shock of such an unexpected revelation make a man of you? I have been tempted to make the trial, at times. Deep down in my heart I have thought that perhaps I should best serve the good man who is growing grey under your waywardness, by opening up before you the past and present agonies of which you are the unconscious centre. But I cannot do this while SHE lives. The look she gave me one day when I approached you a step too near at the church door, proves that it would be the killing of her to reveal her long-preserved secret now. I must wait her death, which seems near, and then—

No, I cannot do it. Mr. Sutherland has but one staff to lean on, and that is you. It may be a poor one, a breaking one, but it is still a staff. I dare not take it away—I dare not. Ah, if Philemon was the man he was once, he might counsel me, but he is only a child now; just as if God had heard my cry for children and had given me—HIM.

More money, and still more money! and I hate it except for what it will do for the poor and incapable about me. How strange are the ways of Providence! To us who have no need of aught beyond a competence, money pours in almost against our will, while to those who long and labour for it, it comes not, or comes so slowly the life wears out in the waiting and the working. The Zabels, now! Once well-to-do ship-builders, with a good business and a home full of curious works of art, they now appear to find it hard to obtain even the necessities of life. Such are the freaks of fortune; or should I say, the dealings of an inscrutable Providence? Once I tried to give something out of my abundance to these old friends, but their pride stood in the way and the attempt failed. Worse than that. As if to show that benefits should proceed from them to me rather than from me to them, James bestowed on me a gift. It is a strange one, — nothing more nor less than a quaint Florentine dagger which I had often admired for its exquisite workmanship. Was it the last treasure he possessed? I am almost afraid so. At all events it shall lie here in my table- drawer where I alone can see it. Such sights are not good for Philemon. He must have cheerful objects before him, happy faces such as mine tries to be. But ah!

I would gladly give my life if I could once hold you in my arms, my erring but beloved son. Will the day ever come when I can? Will you have strength enough to hear my story and preserve your peace and let me go down to the grave with the memory of one look, one smile, that is for me alone? Sometimes I foresee this hour and am happy for a few short minutes; and then some fresh story of your recklessness is wafted through the town and—

What stopped her at this point we shall never know. Some want of Philemon's, perhaps. At all events she left off here and the letter was never resumed. It was the last secret outpouring of her heart. With this broken sentence Agatha's letters terminated. .

. . . . . .

That afternoon, before the inquiry broke up, the jury brought in their verdict. It was:

"Death by means of a wound inflicted upon herself in a moment of terror and misapprehension. "

It was all his fellow-townsmen could do for Frederick.

XXXIII

FATHER AND SON

But Frederick's day of trial was not yet over. There was a closed door to open and a father to see (as in his heart he still called Mr. Sutherland). Then there were friends to face, and foes, under conditions he better than anyone else, knew were in some regards made worse rather than better by the admissions and revelations of this eventful day—Agnes, for instance. How could he meet her pure gaze? But it was his father he must first confront, his father to whom he would have to repeat in private the tale which robbed the best of men of a past, and took from him a son, almost a wife, without leaving him one memory calculated to console him. Frederick was so absorbed in this anticipation that he scarcely noticed the two or three timid hands stretched out in encouragement toward him, and was moving slowly toward the door behind which his father had disappeared so many hours before, when he was recalled to the interests of the moment by a single word, uttered not very far from him. It was simply, "Well? " But it was uttered by Knapp and repeated by Mr. Courtney.

Frederick shuddered, and was hurrying on when he found himself stopped by a piteous figure that, with appealing eyes and timid gestures, stepped up before him. It was Amabel.

"Forgive! " she murmured, looking like a pleading saint. "I did not know—I never dreamed—you were so much of a man, Frederick: that you bore such a heart, cherished such griefs, were so worthy of love and a woman's admiration. If I had—"

Her expression was eloquent, more eloquent than he had ever seen it, for it had real feeling in it; but he put her coldly by.

"When my father's white hairs become black again, and the story of my shame is forgotten in this never-forgetting world, then come back and I will forgive you. "

And he was passing on when another touch detained him. He turned, this time in some impatience, only to meet the frank eyes of Sweetwater. As he knew very little of this young man, save that he was the amateur detective who had by some folly of his own been carried off on the Hesper, and who was probably the only man saved from its wreck, he was about to greet him with some commonplace phrase of congratulation, when Sweetwater interrupted him with the following words:

"I only wanted to say that it may be easier for you to approach your father with the revelations you are about to make if you knew that in his present frame of mind he is much more likely to be relieved by such proofs of innocence as you can give him than overwhelmed by such as show the lack of kinship between you. For two weeks Mr. Sutherland has been bending under the belief of your personal criminality in this matter. This was his secret, which was shared by me."

"By you?"

"Yes, by me! I am more closely linked to this affair than you can readily imagine. Some day I may be able to explain myself, but not now. Only remember what I have said about your father—pardon me, I should perhaps say Mr. Sutherland—and act accordingly. Perhaps it was to tell you this that I was forced back here against my will by the strangest series of events that ever happened to a man. But," he added, with a sidelong look at the group of men still hovering about the coroner's table, "I had rather think it was for some more important office still. But this the future will show, —the future which I seem to see lowering in the faces over there."

And, waiting for no reply, he melted into the crowd.

Frederick passed at once to his father.

No one interrupted them during this solemn interview, but the large crowd that in the halls and on the steps of the building awaited Frederick's reappearance showed that the public interest was still warm in a matter affecting so deeply the heart and interests of their best citizen. When, therefore, that long-closed door finally opened and Frederick was seen escorting Mr. Sutherland on his arm, the tide of feeling which had not yet subsided since Agatha's letters were read vented itself in one great sob of relief. For Mr. Sutherland's face was calmer than when they had last seen it, and his step more assured, and he leaned, or made himself lean, on Frederick's arm, as if to impress upon all who saw them that the ties of years cannot be shaken off so easily, and that he still looked upon Frederick as his son.

But he was not contented with this dumb show, eloquent as it was. As the crowd parted and these two imposing figures took their way down the steps to the carriage which had been sent for them, Mr. Sutherland cast one deep and long glance about him on faces he knew and on faces he did not know, on those who were near and those who were far, and raising his voice, which did not tremble as much as might have been expected, said deliberately:

"My son accompanies me to his home. If he should afterwards be wanted, he will be found at his own fireside. Good-day, my friends. I thank you for the goodwill you have this day shown us both."

Then he entered the carriage.

The solemn way in which Frederick bared his head in acknowledgment of this public recognition of the hold he still retained on this one faithful heart, struck awe into the hearts of all who saw it. So that the carriage rolled off in silence, closing one of the most thrilling and impressive scenes ever witnessed in that time-worn village.

XXXIV

"NOT WHEN THEY ARE YOUNG GIRLS"

But, alas! all tides have their ebb as well as flow, and before Mr. Sutherland and Frederick were well out of the main street the latter became aware that notwithstanding the respect with which his explanations had been received by the jury, there were many of his fellow-townsmen who were ready to show dissatisfaction at his being allowed to return in freedom to that home where he had still every prospect of being called the young master. Doubt, that seed of ramifying growth, had been planted in more than one breast, and while it failed as yet to break out into any open manifestation, there were evidences enough in the very restraint visible in such groups of people as they passed that suspicion had not been suppressed or his innocence established by the over-favourable verdict of the coroner's jury.

To Mr. Sutherland, suffering now from the reaction following all great efforts, much, if not all, of this quiet but significant display of public feeling passed unnoticed. But to Frederick, alive to the least look, the least sign that his story had not been accepted unquestioned, this passage through the town was the occasion of the most poignant suffering.

For not only did these marks of public suspicion bespeak possible arraignment in the future, but through them it became evident that even if he escaped open condemnation in the courts, he could never hope for complete reinstatement before the world, nor, what was to him a still deeper source of despair, anticipate a day when Agnes's love should make amends to him for the grief and errors of his more than wayward youth. He could never marry so pure a being while the shadow of crime separated him from the mass of human beings. Her belief in his innocence and the exact truth of his story (and he was confident she did believe him) could make no difference in this conclusion. While he was regarded openly or in dark corners or beside the humblest fireside as a possible criminal, neither Mr. Sutherland nor her father, nor his own heart even, would allow him to offer her anything but a friend's gratitude, or win from her anything but a neighbour's sympathy; yet in bidding good-bye to larger hopes and more importunate desires, he parted with the better part of his heart and the only solace remaining in this world for the boundless griefs and tragic experiences of his still young life. He had learned to love through suffering, only to realise that the very nature of his suffering forbade him to indulge in love.

And this seemed a final judgment, even in this hour of public justification. He had told his story and been for the moment believed, but what was there in his life, what was there in the facts as witnessed by others, what was there in his mother's letters and the revelation of their secret relationship, to corroborate his assertions, or to prove that her hand and not his had held the weapon when the life-blood gushed from her devoted breast? Nothing, nothing; only his word to stand against all human probabilities and natural inference; only his word and the generous nature of the great-hearted woman who had thus perished! Though a dozen of his fellow-citizens had by their verdict professed their belief in his word and given him the benefit of a doubt involving his life as well as his honour, he, as well as they, knew that neither the police nor the general public were given to sentimentality, and that the question of his guilt still lay open and must remain so till his dying day. For from the nature of things no proof of the truth was probable. Batsy being dead, only God and his own heart could know that the facts of that awful half-hour were as he had told them.

Had God in His justice removed in this striking way his only witness, as a punishment for his sins and his mad indulgence in acts so little short of crime as to partake of its guilt and merit its obloquy?

He was asking himself this question as he bent to fasten the gate. His father had passed in, the carriage had driven off, and the road was almost solitary—but not quite. As he leaned his arm over the gate and turned to take a final glance down the hillside, he saw, with what feelings no one will ever know, the light figure of Agnes advancing on the arm of her father.

He would have drawn back, but a better impulse intervened and he stood his ground. Mr. Halliday, who walked very close to Agnes, cast her an admonitory glance which Frederick was not slow in interpreting, then stopped reluctantly, perhaps because he saw her falter, perhaps because he knew that an interview between these two was unavoidable and had best be quickly over.

Frederick found his voice first.

"Agnes," said he, "I am glad of this opportunity for expressing my gratitude. You have acted like a friend and have earned my eternal consideration, even if we never speak again."

There was a momentary silence. Her head, which had drooped under his greeting, rose again. Her eyes, humid with feeling, sought his face.

"Why do you speak like that?" said she. "Why shouldn't we meet? Does not everyone recognise your innocence, and will not the whole world soon see, as I have, that you have left the old life behind and have only to be your new self to win everyone's regard?"

"Agnes," returned Frederick, smiling sadly as he observed the sudden alarm visible in her father's face at these enthusiastic words, "you know me perhaps better than others do and are prepared to believe my words and my more than unhappy story. But there are few like you in the world. People in general will not acquit me, and if there was only one person who doubted"—Mr. Halliday began to look relieved—"I would fail to give any promise of the new life you hope to see me lead, if I allowed the shadow under which I undoubtedly rest to fall in the remotest way across yours. You and I have been friends and will continue such, but we will hold little intercourse in future, hard as I find it to say so. Does not Mr. Halliday consider this right? As your father he must."

Agnes's eyes, leaving Frederick's for a moment, sought her father's. Alas! there was no mistaking their language. Sighing deeply, she again hung her head.

"Too much care for people's opinion," she murmured, "and too little for what is best and noblest in us. I do not recognise the necessity of a farewell between us any more than I recognise that anyone who saw and heard you to-day can believe in your guilt."

"But there are so many who did not hear and see me. Besides" (here he turned a little and pointed to the garden in his rear), "for the past week a man—I need not state who, nor under what authority he acts—has been in hiding under that arbour, watching my every movement, and almost counting my sighs. Yesterday he left for a short space, but to-day he is back. What does that argue, dear friend? Innocence, completely recognised, does not call for such guardianship."

The slight frame of the young girl bending so innocently toward him shuddered involuntarily at this, and her eyes, frightened and flashing, swept over the arbour before returning to his face.

"If there is a watcher there, and if such a fact proves you to be in danger of arrest for a crime you never committed, then it behooves your friends to show where they stand in this matter, and by lending their sympathy give you courage and power to meet the trials before you."

"Not when they are young girls," murmured Frederick, and casting a glance at Mr. Halliday, he stepped softly back.

Agnes flushed and yielded to her father's gentle pressure. "Good-bye, my friend," she said, the quiver in her tones sinking deep into Frederick's heart. "Some day it will be good-morrow," and her head, turned back over her shoulder, took on a beautiful radiance that fixed itself forever in the hungry heart of him who watched it disappear. When she was quite gone, a man not the one whom Frederick had described, as lying in hiding in the arbour, but a different one, in fact, no other than our old friend the constable—advanced around the corner of the house and presented a paper to him.

It was the warrant for his arrest on a charge of murder.

XXXV

SWEETWATER PAYS HIS DEBT AT LAST TO MR. SUTHERLAND

Frederick's arrest had been conducted so quietly that no hint of the matter reached the village before the next morning. Then the whole town broke into uproar, and business was not only suspended, but the streets and docks overflowed with gesticulating men and excited women, carrying on in every corner and across innumerable doorsteps the endless debate which such an action on the part of the police necessarily opened.

But the most agitated face, though the stillest tongue, was not to be seen in town that morning, but in a little cottage on an arid hill-slope overlooking the sea. Here Sweetwater sat and communed with his great monitor, the ocean, and only from his flashing eye and the firm set of his lips could the mother of Sweetwater see that the crisis of her son's life was rapidly approaching, and that on the outcome of this long brooding rested not only his own self-satisfaction, but the interests of the man most dear to them.

Suddenly, from that far horizon upon which Sweetwater's eye rested with a look that was almost a demand, came an answer that flushed him with a hope as great as it was unexpected. Bounding to his feet, he confronted his mother with eager eyes and outstretched hand.

"Give me money, all the money we have in the house. I have an idea that may be worth all I can ever make or can ever hope to have. If it succeeds, we save Frederick Sutherland; if it fails, I have only to meet another of Knapp's scornful looks. But it won't fail; the inspiration came from the sea, and the sea, you know, is my second mother! "

What this inspiration was he did not say, but it carried him presently into town and landed him in the telegraph office.

. . . . . .

The scene later in the day, when Frederick entered the village under the guardianship of the police, was indescribable. Mr. Sutherland had insisted upon accompanying him, and when the well- loved figure and white head were recognised, the throng, which had rapidly collected in the thoroughfare leading to the depot, succumbed to the feelings occasioned by this devotion, and fell into a wondering silence.

Frederick had never looked better. There is something in the extremity of fate which brings out a man's best characteristics, and this man, having much that was good in him, showed it at that moment as never before in his short but over-eventful life. As the carriage stopped before the court-house on its way to the train, a glimpse was given of his handsome head to those who had followed him closest, and as there became visible for the first time in his face, so altered under his troubles, a likeness to their beautiful and commanding Agatha, a murmur broke out around him that was half a wail and half a groan, and which affected him so that he turned from his father, whose hand he was secretly holding, and taking the whole scene in with one flash of his eye, was about to speak, when a sudden hubbub broke out in the direction of the telegraph office, and a man was seen rushing down the street holding a paper high over his head. It was Sweetwater.

"News! " he cried. "News! A cablegram from the Azores! A Swedish sailor—"

But here a man with more authority than the amateur detective pushed his way to the carriage and took off his hat to Mr. Sutherland.

"I beg your pardon, " said he, "but the prisoner will not leave town to-day. Important evidence has just reached us. "

Mr. Sutherland saw that it was in Frederick's favour and fainted on his son's neck. As the people beheld his head fall forward, and observed the look with which Frederick received him in his arms, they broke into a great shout.

"News! " they shrieked. "News! Frederick Sutherland is innocent! See! the old man has fainted from joy! " And caps went up and tears fell, before a mother's son of them knew what grounds he had for his enthusiasm.

Later, they found they were good and substantial ones. Sweetwater had remembered the group of sailors who had passed by the corner of Agatha's house just as Batsy fell forward on the window-sill, and cabling to the captain of the vessel, at the first port at which they were likely to put in, was fortunate enough to receive in reply a communication from one of the men, who remembered the words she shouted. They were in Swedish and none of his mates had understood them, but he recalled them well. They were:

"Hjelp! Hjelp! Frun haller pa alb doda sig. Hon har en knif. Hjelp! Hjelp!"

In English:

"Help! Help! My mistress kills herself. She has a knife. Help! Help!"

The impossible had occurred. Batsy was not dead, or at least her testimony still remained and had come at Sweetwater's beck from the other side of the sea to save her mistress's son.

......

Sweetwater was a made man. And Frederick? In a week he was the idol of the town. In a year—but let Agnes's contented face and happy smile show what he was then. Sweet Agnes, who first despised, then encouraged, then loved him, and who, next to Agatha, commanded the open worship of his heart.

Agatha is first, must be first, as anyone can see who beholds him, on a certain anniversary of each year, bury his face in the long grass which covers the saddest and most passionate heart which ever yielded to the pressure of life's deepest tragedy.

THE END

Copyright © 2021 Esprios Digital Publishing. All Rights Reserved.

Lightning Source UK Ltd.
Milton Keynes UK
UKHW011536020921
389909UK00001B/56

9 781006 604744